After Helen

After Helen

✳

Paul Cavanagh

HarperCollins*PublishersLtd*

Published by HarperCollins Publishers Ltd

HarperCollins Publishers Ltd
2 Bloor Street East, 20th Floor
Toronto, Ontario, Canada
M4W 1A8

www.harpercollins.ca

Library and Archives Canada Cataloguing in
Publication

Cavanagh, Paul, 1962-
  After Helen / Paul Cavanagh. — 1st ed.

ISBN-13: 978-0-00-200605-7
ISBN-10: 0-00-200605-7

I. Title.

PS8605.A918A64 2006 C813'.6
C2005-905501-4

HC 9 8 7 6 5 4 3 2

Printed and bound in the United States
Set in Dante

to Amy,
to Dad,
as well as to all those in search of a
passage of their own

Ah, for just one time I would take the Northwest Passage
To find the hand of Franklin reaching for the Beaufort Sea;
Tracing one warm line through a land so wide and savage
And make a Northwest Passage to the sea.

—Stan Rogers

Chapter 1

I began teaching again one week after Helen died. The principal at my school, Abbie Sullivan, was willing to let me stay out longer. I still had to be in shock, she insisted. No point in forcing things. Of course, her real worry was that I'd melt down before the end of my first class and irradiate the kids with unresolved grief. She was picturing herself scrambling to contain the fallout, the calls from parents. I could tell. But I was resolute. My first class proceeded without incident. Then the next. And the next. After a while, Abbie stopped "accidentally" bumping into me in the corridors and assessing my responses to her forced casual remarks. Not that she seemed relieved. Actually, I sensed her wariness hardening into disappointment—or was it disapproval?—as if she somehow believed that by getting on with my life, I was declaring Helen easy to forget.

If she only knew.

Few people at school had known Helen other than by reputation. To them, she was my miscast wife: six feet tall to my five-foot-eight; smouldering red hair to my receding charcoal; faded freckles to my indelible crow's feet. More rumoured than seen. She was the woman who had once charmed a reluctant Farley Mowat into delivering a soliloquy on Canada's North to my

1

grade ten history class. The woman who had parked her car in the foyer of the big-box outlet that had put the bookshop she'd inherited from her father out of business. This was the Helen I tried to remember, the indomitable, larger-than-life version. Helen before her cherished red locks fell out in clumps, before she shrunk in on herself, her world collapsing into a small sphere of pain and nausea.

Teaching's a relief for me. It forces me to live in the present. There's no way I can teach anything of consequence to a room full of fourteen- and fifteen-year-olds without being fully alert to their shifting hormonal moods and adapting my lesson plans on the fly. No time for reliving those last days in the hospital, when Helen's body was so ravaged by cancer that she was barely recognizable. The classroom is my refuge. Home is where the past swallows me, where reminders of her absence—the closet full of clothes I can't bring myself to give away; the half-used tube of toothpaste in the medicine cabinet; the renegade strands of hair that keep appearing in the dustpan—lie in wait.

And then there's Severn, the most undeniable reminder of them all. Even last night, when she sullenly avoided my gaze at the dinner table, I saw afterimages of Helen in her. It wasn't so much the facial resemblance any more—the upturned nose, the lips so quick to pout. "Why are you staring at me like that?" she complained, as if a man wasn't supposed to look at his own daughter. But of course, it wasn't only her I was staring at. She'd just picked the heart out of a slice of bread and left the crust, exactly as Helen used to do.

With other people's children, I've learned how to see past their affected indifference and catch glimpses of their inner clockwork. From there, it's just a matter of gently jiggling the right springs and letting their potential unwind. With each year that passes, I quietly appreciate my handiwork when one or two dark-horse students of mine go on to surprise their critics in the teachers' lounge. It's easy when your stake in a child is professional and not personal, when you see your protégés for only an hour each day. With Severn, I have no such luxury. Like any father and daughter, we know how to push each other's buttons, and frequently do—more so now that it's just the two of us. My powers of gentle persuasion are useless with her.

Last night we were eating late because she hadn't got home until nearly eight—no call to let me know where she was, no apology once she walked in the door. It had become a regular occurrence, so much so that I'd given up chewing her out and generally started eating without her. Yesterday I'd waited for her, though.

"Where were you this afternoon?" I asked her as she poked at the egg noodles on her plate.

The response was predictable. She rolled her eyes, not even bothering to answer. Clearly my question was an invasion of her privacy. Why did I have to know where she was every second of the day? A week earlier, I might have backed off, chided myself for not trusting her more.

"Were you with Avery?" I asked.

Now I'd done it. I'd crossed the line. She shoved her chair back from the table. Its feet scraped across the hardwood floor, an effect designed to irritate me, I knew.

"I'm not hungry any more," she declared to the kitchen table and tromped off, leaving the overcooked fish I'd prepared for her.

I forced myself to finish what was on my plate, even though the knots in my stomach had cinched my appetite. The green beans squeaked between my teeth. The empty chair where Helen used to sit stared back at me. Severn resented the pretense of the family meal. She thought that I was trying to teach her a hackneyed lesson about how life goes on by cooking her pale imitations of Helen's meals. To her, I was the two-headed impostor, the father who wears an apron and pretends to be her mother.

I shovelled Severn's leftovers into a Tupperware container. Then I heard the front door thump shut. She'd gone again, probably to see Avery.

I have my grade ten students write me a short essay near the beginning of the year. I know that most of them look on history as a collection of boring things that happened to dead strangers in the dull and uninteresting reaches of time, before TV was invented. To help them understand their connection to the past, I get them to describe one of their own relatives, and to list some of the things that were going on in the world when these predecessors were growing up. I tell them they can choose a parent, a grandparent, an uncle, an aunt, whomever. Alive or dead, it doesn't matter. Of course, I get the usual wide range of efforts— from the students who try to pass off a thumbnail sketch of their twenty-year-old uncle to those who cite published biographies of a famous distant relation. No matter how well or how poorly written, each essay tells me a little something about the kid who wrote it that I can salt away for future reference.

This year when the essay was due, one girl didn't hand it in. Her name was Holly. She was Korean, but her parents, whom I'd met at parent–teacher night, were white. She seemed a lot like many of the second-generation Asian students I'd taught: utterly North American in her manners and attitudes; eager to fit in with all the other girls at school. Maybe too eager, at times. She wasn't the first adopted kid I'd ever had in my class. I'm always careful to stipulate to my students that the person they choose to write about doesn't have to be biologically related.

When I noticed she didn't have a paper to give me, I asked that she stay after the bell. At first she pretended that she'd forgotten when the assignment was due. But when I asked her whom she'd planned to write about, she looked away uncomfortably. It took me a while to get her to open up. I knew that the whole exercise was reminding her of how inescapably different she was from her classmates, despite her attempts to blend in. Eventually, she admitted that she wanted to write about her birth mother but knew nothing about her. I said that if that's what she wanted to do, I'd be willing to change the requirements of the essay for her. She could concentrate entirely on telling me about life in South Korea after the war, and thus—indirectly, at least—get a sense of the world in which her birth mother grew up. I gave her a couple of references that I thought she'd find useful and told her she had a month's extension.

What she eventually handed in was practically a dissertation. The essay included accounts of children orphaned by the war and families fractured by the country's partition, along with a description of how the country had changed in the years since then, having emerged from martial law and bloody student demonstrations to become a modern nation with an enduring sense of tradition. I gave her an A plus.

She kept doing research on her own after that. Last week, I spotted her in the library after school, browsing adoption websites, scrolling through messages from kids who were trying to locate their biological parents overseas. When she noticed me reading the screen from across the room, she quickly clicked to Amazon.com.

"Any luck?" I asked.

She was evasive to begin with. Finally, she admitted that her mom had caught her on the computer at home, then had tried to act as if it didn't bother her. "I felt like I was cheating on her or something," she told me.

When Holly was growing up, her parents had gone out of their way to make sure that she learned about her heritage. They'd sent her to Korean classes on the weekends, even packed her off to a special Korean culture camp one summer. But now that she was showing signs of wanting to know who her birth mother was, her parents had grown vaguely uneasy and started treating her with kid gloves.

"Stands to reason," I said. "They've raised you from a baby. They don't want to lose you."

Holly frowned at me for not being firmly on her side. After all,

I was the one who'd started her down this path. "It's not like I'm planning to hop the next flight to Seoul, you know," she said.

I was about to make her reflect a little more on her parents' point of view when Abbie walked into the library. She fixed me with one of those serious looks that principals are known for. I tried to wave her off with my eyes, telegraph that now was not a good time.

"Excuse us," she said to Holly, moving in to snatch me away.

I apologized to Holly and suggested that we pick up our discussion later. I might as well have jilted her. I could see it in her eyes. All she knew was that she'd shared her secret troubles with me, but I couldn't be bothered to stick around and talk them through.

I followed Abbie to her office, asking her what was so important that it couldn't wait. She wouldn't tell me anything until she'd closed the door behind us.

"It's Severn," she said ominously. "The police called a few minutes ago."

Various catastrophes flashed through my brain, all involving Severn maimed or dead.

"She's all right, Irving," she added quickly, reading my mind. Then: "They want to talk to you."

There was something in Abbie's tone that didn't fit with the doomsday scenarios I'd painted for myself. Something almost apologetic, embarrassed on my behalf.

"What's happened?" I asked her. I felt naked.

"She's been caught shoplifting."

I stood there inert.

"They didn't want to tell me at first," she explained, still waiting for me to react.

And then I wondered why I was so surprised. In retrospect, the pattern had been obvious, if I'd wanted to recognize it. Two days after Helen was diagnosed, Severn had got shit-faced and thrown up over one of her friends at a school dance. One month into chemo, when Helen's bravery act began to crumble, Severn had "inadvertently" shattered the mirror in her bedroom. I'd dismissed these outbursts as temporary short-circuits, excusable at the time.

Abbie offered to step out of the office so I could use her phone in private. Just before she closed the door behind her, I thought to ask her, "Did they say where she was?"

"Imprint Books," Abbie said.

The police cruiser was parked in front of the store when I pulled into the parking lot. Severn was sitting in the back seat, eyes downcast. A chunky boy in a baggy jacket was there with her. Avery Costello. The cop behind the wheel was filling out some paperwork, his window rolled up against the raw February wind. I stood by his door, my ears freezing, waiting for him to notice me. Shoppers passing by eyed me curiously, exchanging little smirks with one another. I tapped on the window. Finally, the cop looked up and got out of the cruiser.

"Mr. Cruickshank?" he asked. He was in his late twenties, brush cut, neck like a tree trunk. He looked vaguely familiar. I wondered if he'd been one of my students.

"Is this really necessary?" I said, shooting my eyes to Severn caged in the back seat.

"Shoplifting's a crime, Mr. Cruickshank. It has consequences."

The pedantic ass. "My daughter's going through a rough time," I said. "Her mother passed away last year."

He slid his lower jaw forward as he considered my story. "You know the boy with her?"

Before Helen got sick, Severn spent all her time with other girls from school, mostly at the mall or on the phone, talking about the things that teenage girls talk about and middle-aged fathers find bone-achingly trivial: clothes, boys, makeup, hair. Back then, I had wished she'd find new friends with interests that wouldn't turn her brain to mush. Now all her old friends had mysteriously vanished. If she wasn't at home or in class, she was with Avery. What his appeal was I still hadn't figured out. I glanced at his splotchy face, beefy hands. His body had grown so fast in all directions, it had surprised even him, forcing him into a stoop that, in the back seat of the police cruiser, made him look like a question mark with a gland problem. Severn had never brought him home, never introduced him to me. I'd had to gather intelligence from my confederates at their high school. He was a loner with good grades in math and sciences and a collection of Lord of the Rings artwork in his locker, they told me. Someone who grows up and walks into his dead-end, white-collar job one day with a rifle, I thought. Not anyone you'd want your daughter hanging around with.

"They go to school together," was all I told the cop.

"The manager caught them outside the store with a book they hadn't paid for," he said.

"Look, if it's just one book, I'll pay for it."

He looked at me as if I'd just said something incredibly stupid and he was waiting for me to reconsider.

"Okay," I said. "I know what she did is serious. But do you have to charge her?"

I must have grovelled just enough, because then he eased off his by-the-book routine. "Here's what I'll do," he said, as if he was doing me a big favour. "There's this program we've got for first-time offenders now." He handed me a card with a social worker's name on it. "Just make sure she shows up."

Great. Some social worker was going to poke into Severn's childhood and blame everything on her parents. "Thanks," I said. "I appreciate it."

He reached for the back door of the cruiser, but before he opened it, he turned to me and said, with a coy smile, "Grade ten history. You gave some pretty tough tests, Mr. Cruickshank."

The bugger. He'd had to put the screws on me before he let on.

On the ride home, I asked Severn what the hell she was thinking. I asked her to explain to me why a girl who'd grown up in a house filled with books would want to steal one from a store. Of course I realized that shoplifting wasn't about taking something you needed, or even valued. It was an act of rebellion. As a young girl, Severn had read voraciously. But recently it seemed that the notion that one could find useful knowledge in or inspiration from a book had become unbearably hokey to her.

"I don't want you hanging out with Avery any more," I told her.

Up to that point, her strategy had been to stare stone-faced out the window and weather my barrage. Now she sat ramrod straight and trained her withering sights on me. Like her mother, she tops me by a few inches. She likes to remind me of the fact when I really piss her off.

"You'd love it if I had no friends at all," she said, her voice trembling between rage and tears. "No life. Just sitting at home every night like you."

Her melodramatic tone was more than a little irritating. I thought of all the soccer practices, birthday parties, and sleepovers I'd driven her to as a girl. "I have papers to mark, lessons to prepare," I said.

"You're such a control freak."

"I'm not the one who got picked up by the cops," I reminded her.

She glared at me as if I wasn't fighting fair, as if I was dumping on her. What was I supposed to do? Pat her hand and tell her that I understood? Because I didn't.

"And why *that* particular store?" I said.

She gave a little snort. Obviously I should know, and I was just being dense.

"Was this stunt supposed to be some kind of whacked-out tribute to your mother?" I asked.

I remembered the last time I'd visited the store, years before. Seeing the back end of our Toyota sticking out through what was left of the front doors, the lights of emergency vehicles flashing all around me. I'd found Helen sitting in the back of an ambulance and wearing a mischievous, self-satisfied grin as a paramedic

tended to a gash on her forehead. Since then I'd carefully avoided
that parking lot, worried that I would come face to face with the
store manager again. I was surprised she hadn't cottoned on that
Severn was Helen's daughter, come to wreak further vengeance in
the family name.

"So what are you saying?" Severn said. "That Mom embarrassed you?"

"I loved your mother."

She gave another little snort.

"This isn't some competition about who misses her the most,"
I said.

She turned away, shutting me out, her arms crossed tight. We
didn't talk for the rest of the drive.

I'd only ever spoken to Avery's mother over the phone, usually
to confirm Severn's whereabouts and the presence of an adult
in the house. I got the impression from our brief exchanges
that she was raising Avery on her own, Mr. Costello having
flown the coop. We never strayed into chit-chat—partly
because we were both embarrassed that our children had
become such outcasts that they could claim only each other as
friends, and partly, I suspect, because Mrs. Costello didn't want
to say anything to set me off, given that I was presumably still
grieving the loss of my wife.

Our phone conversation after we'd both collected our children
from the police was awkward, to say the least.

"It must be tough for you, raising Severn on your own," she
said to me. Perhaps she meant it as commiseration from one single parent to another, but I didn't hear it that way. I detected a subtle rebuke, a suggestion that I'd let Severn get out of hand, that as
a man I couldn't possibly understand what made a sixteen-year-
old girl tick.

"I think it would be better if Severn stopped hanging out with Avery," I said.

"Fine," she said, as if I was hopelessly naive to think we could control what they did.

Chapter 2

It's now 3:00 a.m., and Severn isn't home. This isn't the first time I've waited up for her like this, contemplating all the horrific things that can happen to a girl of sixteen who's bent on putting herself at risk just to annoy her father. Half a dozen times I've tried her cellphone, the one I insist she carries but she never turns on. I've even called the parents of most of her old friends, just to see if they have a clue where she is, but most of them simply say that they haven't seen Severn for a long time, and that they're so sorry about her mother and hope I'm doing all right. I murmur back my thanks, just as I always do when platitudes are cast my way like spare change to a beggar.

The last time I waited up for her, she finally arrived home at two-thirty. Instead of making excuses, she rolled her eyes and asked me what the hell I thought I was doing sitting up in the living room. Everyone else she knew stayed out late, and none of their parents stared at their watches all night waiting for them to come through the front door. I told her that I knew it had to be rough living with a father who actually cared where she was, but she'd have to get used to it, as embarrassing as that might be for her.

Although the thought makes me sick, I know that during one of her late-night excursions, my little girl has almost certainly found herself pressed against some boy with a hard-on and no fully formed idea of what to do with it. Maybe even Avery. Sure that Helen had talked with her about it before, I asked her once whether she was taking precautions. She looked at me like I'd propositioned her, like I'd violated the bounds of what any man should ask his daughter.

"Not that I think you should be in a position where you actually have to use precautions," I sputtered.

God, whatever happened to that little girl I held in the crook of my arm at festivals in the park and sang silly songs with? The girl who wrapped her arms around my neck when I came home from school and blew wet raspberries on my cheek? Sometimes when I look at Severn now, she becomes unstuck in time, and I see her at sixteen, ten, and six all at once, her present and past selves superimposed, each blurring the other.

My first class is at eight-thirty. I've changed the lesson plan, and I know I won't be able to sleepwalk through it. I should go to bed, I tell myself. What will another late-night faceoff resolve? I'll demand that she give me a full accounting of where she's been. She'll stonewall me, then seal herself in her bedroom before I get the full story. She knows I'm growing weary of the fight, and I think she resents me all the more for it.

It's at times like these that I sense Helen looking over my shoulder. She wouldn't have let Severn brush her off so easily. There was a kind of détente between the two of them. They had their yelling matches, but they also had a tacit understanding of when an argument had gone too far. Within hours of a blow-up, I'd find Helen curled on Severn's bed, offering her fashion advice or helping her rehearse lines for the school play. The ebb and flow of the relationship between a mother and her daughter is something no man can fully comprehend, much less replicate. My problem is that Severn and I have no neutral territory, no middle ground where we can meet under a flag of truce, and so we remain locked in an unrelenting war of wills.

I pour myself another cup of coffee and pretend to mark grade ten history tests at the kitchen table. My mind plays tricks on me at this time of night. As I shuffle through my papers, I see a shadow move out of the corner of my eye, and my brain reflexively concludes that it's Helen investigating why I haven't come to bed yet. She's been so long a part of my life that all but the most conscious part of me is convinced she'll suddenly reappear. At this point, I usually remind myself that it's just an illusion, like the phantom pain of an amputee whose foot was long ago consigned to medical waste. This time, though, I let the fantasy linger before I shatter it, and memories coalesce until she almost becomes whole before me. I feel her touch, smell the warmth of her skin. She wants me to put the papers away. She takes my face in her hands, lowers herself onto my lap. And then it all evaporates, and I feel the same sickening sense of free fall I did when I drove home from the hospital the morning she died.

A cold sweat clings to the inside of my shirt. It was at this very table that Helen first told Severn about her diagnosis. Helen explained to her as best she could about the surgery and the chemotherapy treatments, about how the doctor said there was still hope they'd caught it in time. I could see the fear in Helen's eyes as she tried to convince us that everything would be all right. Severn could see it too. She looked at me, seeking reassurance that Mom had got it wrong, that it was all a misunderstanding that could be explained away. When Severn read the forced optimism on my face, I think she stopped hearing anything Helen was telling her. I saw a panic building inside her. Her eyes converged on empty space as she tried to grasp how this could possibly be happening to *her* mother. All she could comprehend was that her world, with all its unassailable assumptions about the future, had just fallen into the sun. Shaking with shock and anger, she turned and left the room. Not a word of solace or comfort for her mother. As we heard Severn's bedroom door slam shut, Helen's brave facade dissolved and she collapsed into a series of heaving sobs. The two of them couldn't face each other for a long time after that. I'm not sure that I've fully forgiven Severn for her behaviour that day.

I should sell the house, I tell myself. Escape the apparitions that drag me into a pit of stillborn futures. I should leave town, find a new home for us. Somewhere they never knew Helen, and where Severn isn't simply the poor, motherless girl. I imagine myself sitting in another kitchen, at a table I didn't buy with Helen, looking at walls that aren't covered with her wreaths or copper moulds or stencilled borders. But the walls of this imagined room are bare, as sterile as an oncologist's waiting room. And where once an unrelenting throb of memories filled me with pain, a consuming emptiness now exists, like a cosmic black hole the size of a nickel, swallowing me from the inside.

I check the clock on the microwave. Five-fifteen.

She's been run down by a drunk driver. Some paroled sex offender's raped her and slit her throat. The police will be calling any second, wondering why I didn't bother to pay closer attention to my only daughter's safety.

As much as I despaired of the possibility earlier in the night, I begin to hope she's with Avery, who's become the least of all the evils I can imagine. I'd called his mother at about ten-thirty, after ruling out all Severn's old friends. It was a conversation I hadn't been looking forward to. I was almost glad there was no answer, except that it left me no closer to finding Severn.

I've worked myself up too much, I tell myself. Severn will walk through the front door the moment I've given up on her, as if to prove a point. This is another one of her tests. She's waiting for me to blink first, just as I always do. I should go to bed and turn off all the lights. That would show her.

Instead I pick up the phone again.

Avery's mother answers after only a couple of rings. I expect her voice to be thick with sleep, but it's not. When I tell her that Severn hasn't come home, there's a wary pause.

"I thought so," she says, as if I've just confirmed some suspicion she hasn't bothered to share. She tells me that when she got home after work, both Avery and the car were gone. His toothbrush and contact-lens case were missing from the bathroom. He'd taken clean underwear, socks, a few shirts, and a tote bag.

"I don't suppose you've noticed if any of Severn's clothes are missing," she asks, knowing full well I wouldn't have, even if I'd looked. Because I'm a man. The implication is that I'm negligent for not having an inventory of her wardrobe ready for just such an emergency. It's not as if I buy her clothes for her. Nor would she want me to, thank God. And when it comes to laundry, she'd be mortified if I handled her bras and panties, which is just fine by me.

Avery's mother and I promise to call the minute one of us uncovers a clue that points to where our kids have headed. After we hang up, I go and stand in Severn's bathroom, trying to decide whether the right numbers of lotions and hair clips are sitting on the vanity.

I'm not sure what I thought would be waiting for me when I stepped inside that Imprint store two days ago. Maybe an eagle-eyed security guard on the lookout for Cruickshanks set to storm the battlements one more time. Jittery staff who'd recognize me as the husband of that lunatic woman with the car. An irate manager eager to finally extract her pound of flesh. At least some lingering scars from the fury our late Toyota brought down upon them. But there was none of that. Instead what I found was a cheerful display trumpeting new arrivals near the entrance where our front bumper once came to rest, as well as a company of fresh-faced young staff, most of whom were probably still in high school when Helen mounted her glorious assault. The place was obliviously going about its business, with no thought to the past. I was just another customer. It was like being a veteran in a

Remembrance Day parade that nobody had come to watch. The least the store could have done was have someone give me a dirty look, something to show me that Helen had stung them hard enough that they couldn't simply forget her after a quick repair job and a fresh coat of paint.

A young woman in an Imprint golf shirt greeted me with a standard-issue smile at the information desk.

"I'd like to see the manager," I told her.

As I waited, I surveyed the store. Past the magazine racks, in the upscale coffee bar, university students pretending to study were on the make. I'd heard tell that some arts students bought second-hand anatomy books and carted them to places like this just so they would be confused for medical students by eligible members of the opposite sex. Pretending to be something they're not. In a way, this whole town was about being mistaken for someone or something else. London, Ontario. Not to be confused with the other London, the real London. Certainly not by airline ticket agents and baggage handlers. John Graves Simcoe must have been awfully homesick when he named this place. What possessed him, as he gnawed on that first supper of porcupine, to ennoble a mosquito-infested tract of wilderness with the same name as the capital of the empire he served? Not a castle, cathedral, or manor home in sight. His homeland so far removed in time and space that it could be only a faint, teasing memory. Perhaps it was his attempt at satire, a veiled record of his dissatisfaction with his superiors at home.

"Irving?"

The voice sounded familiar but out of place. I turned to see Will Graham, Helen's right-hand man from the days of the family bookshop on Richmond Street, in a yellow Imprint golf shirt. He was a little greyer around the edges than I remembered. Yellow wasn't his colour.

"It's been a while," he said, shaking my hand and patting me on the arm.

Will had jumped ship and gone to work for the competition when the family bookshop was going under. Not that he'd had much choice, given how few hours Helen was offering him near the end. Still, to Helen it had been an act of betrayal rivalling Macbeth's. I knew that Will hadn't made the move without remorse. Small and intimate, Donnelly's Books had been home to him, the kind of quirky place he'd wanted to own himself one day.

"So you're manager here now," I said.

"Assistant," he said, correcting me politely, and overlooking my unintended reminder of how short of his goals he'd fallen.

"You know why I'm here, don't you?" I asked.

He took me gently by the elbow and steered me past the magazine rack. "Let me buy you a coffee," he said.

Will is a purebred book hound. He's one of a dwindling species of book merchants who read everything they sell. I used to play a game with him back at the old shop. Each time I had a few minutes to kill before Helen knocked off, I'd drag out an obscure volume from the back shelves and ask him whether he'd read it. Without fail, he'd give me a synopsis of the text, offer his sly appraisal of the work, and throw in a few shocking tidbits about the author. It didn't matter if it was the latest new-age take on the Kama Sutra, a Mavis Gallant anthology, or a medieval pilgrim's guide to cathedrals. I used to think he was snowing me, until I perused a few of the books at home. Then I didn't question it any more.

He sat me down in a quiet corner, at one of the few tables not taken over by students. Before he started talking, he studied my face, assessing the ravages of my year as a widower and single parent.

"I want to apologize, Irving. They'd already called the cops when I came on for my shift. When I saw it was Severn—"

"She didn't deserve any special treatment," I said, perhaps a little too abruptly.

"What's it been now?" he ventured. "A year?"

I remembered then that he'd spoken to me at the visitation, sounding equally earnest in his sympathy. To be perfectly honest, I couldn't recall much about that day, except the closed coffin and Severn stiff and brittle beside me as we endured wave after wave of condolences.

"How are things at home?" he asked. He expected the real story, unlike most people who asked.

I shrugged. "She's a teenager who's angry with the world. Hardly sets her apart from the crowd." I realized I was drumming my fingers on the table. I curled them in a fist and set them on my lap, out of view.

I could see that my answer didn't satisfy him. I was being too glib for his taste. But I wasn't about to relive the past year with him.

"There was a boy with her," I said, getting back to business.

He blew on his coffee. "You want to know if he put her up to it."

I said nothing. I didn't have to. He understood me.

"No," he said. "I don't think so."

"Why not?"

"You want a biscotti? I should have asked when we were getting the coffee."

"Will," I said impatiently.

He let his eyes wander through the store as if he was looking for a volume that would help him find the right words for what he had to tell me. But there was no inspiration on the shelves. His gaze settled back on me.

"I don't think the boy was all that interested in the book," he said. "But Severn was."

"How can you be so sure?"

He sat there sizing me up, deciding whether to be straight with me. Finally he got to his feet. We left our coffees on the table, and he led me back through the stacks to the information desk. He pulled a hardcover from the shelves where they kept special orders.

"I set it aside," he said, then handed it to me. "Have a look at the author."

The title was *Northwest Passage*. I read the name below it and felt my cheeks burn.

"He was in the store autographing copies that day," Will explained.

It was as if a long-buried prehistoric beast had reached out of the dirt and grabbed me by the ankle, pulling me down into a terrible volcanic layer of my past. Jack Livingston's smug face smiled back up at me from the jacket flap. His photo was an old one, even though the novel was new. He looked just as he had the night Helen brought him home all those years ago—a man of forty, with Samson-like hair and a supercilious glint in his eye.

Will's lips twitched sympathetically. He knew that Severn's shoplifting was the least of my concerns now. "He signed it."

I opened the front cover. There was Jack's signature, and above it the words "Dear Irving—Glad to have you on the voyage."

Will eyed me cautiously. "The book's outselling Atwood and Ondaatje," he told me. "It'll probably be nominated for the Governor General's Award. You can take it, no charge. With the inscription, it can't be sold or returned to the publisher anyway." And then he added meaningfully, "I think you'll be interested in the story."

I handed it back to him without even reading the synopsis on the inside flap. It wasn't hard to figure out from the book's title where Livingston had got his inspiration, but I wasn't about to let the bastard taunt me any further. Not after nearly twenty years.

I've just hung up from calling in sick to school when the phone rings. It's Avery mother.

"They're in Toronto," she says.

She explains that she remembered Avery has a debit card for one of her accounts. She checked the Web for recent transactions and found that he spent fifty bucks at a bistro in Toronto. In the

Beaches, to be more precise. It was more than he'd spend on a meal if he were on his own. A piece of shrewd detective work I wouldn't have expected from a woman I'd always taken for a bit of a flake.

"It's not far from his dad's place," she says. Avery normally visits his dad on weekends, she adds. She's tried the condo, but there's no answer. Dad's often out of town on business, but Avery has a key.

"What's the address?" I ask.

"We still can't be certain that Severn is with him," she says.

"It's a place to start."

I can tell that she's not keen to have me banging on the door to her ex's condo. "There's a blizzard on the way," she says. "They're advising people to stay off the roads."

"I've already booked the day off work," I tell her.

Despite her misgivings, I can sense that, like me, she's not happy simply waiting by the phone. "We go together, then," she says.

I'm not particularly enthusiastic about having her along for the ride. At the best of times, the drive down the 401 takes two hours. We'll feel obliged to fill the long silences, to try explaining our messy lives to each other without really wanting to. Still, I don't see a way around it. She's not going to let me look for her son without her. And without the address, I might as well be searching for a contact lens in a snowstorm.

"I'll pick you up in ten minutes," I tell her.

Chapter 3

As I grab my car keys from the dresser, I ask myself why I never confronted Severn once I discovered who she'd gone to see at the bookstore. Maybe I figured the only thing I'd get from her was an impenetrable scowl. Deep down, though, I knew the opposite was true; I was afraid she'd tell me exactly why she'd had him sign his new book for me. It was my nightmare scenario come to life.

I sink to the bed, overcome with exhaustion. The bedcovers are still twisted into the same knots I left them in yesterday morning. My pillow is mashed and herniated from its case. Helen's pillow is plump and undisturbed. Even during my roughest nights, I avoid her half of the bed like it's a foreign land from which I've been deported without appeal. It's the same bed that Severn used to come to in the middle of the night, seeking refuge from the monsters in her closet. She'd curl up, the warmth from Helen and me sheltering her on either side. Snug as a bug in a rug. Was it ever really like that? I begin to wonder. Or is nostalgia playing tricks on me, colouring my memories in warm sepia tones?

"I hear that Jack Livingston goes through wives like he goes through ballpoint pens," Will told me. "Word is he's shacked up with some bohemian painter with a thing for older men." According to him, Livingston still lives in Toronto.

Severn doesn't have a driver's licence. The train and the bus cost money. Avery would have offered to take her to Toronto for free, although he likely would think himself entitled to payment of a different kind.

I get back up, but the axis of the room slips in my brain, and the floor suddenly pitches under my feet like the deck of storm-tossed ship. I steady myself against Helen's dresser, leaving finger tracks in the veil of dust that's settled on it over the months. I wait for the gyroscope in my head to stop malfunctioning and swear at my body for failing me. I'm forced to stare at Helen's knick-knacks, her jewellery, her old perfume bottles—things I've never had the energy or courage to clear away. I notice the footprint left behind in the dust by the framed photo that I now realize is gone. It's the one of Helen jubilantly raising a glass of ouzo to the camera on the day we celebrated the acceptance of her first short story for publication. A day she'd imagined for twenty years and had despaired would never come. Her smile was transcendent, bursting from inside her, joy and vindication fused together. She had no way of knowing that the magazine that had accepted her story would fold before printing it, or that by then she'd be struggling to make it through a day without throwing up. Severn obviously thought this memento of Helen was rightfully hers. She'd assumed I wasn't using it, didn't want it, didn't deserve it. I wasn't to be trusted with her mother's memory any more.

My equilibrium finally returns, and I venture back into Severn's room. Among the clothes, books, and CDs strewn about, I spot the family photo albums. Severn had always hated having her picture taken as a child, but lately I'd caught her mooning over old photos of herself with Helen: at the church when she was christened, at the beach when she was four, in the backyard making a snowman when she was nine. Severn had slapped the album shut when she noticed me spying on her from the hallway, then pointedly closed the door on me.

I pick up one of the albums and open it now. The pages are blank. She's taken the pictures with her. At my feet, I notice the ones she's discarded, scattered across the floor. They're all ones with me in them.

I waste fifteen minutes finding the Costellos' house. Avery's mother's directions prove indecipherable, and I end up trolling their convoluted subdivision in the pre-dawn until I finally stumble on the right street. Fordwich Place. Not to be confused with Fordwich Drive or Fordwich Crescent or Fordwich Court. Their house is the only one with the front porch light on. It's a raised ranch, built in the days when houses had single-car garages because families had only one car and Mom stayed home to look after the kids. It even has one of those little square recesses where the milkman used to leave milk bottles twice a week. I remember telling Severn about milkmen once. She looked at me as if I had grown up on some backward planet orbiting a very dim sun.

As I pull into the driveway behind a rusty minivan, the porch light switches off and the front door opens. Avery's mother descends the front steps like a shadowy wraith. The glow of my headlights bleaches her features, turning her long hair silver and her skin translucent like a bean sprout. In her anorak and insulated boots, she seems more prepared for an Arctic expedition than a drive to Toronto. I get out of the car. She pulls off a mitten and extends her hand to me.

"I suppose we should know each other's first names," she says. "I'm Marla."

"Irving."

We shake. She has a firm, bony grip, more like a man's than I expected. This close to her, I realize that I've overestimated the intensity of the headlights. Her hair really is silver, not the blond I'd assumed it would prove to be in a truer light, and her skin has lost none of its spectral sheen. We stand there for a moment, steam seeping from our nostrils in the cold morning air, waiting to see who'll speak next.

"Well," I say, extending my arm towards the passenger door like a reluctant maître d' guiding a patron to an open table.

She hesitates. "You okay to drive?" she asks. She's noticed the bags under my eyes.

I tell her I'll be fine once we drop by a Tim Hortons and get a coffee. This doesn't reassure her much, but she sees that I'm determined to get going, so she doesn't press the point. It takes her forever to get settled in the passenger seat. She's brought a knapsack stuffed with God knows what. She can't decide whether to leave it by her feet or hoist it to the back seat. The car suddenly feels cramped. I back out of the driveway before she gets around to fastening her seat belt.

"So where does Avery's father live?" I ask her.

"I'll give you directions once we're in Toronto," she says. Perhaps she thinks I'll leave her at the side of the road if she tells me too soon. A wise precaution, under the circumstances.

The next time we say anything to each other is when I ask her what she'd like as we're going through the Tim Hortons drive-thru on the way out of town. She tells me she has a bottle of water and some oranges in her bag. I order a large coffee for myself and set it in my cup holder.

"I hear you're a teacher," she says, the impulse to make small talk finally overcoming her.

"That's right," I say, offering her no more details.

"What subjects?" she asks.

"History and geography."

"Ah," she says. "I was never very good at remembering dates or capital cities."

I make no comment, even though hearing someone sum up the subjects I love as a bundle of sterile facts never fails to annoy me. Flecks of snow speckle the windshield. The wipers smear them, so the lights of the occasional oncoming car bleed across the road ahead.

"Did you major in history?" she asks.

"Listen, Marla, I don't mean to be rude, but I really need to concentrate on the road."

"Sorry," she says, miffed but trying not to show it. She stares out her window at the passing strip malls and gas stations. A few blocks later, she grows uncomfortable with the silence again. "So does Severn know anyone in Toronto?" she asks.

I cast a quick sideways glance at her. "Why do you ask?"

She looks down her nose at me, feeling no compulsion to defend what she obviously considers a perfectly reasonable question.

"No," I say. "I don't know anyone she'd want to see there."

"Ah," she replies, as if she knows I'm lying but is far too polite to call me on it. At least not yet.

Chapter 4

I was still an eager young teacher when I first walked into the store on Richmond Street. It was 1984. Farley Mowat was there that day, copper beard as big as Santa's, signing the latest reprint of *Never Cry Wolf,* which had just been released as a movie. I'd already seen it three times. Like three-quarters of the people in this country, I'd spent my life in a 3,400-mile strip of land hugging the southern border, never out of range of American TV signals. The North was something Canadians only dimly understood but were quick to crow about to unsuspecting tourists who had trouble pronouncing "Saskatchewan." Here was a man who'd lived the geography I struggled to teach from uninspiring textbooks, who'd made it his life's work to explain our own country to us. A man who was crazy enough to wear a kilt to a book-signing in March, when the snow was still a foot deep outside.

I was covering the search for the Northwest Passage that week in class. I'd come armed with my well-fingered copy of his book *Ordeal by Ice*. But when I saw the great man himself, dutifully scribbling inscriptions when it was clear that he'd much rather be drinking rum in the nearest tavern, my resolve faltered. I pretended to browse the biography section as I rehearsed my lines in my head, waiting for my nerve to return.

"*Ordeal by Ice*, eh?" I heard from behind my right elbow. "Maybe you'd be interested in this."

That was how I first met Will. Even then, he was a skilled book hustler. He had to have been in his late-twenties—he's only a few years older than I am—but already a pair of reading glasses hung from a chain around his neck.

He pulled a biography of Sir John Franklin, the Arctic explorer, off the shelf and handed it to me. "A classic British explorer," he said. "Glorious in his failure."

"Known affectionately in his day as the man who ate his boots," I said.

Will smiled, recognizing me as a Franklin aficionado. "Did you know that more than twenty expeditions went looking for him?"

"And in the process charted the passage he died looking for," I added. "Some say it was the largest search-and-rescue operation to this day."

"History teacher," he said, his first impressions of me confirmed. "Am I right?"

"Guilty," I confessed. It wasn't often that I met someone who could quote Franklin back to me chapter and verse. For most people, he was a footnote in Canadian history, the central figure in a vaguely familiar tragedy that hadn't been important enough to make its way onto any test they'd taken in high school.

"Did you get Farley to sign that for you yet?" he asked, eyeing the book I'd brought with me.

"Not yet."

He sensed my hesitation. "He won't bite," he assured me. "At least, I haven't heard of him doing it recently."

"Thanks," I said. He was right; I should just get it over with.

"Let me know if you need my help with anything," he said and moved to another customer, leaving me to get on with it.

There was a lanky red-haired woman talking to Mowat as I approached the special table they'd set up for him. By the way she sat, with one leg swinging idly off the edge of the table as she chatted him up, I could tell she wasn't a customer. His eyes twinkled the way men's eyes do when a younger woman flirts with them. I was having second thoughts again, afraid that interrupting them might not put me in Mowat's favour.

The woman noticed me hovering. She leaned over to Mowat. "A member of your public awaits," she said, patting him affectionately on the hand. She stood up, making way for me with a polite smile. Now I could see what had made his eyes twinkle. There was something very direct and unapologetic about the way she looked at me, as if for that instant I was the sole focus of her attention, the only man on earth as far as she was concerned. And then, just as quickly, her focus shifted away, and I felt strangely abandoned.

"Hello there," Mowat said to me, inviting me to come closer.

I felt like a six-year-old who's too shy to step up and deliver his only line at the Christmas pageant. I shuffled forward and awkwardly extended my hand.

"Mr. Mowat," I said. "I'm a big fan." How original of me. I wondered how many times he'd heard that line.

Mowat shook my hand and smiled graciously. "Glad you enjoy my work."

For all my rehearsing, I couldn't decide what to say next. We looked at each other like two strangers at a party who've run out of small talk. Then he saw the book I was clutching.

"Would you like me to sign that for you?" he asked helpfully.

I handed it to him. "The name's Irving," I said.

The cover of the book almost came loose as he opened it. "It's nice to see one of my books so well used," he said as he signed.

He handed it back to me, hoping, I'm sure, that I'd thank him and move on. Instead, I kept standing there, looming over him in my overstuffed parka like a dark cloud.

"Was there something else?" he asked, peering at me over the rim of his glasses.

"I'm Irving Cruickshank," I said. "I wrote you a few weeks ago. Right after I found out you'd be coming to town today."

"Ah, the schoolteacher," he said warily. He could see what was coming. He was figuring out how to let me down gently, I could tell.

"We're doing the search for the Northwest Passage this week in class," I said. *"Ordeal by Ice* blows away any of our history texts. As I said in my letter, I was hoping you might find half an hour in your busy schedule to drop by and talk with my class."

His smile verged on a wince. "Irving," he said, "I'm flattered you asked, but—"

Before he could finish, I'd fished into my jacket pockets and pulled out my insurance. I laid a dozen crumpled letters on the table in front of him. "These are from my students," I said. "Addressed to you. I told them I'd deliver them personally. They're really hoping you will come."

My appeal had caught the attention of the woman who'd been talking with Mowat. I felt the warmth of her gaze shine back on me as she looked on in amusement from the nearby cash register. Mowat slouched back in his chair, his kilt creeping up, further exposing his knobby knees. I wasn't making it easy for him. He placed his glasses on the table and massaged the bridge of his nose.

"I'm sorry," he said with a sigh. He felt ambushed. There was a mixture of regret and irritation in his voice. "I tell you what, though. When I get home, I'll write your class a reply to their letters." He shuffled them into a stack and tapped the bottom edge of the pages against the tabletop as if to signify that the matter was resolved. "It was nice to meet you, Irving. I wish more teachers were as dedicated as you."

I'd been politely dismissed. I didn't know what I was expecting. He was a busy man. He couldn't rearrange his entire schedule just to help a crackpot teacher entertain his students. I thanked him and turned for the door. I was like one of those failed Arctic explorers, casting off with grandiose ambitions only to crash into the reality of the polar ice pack.

As I twisted the rickety old doorknob to leave, I heard the

woman call after me from the cash. "Wait," she said. "You forgot to fill out one of our ballots."

I looked back at her. She sat perched on the tall stool behind the counter, her fingers interlaced across her knee. The sleeves of her Icelandic sweater were pushed up to her elbows. She acted like she owned the place, which I might have thought possible if it weren't for the fact that she didn't look any older than me.

"I didn't buy anything," I said apologetically.

"Doesn't matter," she said. "Maybe you will next time." She held out a pen.

I had the feeling she was toying with me like a cat does with a wounded mouse. Still, I couldn't resist the pull of her green eyes. I approached the counter and took the pen from her. I was acutely conscious of the salt stains on the sleeve of my parka. She slid a blank scrap of paper in front of me.

"Just write your name, address, and telephone number," she told me.

"This doesn't look like a ballot," I said.

"We ran out. This will do."

I carefully wrote out my name and address. For a moment, I couldn't remember my telephone number.

"What's the prize?" I asked.

"We haven't decided yet," she said with a sly smile.

A few moments later, I found myself out on the sidewalk, as giddy as a wallflower who has just been asked to dance by the prettiest girl at school. The wind chill was minus twenty, but I didn't feel the cold.

The way Helen told the story later, it was the look of pure disappointment on my face after I so ineptly blackmailed Mowat with my sheaf of student letters that intrigued her. She could tell how much I'd hung my hopes on his goodwill. It was my lack of guile that charmed her.

She took Mowat across the street to a pub after the book-signing and convinced him to reconsider my request despite his secret fear of speaking in public. Helen had known him since she was a little girl. He and her dad had served in Italy together during the war. Whenever "Uncle" Farley had paid a visit to the house, she'd crawled up on his lap, played with his beard, and asked him to tell her a story. He'd never refused. Even though she wasn't a little girl any more, he was still susceptible to her charms. She promised to come with him to my class. They'd pretend they were in her parents' living room. She'd ask him to tell her a story, except this time she wouldn't crawl up on his lap and a few extra people would be listening in.

"The key is not to spook him," she told me over the phone.

I felt queasy. I was stunned that she'd taken such an interest in me, and terrified of saying anything that would reveal me to be the hayseed I knew I was. "I can't tell you how much this will mean to the kids," I said.

"It's not the kids I'm doing it for," she said.

Even though men aren't supposed to swoon, I came pretty close right then.

I don't remember how I managed to get through my first class that next day. I was in a complete fog. Helen was bringing Mowat for fourth period. I told the front-office secretary to let me know the moment they arrived. It wasn't long before the whole staff knew. A couple of my colleagues from social studies and English intercepted me in the hall between classes. Why hadn't I talked to administration about scheduling a special assembly so everyone could hear Mowat speak? At the very least, I should open my class to any staff members who weren't teaching that period.

By the time Helen brought Mowat in the front door, Pritchard, the principal at the time, was there with his coterie to greet them. I came upon the scene just as he was explaining to Mowat that a reporter from the *London Free Press* would be arriving shortly to cover his historic visit to the school. If it weren't for Helen, I think Mowat might have bolted right then and there.

"Farley's really looking forward to speaking with the kids in Mr. Cruickshank's class," she said. "But I'm afraid he has to leave town right after." She danced Mowat through the crowd with the grace of a toreador. "Ah, Irving. Our gallant host. Show us the way."

Man, what a dish she was, in her Italian leather jacket with those fluorescent, skin-tight leggings and ankle-high hiking boots. She had an edgy sense of style, as if she were from cosmopolitan Montreal, not white-bread London, Ontario. I could tell that Pritchard felt jilted, but he knew enough not to tangle with her. His envious gaze lingered on us as she linked arms with Mowat on one side and me on the other. I knew I'd be getting a lecture on proper protocol in Pritchard's office later that afternoon, but at that moment, I couldn't have cared less.

"Who said anything about a reception committee?" Helen whispered, elbowing me in the ribs. She smelled of lavender, a scent that transported me to my grandmother's house when I was five, and that Helen made confusingly arousing.

"Sorry about that," I said. It was then that I noticed my eyes were level with her lips. "Word got out."

Mowat winked at me. "Best not disappoint her, Irving. Believe me." This tongue-in-cheek remark drew a jab from her other elbow. "You see what I mean?" he said in mock distress.

There was a buzz from the students the moment Mowat walked into the classroom. He was hard not to recognize, especially since he was wearing the requisite outdoorsman's parka, which, by the look of it, had seen more of Canada in the past ten years than I could hope to see in my lifetime. The kids were so juiced up that they completely ignored the elaborate introduction I'd spent the whole night pulling together. When I handed the class over to Helen, she attracted as many looks as Mowat did, especially from the boys. She explained to the class how persuasive

I'd been on their behalf, leaving out the bits where Mowat turned me down and she plied him with booze to change his mind. She invited Mowat to join her at the front of the class, and the two of them sat on the edge of my desk like two jawing cowhands perched on a corral fence overlooking the herd. After settling Mowat in with chit-chat about his recent travels, she looked over at me with a glint in her eye, then asked her uncle Farley, one of the country's literary icons, to tell her the story of Sir John Franklin and his lost expedition. I'd never mentioned my interest in Franklin to her. She'd obviously pumped Will for information about me. The thrill of her attention was turning me to Jell-O.

Mowat described Franklin's final expedition as the nineteenth-century equivalent of an Apollo moon mission. The British Admiralty had already figured out that any shortcut to the Orient through the frozen channels of the Arctic would be too treacherous to have commercial value. It invested so heavily in Franklin's attempt simply because of national pride. Britain wanted to demonstrate its scientific superiority to the world just as twentieth-century America did when it planted its flag on the lunar surface.

"So following your analogy, that would make Franklin an astronaut," Helen interrupted. "Wasn't he a bit too old and podgy?"

"Like me, you mean?" Mowat said.

The class cracked up.

"All right," he admitted. "He wasn't exactly the Admiralty's first choice. But he was the most eager to go."

"Why?" she asked. "I mean, surely taking a rat-infested wooden ship into the coldest place on earth couldn't have been his idea of fun."

"His wife put him up to it," Mowat replied with a mischievous grin. He was trying to get a rise out of Helen, I could tell.

Helen realized it too, but she wasn't about to let a sexist remark like that go unchallenged. "Oh, I see. Blame it on the wife," she said.

"Don't you believe there are women in this world who can get a man to do almost anything?" The irony was dripping from his voice.

For the remainder of the class, Helen gave as good as she got. When Mowat said that Franklin had relied too heavily on the Royal Navy's misleading charts, and that he'd failed to learn from the Inuit who had lived in the Arctic for thousands of years, Helen cited it as historic proof that men would sooner die than ask a local for directions. Later, Mowat described how Lady Franklin shamed the Admiralty, the emperor of Russia, and the president of the United States into helping her learn the fate of her husband, then subverted history so that Sir John was unjustifiably praised as the hero who'd discovered the Northwest Passage. Helen called it a refreshing change that for once it wasn't a man who'd rewritten history. She told Mowat that he of all people should appreciate the importance of never letting the facts get in the way of a good story.

After the bell, Helen drifted to the back of the classroom, where I was standing, and watched Mowat sign autographs for a clutch of students. She sat on a vacated student desk, her long legs dangling over the edge. "What do you suppose the attraction was?" she asked me.

"Attraction?"

"John Franklin and Lady Jane," she said. "She had her pick of suitors. Why choose such a lump of a man?"

"You make him sound like the Pillsbury Doughboy," I said.

"I'm sorry. I forgot he was your hero," she said, titillating me with her teasing. I realized I was being evaluated, and not just for my views on history.

"Lady Jane wasn't all sweetness and light, you know," I said.

"Meaning?"

"I suspect that Franklin was one of the few men who found her bossiness endearing," I said.

She folded her arms in a parody of indignation. "Do you have a problem with bossy women?"

"I'm beginning to sense I don't have much chance of winning this argument."

"You've got that right," she said.

Mowat signed his last autograph. He peered over at us with the curiosity of a field biologist observing the courtship behaviour of two wolves on the tundra.

"The two of you seem quite pleased with yourselves," he said.

Helen retrieved his parka from a nearby chair. "You managed to survive unscathed, I see," she said to him dryly.

Mowat grunted as he let her help him on with his coat. "I should write a sequel. *Ordeal by Helen.*" Despite his grumbling, I could see that the whole experience had put a spring in his step. Beneath his gruff whiskers, he plainly wore the exhilaration of a man who'd faced his fear and prevailed.

"You were great," I told him. "The kids will never forget this day. Neither will I." In a distracted sort of way, I knew this was one of those golden experiences that I might never capture again in my teaching career. But at that moment, I was more concerned with asking Helen to see me again without coming across as a tongue-tied geek.

I escorted them out to the parking lot. A fine dusting of snow had settled on Helen's car, and I helped her brush it off. The cold made me feel like a snotty-faced boy on a toboggan run. Mowat quietly handed me a Kleenex so I wouldn't have to wipe my nose with the back of my hand in front of Helen.

"Thanks," I whispered.

Helen was leaning across the hood, scraping away a stubborn patch of ice on the windshield with one leg extended like a ballerina. She left a wispy imprint where her breasts had gently brushed against the powdery snow.

Mowat noticed my spellbound gaze. "Don't get your hopes up," he said under his breath. It was offered to me as sage advice. He gave me a fatherly pat on the shoulder. "I've seen many unfortunate souls brave these waters before you."

My cheeks flushed despite the cold. I felt strangely betrayed. I'd almost begun to see myself as Mowat's comrade, a confidant, a fellow member of Helen's inner circle. But as they drove out of the ice-rutted parking lot and I waved goodbye, having lost my nerve to ask Helen out, I sensed I'd been put back in my place, no matter how kindly.

Chapter 5

"You should really let me drive," Marla says.

The sun is a pale silvery smudge just above the horizon ahead of us. Everything outside is shades of grey—the other cars encrusted with road salt, the heavy sky. The windshield wipers pound furiously in a vain attempt to clear the thick spray thrown up by the unending parade of trucks churning along in the slow lane. I crane my neck, straining to make out the lane markers ahead, tugging on the steering wheel when the shadow of the concrete median suddenly presses in on my left side from out of the dirty mist. I estimate that we're almost to Woodstock, about a half hour out of London on a good day, but I have no way of knowing for sure. All the normal landmarks are indiscernible, the road signs caked with snow.

"There's a service centre somewhere around here," she says. "We could switch there."

We close in on the tail lights of another car in the fast lane. Out of the corner of my eye, I notice Marla's foot instinctively pressing down on an imaginary passenger-side brake. I slide into the middle lane, in front of a flatbed truck that's carrying stacks of automobile chassis, and pass the car on the right.

"Is my driving making you nervous, by any chance?" I ask.

"Now that you mention it . . ." she says.

"Traffic in Toronto's going to be a mess," I say. "I want to make up time while I can."

Through a momentary parting in the mist, we see a minivan in the ditch alongside the westbound lanes. Its shell is battered and scratched, the windshield spider-cracked, telling me it went for a roll before landing back on its wheels. At least an hour's worth of snow has settled on the wreckage. The driver's door yawns open. There's no one inside. Passing cars crawl by like mourners viewing the casket at a funeral home.

Marla stares at me once the accident's behind us. I sigh and ease my foot off the accelerator.

"All right," I say. "I'll slow down."

"There's an exit sign coming up," she says.

"I'm fine," I insist.

"Well, I need to pee."

I silently curse women and their microscopic bladders. In contrast, I pretend to be a camel, drinking only the occasional cup of coffee and fossilizing my kidneys in the process.

I pull off at the next service centre behind an empty garbage truck. Snagged remnants of grocery bags, junk mail, and diaper liners wave at us through the truck's thick wire mesh. The driver's probably dumped his load in a Michigan landfill and is headed back to Toronto for a refill. He pulls onto the exit ramp's shoulder and rumbles to a halt behind a long line of rigs. He's not the only trucker who's pulled off the highway because of the weather. Fortunately, the parking lot reserved for cars is only half full.

The floor mats inside the entrance to the service centre are so thick with slush that the doors won't close properly. Marla makes a beeline for the washroom while I line up at the Tim Hortons counter behind a heavy-set trucker in a Detroit Tigers ball cap and an insulated vest. He smells of stale cigarettes and wet woollen socks. When it's finally my turn to step up to the counter, I order a couple of large coffees, along with a box of assorted Timbits. By this time Marla's done her business, and she waves to me from a table she's laid claim to.

I give her one of the coffees. "I thought we'd drink these on the road," I say.

She stays rooted to her seat and holds out her hand, palm up. "The keys," she says.

"I've got my caffeine," I say. "I'm fine."

Her hand remains extended.

"I'll drive slower," I tell her. "All right?"

She snorts. "Did you even sleep last night?"

"Did you?"

A man with stubby fingers and paint-spattered coveralls eyes us with sullen curiosity from the next table. His hair is speckled with plaster dust. The shadow of his beard looks permanent, as if he started shaving when he was five. He probably thinks Marla and I are a married couple having a fight. I'm tempted to tell him to mind his own business.

"The snow's getting heavier," she says.

"I've driven in worse," I reply.

She pulls an orange out of her knapsack and starts peeling it. "Sit down," she says, no longer bothering to conceal how thin I've worn her patience.

I plunk myself in the chair across from her in exasperation. "Does Avery do this kind of thing often?"

She keeps peeling, ignoring my question.

"I'm only asking because you seem awfully calm about the whole thing," I say. "Like you're an old hand at this."

"Have an orange slice," she says.

"Tell me about him," I say. "We've never actually met, he and I. Unless you count last week, when he was sitting in the back of a police cruiser."

She sets the orange down and scorches me with a dirty look.

"I'm sorry," I say. "Am I being a little too inquisitive? How impolite of me. Must be because he's run off with my daughter."

She slowly wipes her fingers with a paper napkin. I can see her jaw muscles twitching. "I'm as concerned about them as you are," she says.

"That's good to hear," I tell her, getting back to my feet. "Because I'm heading back out to the car."

As I stand, the blood drains from my head, causing the room to tilt and the babbling voices around me to suck into the distance. Marla's face slips out of focus. I feel submerged, as if I'm staring up at her from the bottom of a pool of water.

"Are you okay?" I hear her ask from a million miles away, her voice both annoyed and concerned.

I turn towards the exit, trying to mask my disorientation, spilling part of my coffee on the floor in the process. My internal compass is still spinning as I stagger through the doors into the teeth of an Arctic wind. I don't look back to see whether Marla is following me.

The snow covering the parking lot is the consistency of brown sugar blended with butter. My shoes can't get a firm hold. I wade into the morass, searching for the familiar outline of my car under the new layer of snow, unable to remember where I parked it. I trip over a curb obscured by the drifts and topple into the path of an SUV that's searching for a parking spot.

Marla's bony fingers grab me by the bicep. She yanks me back to my feet while staring down the driver of the SUV. "The car's the other way," she says.

My cup of coffee is now a warm brown splat in the snow. My ears are stinging from the wind. Snow is melting inside my shoes. "They should spread salt in this parking lot," I mutter.

I let her lead me to the car like I'm a wayward child. I start to shiver uncontrollably. She wrests the car keys from my hand and helps me in the passenger side.

"Here," she says, taking off her scarf and wrapping it around my neck. It's one of those long crocheted jobs with tassels on the ends. I feel like I'm in drag.

"It doesn't go with my outfit," I say. Its warmth feels good against my cheek.

She starts the engine and runs the heater full blast. My shuddering subsides to an occasional spasm. Marla adjusts the seat and rear-view mirror so she can drive.

"You know," I say, "this could be construed as a carjacking."

"If it were a carjacking, I'd have left you in a snowbank." She gets out and grabs the brush and ice scraper from the back seat, casting a warning glance my way as she does. "Don't get any ideas about slipping behind the driver's seat while I'm out there."

She slams the door shut and begins cleaning snow off the windshield. I lean back and close my eyes—only for a minute, I tell myself. The sound of chipping ice blends into a gauzy background of white noise. As sleep rushes in to ambush me, the book-jacket picture of Jack Livingston comes alive in my head. I see him sitting with Helen at our old dining-room table, pleasantly pissed, seducing her right in front of me with tales of his randy adventures in Europe. And then I look again and realize that it's not Helen he's talking to but Severn.

Chapter 6

I returned to the bookshop on Richmond Street the Saturday after Farley Mowat's visit to my history class. I was hoping to find Helen behind the counter, but no such luck. A man who could have passed for the sinister schoolmaster in a Dickens novel was presiding over the till. His greying beetle brows cast a perpetual shadow over his eyes. He seemed to be all bone and sinew, angular in appearance and acute in demeanour. I learned a little later that he was Helen's father, Walter Donnelly, the man whose name was so meticulously painted in the bottom corner of the storefront window, above the word "Proprietor."

I'd just bought Helen a bouquet of spring flowers, a thank-you for working her charms on Uncle Farley. Walter peered over his half-lens glasses at me as I entered. It was a look designed to turn a man to stone. I know now that it's an instinct all fathers possess: the ability to smell out men who intend to pursue their daughters. Not that the bouquet didn't flag me as a pretty obvious threat. I momentarily considered turning tail and heading back out to the street, but I elected instead to drift casually to the shelves in the back and pretend I was just another weekend shopper passing through on his way to meet his sweetie at a café up the block.

It was one of those quirky little shops with uneven wooden floors and a pressed-tin ceiling. A calligraphy sign warned "Watch Your Step" where more than a few patrons had likely failed to do so. As I peeked around the bookcase that held the titles on philosophy, art, and architecture, I saw a faded floral-print curtain drawn across the opening to a closet that contained a narrow set of stairs. They led sharply upward, almost like a ladder. It looked like a portal to the Land of Narnia.

Will was giving a woman in a red vinyl raincoat who'd picked up *Don Quixote* an unsolicited lesson on the life of its author. After working the full measure of his charm and convincing her to add *The Canterbury Tales* to her purchases, he made his way over to me.

"Let me guess," he said, seeing the flowers. "For Helen."

"I wanted to thank her for coercing Farley," I said.

"Ah. Yes, well . . ."

"Is she around?" I asked, trying not to show my nerves.

Will gestured towards the ceiling. "She's in her writing garret."

"I'm sorry?"

"The little room upstairs," he explained. "Where once she plumbed the depths of her creative soul. Not that she's been using it for literary pursuits lately."

As if on cue, I heard the sound of footsteps from inside the closet. Surprisingly heavy steps. A man with a precisely clipped beard and shiny pate emerged from behind the curtain. I immediately sensed that he fancied himself a Sean Connery clone. His face was flushed, but somehow I doubted that was simply from climbing down the stairs. He leaned back into the closet and looked up the staircase.

"Well, are you coming?" he called.

In an imitation of gallantry, he held back the curtain and offered his hand to Helen as she descended the stairs. She paused on the last step to polish the top of his head with her sleeve.

"I can see myself," she exclaimed, pretending to admire her

reflection. "Except that the lumps on your head make my face look fat."

"Very funny," the man said, accepting the dig with a lover's forbearance.

"Hello, Helen," I say.

Her smile snagged when she saw me standing there with the bouquet. She quickly recovered her grace, though, sliding her hand down her middle-aged boyfriend's arm before gliding towards me.

"I just wanted to thank you," I said. The flowers were an embarrassment to me now, a badge of gullibility.

"How sweet," she said, seeing the hurt in my eyes but choosing not to acknowledge it to spare me further humiliation. I felt like a peevish first-grader pining for the attentions of his teacher.

She made her balding Romeo wait while she found a vase for the flowers. He squinted at me, sizing me up, wondering just what I was thanking Helen for. I could tell that he didn't appreciate my interruption. He picked out a book from a nearby shelf and started flipping through it to show me I wasn't worth his interest any more.

When Helen returned, she thanked me again for the flowers and apologized for not being able to stay to chat. I tried to sound magnanimous, saying I understood. She took her boyfriend by the arm and said goodbye, tossing me one last rueful glance as she stepped to the front of the shop.

Will had apparently seen my crushed look on the faces of other men before. "He's a biology prof at Western," he explained. "Divorced and fighting a mid-life crisis."

"That's his sports car parked out front, I take it."

Will nodded. "He's lasted longer than most. This is his second week."

Helen slid behind the front counter and gave her father a goodbye peck on the cheek. Walter's scowl didn't soften. His Medusa gaze bore down on Helen's middle-aged beau.

"Why do you suppose daughters so enjoy tormenting their fathers?" Will asked me.

Helen was rubbing up against her biology prof like a purring kitten now, trying to convince him to let her drive his car. I could tell it was eating away at Walter to watch her fondle a man who was almost as old as he was. On the way out the door, Helen rooted in her boyfriend's pants pockets for the car keys. Old baldy looked annoyed, but I knew her groping was probably giving him a hard-on.

Will glanced at his watch. "And so ends Helen's workday," he said wryly. "Early as usual." He picked up the book that her boyfriend had tossed on a display table and returned it to its proper place. His fingers trailed gently along the covers of the other books on the shelf. "Someday all this is supposed to be hers. Walter wants to pass the shop to another Donnelly, and she's all he has." A crooked smile crinkled his lips. "I doubt she knows even half of what we have on the shelves."

I realized then that we were both failed suitors—in my case for Helen's affection, in Will's case for Walter's favour. His was a hopeless love for books, mine for an errant woman.

"She's not worth it, Irving."

Will excused himself to serve a customer perusing the coffee-table books. I lingered at the back of the shop, wanting to make sure that Helen and her date had driven off before I stepped outside. I found myself staring at the titles in the self-help section: *Fifty Ways to Find Your Lover*, *Beyond Sergeant Pepper*, *Checking Out of Heartbreak Hotel*. Pithy, tuneful advice for losers like me.

I spent that night marking tests at my garage-sale kitchen table, a bag of Oreo cookies at my side. To get through such mind-numbing jobs, I generally bribed myself with petty rewards, including the carrot of slumping in front of the TV once I was done to watch "Hockey Night in Canada." At the rate I was going, I'd be lucky to catch the late game from the West Coast. I kept picturing Helen upstairs in her bohemian garret, exchanging bodily fluids with her overage lover.

My own career as a lover had been short and unspectacular. The only woman I'd ever taken to bed had been a year ahead of me in teachers' college. When I met her, I knew she was one of those teachers boys would have wet dreams about, not because she was gorgeous—although she did have a certain country-girl appeal to her, like Mary Ann in "Gilligan's Island"—but because she was the type of woman who couldn't help taking pity on stray dogs and helpless little boys. She first spotted me sitting by myself at an orientation week party and naturally took me under her wing. From there, we started meeting each other for meals in the residence cafeterias, then hanging out in her room at the women's dorm. Eventually, I started staying overnight, slipping out early in the morning, when we figured the proctor wasn't looking. As a lover she was patient with my clumsy efforts, guiding me where I needed to go in a land I had knowledge of only from books. We became inseparable. Soon, it became too comfortable for me, like being smothered in a warm blanket. I started looking for excuses not to see her. Sensing my distance, she called me at all hours, imploring me to tell her why. Her neediness began to embarrass me. By the time I left for my out-of-town practicum, I'd entirely turned my back on her. I knew I was being an asshole, spurning the very girl who'd taken me in, but I didn't have a vocabulary for graceful exits. I let callousness be my messenger.

I became accustomed to celibacy after that, as I possessed neither the charm nor the machismo to strike up conversations with women in bars or supermarket lineups. Not to say that I didn't develop infatuations, and even try to act on them in my own shy and inept way. But for whatever reason, I never got further than a bashful kiss goodnight at the door and a decided lack of response to the awkward little messages I left on various answering machines, asking for another date. I formulated theories to explain my stunning lack of success. One was that when my dates found out I was a teacher, they immediately remembered some anal grammarian haranguing them in grade school and worried that I'd parse every sentence they uttered. That certainly would have explained why our conversations tended to peter out so early in the evening. Another theory was that they were unnerved by how intently I listened to them when they talked about themselves—a rather counterintuitive hypothesis, considering the number of inattentive men they had to have suffered through before me. They distrusted the motives for my interest, it seemed. Perhaps I came off as too eager to unlock their secrets, or, worse yet, unctuous. I'm afraid that back then, when I first started as a teacher, I had a tendency to use the same overly earnest tone on everyone, both students and women I was trying to get in the sack. Whatever the true explanation for my failures, the only "action" I'd been able to count on since teachers' college was the occasional jack-off in the shower.

And so, on Saturday night I sat in my basement apartment marking papers as the Western students upstairs stumbled out to the pubs. I dropped my marking pen in disgust and pushed myself away from the kitchen table. My gloomy bachelor pad wasn't big enough for pacing. I sat taking stock of my worldly possessions: a lumpy couch, a Salvation Army floor lamp, a discount microwave, and a thirteen-inch TV perched on an overturned milk crate. My postage-stamp bedroom was hardly big enough to hold my bed. My only solace came from the hundreds of books that lined my walls, crammed onto makeshift plywood-and-cinderblock shelves that rose precariously to the ceiling.

I got up and crossed the room in two steps, scanning the shelves for something to transport me someplace else. I pulled out my atlas of discovery maps of the New World and began leafing through it, careful not to further loosen the worn pages from the binding. The upper corner of a Venetian chart from 1556 showed a large blank space marked *"Parte Incognita"* to denote all the undiscovered lands west of what was then New France. I realized that I'd lived much of my life in that blank space.

I thought of Helen looking back at me as she left the shop with her biology professor. For a split second, I'd wondered whether she was waiting to see if I'd come after her, attempt to rescue her from the spectacle she was making simply to annoy her father. The moment had been so fleeting that in hindsight I couldn't even be sure it had actually happened. Just the same, I hung on to the thought, embroidering it until I was offering to buy them both a drink at a bar across the street, then ducking out with Helen when her balding beau was called to the washroom by his aging prostate.

I considered making some popcorn, maybe even renting a movie—something in black-and-white, where the hero overcomes all odds to save the girl from the dastardly, fifty-something villain. But I decided that all the good videos would probably have been taken out already, and besides, I'd also have to rent a VCR and spend half the night trying to figure out how to hook it up.

As I put the atlas back, I spotted my vintage nineteenth-century bubble sextant sitting on the top shelf. I took it down and turned it over in my hands. A clump of dried mud clung to the arc. I believed in living history, in getting kids to feel things with their own hands. That's why I didn't mind letting them use my antique, to understand for themselves what it was like for the early explorers who ventured into those blank spaces on the map. I showed my students how to take a reading from the sun and explained what it told them about where they were. Franklin would have had a sextant like mine, I told them, as he tried to find the passage through the ice-clogged channels of the Arctic archipelago.

It was easy for us to second-guess men like Franklin, with all that we knew now from history. Sitting in our warm homes and classrooms, none of us could possibly understand the privations he and his crew endured, the miserable deaths they suffered for the sake of discovery. We criticized him for his arrogance, but in doing so, we proved our own conceit.

I imagined Franklin's two ships, the *Erebus* and the *Terror*, creeping through the Arctic fog, drawn forward as if a siren was promising them a path to the Beaufort Sea. I thought of all the men who'd followed, searching the vast unknown for some clue to Franklin's fate, shamed and inspired by the unwavering devotion of his wife, each adding his own lines to the maps of the time. It wasn't until more than fifty years later—long after the cairn containing confirmation of Franklin's death was discovered—that a Norwegian named Amundsen finally sailed through the elusive passage. He was the same man who later would beat Scott to the South Pole. But rather than belittle Franklin's efforts, Amundsen cited the British explorer as a boyhood hero, his inspiration, and his guide.

And then it became clear to me. I saw the path to reach Helen.

Chapter 7

I don't realize that I've fallen asleep until I open my eyes and see that we're not on the highway any more. Through my salt-sprayed window, I make out what looks like the geodesic sphere of Ontario Place. As I widen my gaze, I notice that the snow has eased off for the moment, but the clouds are still hanging low and heavy, obscuring the observation deck of the CN Tower ahead.

My neck has a kink in it the size of a grapefruit. "Jesus," I say, tasting the sour, milky residue of sleep in my mouth. "How long have I been out?"

Marla's grip tightens on the steering wheel as the car passes through a fresh drift of snow that's blown across the road. "Your throat must be sore from all that snoring," she says, her eyes fixed firmly on the car ahead of us.

I finish taking my bearings, ignoring her complaint. Just ahead I see Exhibition Place's giant wind turbine, looking like a forlorn propeller for a gargantuan plane that someone had the good sense not to complete. "Lakeshore Boulevard?" I ask.

"The Gardiner was solid," she says. "This'll get us there faster."

I survey the frozen surface of Lake Ontario. We're not far from our destination now, I realize. Despite all my urgency, I'm woefully unprepared for the moment when I see Severn again. I have no idea what I'm going to say to her, particularly if she's come to meet up with Livingston, as I'm almost certain she has. Now I regret not taking the copy of *Northwest Passage* that Will offered me. I can only imagine what Severn saw in the story—people and events too familiar to be the invention of a stranger; support for suspicions she'd begun to harbour about the official version of our little family's past. I feel as if I'm about to go into the most important final exam of my life without ever having read the text for the course.

"Have you tried calling the condo lately?" I ask, pushing aside my trepidation.

"I've been a little busy," she says testily.

I pull my cellphone out of my jacket pocket. "What's the number?"

Her lips crinkle.

"What?" I say.

"I'll call when the driving's not so bad," she says.

"That's not going to happen until you park the car." I read the pinched lines on her face. "You don't want me talking to Avery, do you?"

She doesn't answer.

"Afraid of what I might say to him?" I say.

She takes her eyes off the road just long enough to give me a dry, what-do-*you*-think look.

"I work with kids his age every day," I tell her. "You think I can't control myself just because he spent the night with my daughter?"

Marla kneads the steering wheel. "You make it sound like he kidnapped Severn," she says sharply. "Like she didn't have a choice."

"What are you saying? You think this was *her* idea?"

She pierces me with a penetrating stare. "I think you know it was."

I narrow my eyes, trying to decide whether she's simply pushing back or knows more about Severn than I've imagined. Before I can make up my mind, her arms go rigid. She slams on the brakes. I grab the dashboard for dear life as I feel the car fishtail.

"Jesus Christ!" I exclaim.

She fights with the steering wheel. I feel my seat belt digging into my shoulder. My head pops back as the car behind us kisses our bumper. I brace myself, waiting for the next impact, but it doesn't come. We're stopped now, aimed askew, straddling two lanes. A wisp of snow blows across the hood. I look over at Marla. Her hands are shaking.

"What was it?" I ask. "A patch of ice?" My impatience is bubbling at the surface. I'm thinking of the police, tow trucks, all the time we'll waste here while Severn becomes increasingly lost to me.

Her eyes are round with panic. "Something ran out," she says, her lips continuing to move, but her voice failing.

"What?"

"I . . . I don't know," she says, gulping air like a goldfish.

I unbuckle myself in disgust and get out of the car, stepping ankle-deep into the slush. It's a cab that's rear-ended us; the driver glaring at me. He has to wait for the traffic to clear before he can open his door and begin his cries of bloody murder. In the meantime, I scan the pavement for signs of roadkill—a dog, a cat, a squirrel—but see nothing, just a steady progression of annoyed drivers edging their way around our accident.

"You crazy?" yells the cabbie, now out of his vehicle. "Why you stop in the middle of nowhere?" He has a Middle Eastern accent. He must hate winter driving even more than I do, I realize.

"Something ran out in the road," I say, despite having no evidence to support my claim.

"What ran out in road?" he says, waving his arms. "Nothing ran out in road."

I examine our respective bumpers. "Doesn't look too bad," I say, trying to cut a quick deal. "Maybe we don't need to get our insurance companies involved."

He's still angry, but I can tell he'd just as soon not wait for the police or see his premiums go up. "Papers," he says with a modicum of compromise. "Show me your papers."

"They're just in the car," I say, sensing that I may be able to talk my way out of this mess after all. "I'll get them for you."

He follows me, perhaps worried that I'll try to make a break for it. I open the passenger door and reach for the glovebox. Marla is gasping for air now, her hands splayed across the dashboard.

"Are you okay?" I ask her, knowing full well that she's not. There's a panic in her eyes that I recognize. I last saw it in Helen in the weeks before she died.

The cabbie sees it too. "Hey, lady, I not hit your car so hard," he says, suddenly worried that a case for personal injury is about to be made against him.

"Just try to take a deep breath," I tell her.

It's no good. Her translucent complexion is turning an even more ghostly shade of white.

I realize this has nothing to do with our trivial collision.

I turn to the cabbie. "Where's the nearest hospital?"

"You follow," he says, heading back to his taxi. "I take you there."

As I help Marla around to the passenger side, I wonder whether I should have asked him to call an ambulance instead. She grips my arm like a vice, her lungs straining, fear still floating in her eyes. At one point, she leans against me heavily, and I'm afraid she's about to pass out, but then she recovers. The cabbie's already edging back into traffic by the time I get her strapped in, so I scramble around to the driver's side and slide behind the wheel, not even bothering to adjust the mirrors.

Chapter 8

If my plan to reach Helen was to succeed, I knew I'd need help. I walked by the bookshop several times after school the following week, casting nonchalant looks through the window as I passed, before finally entering one snowy day when I was reasonably certain that Will was looking after the place on his own. He greeted me with his customary conviviality, rubbing his hands at the prospect of challenging me to another round of historical trivia. Between customers, we debated Peary's questionable claim of being the first explorer to reach the North Pole. We each offered competing theories on how the ancient Egyptians could have built the pyramids. Then, once I thought he was sufficiently softened up, I made my pitch. At first, I could see that he thought I was pulling his leg. But when I didn't show signs of getting to any kind of punchline, he looked at me as if I were some kind of amiable lunatic.

"You're serious," he said.

"It'll be a hook to get more kids into your shop," I said. "And their parents."

"You think you'd be that much of a draw?" he said sceptically.

"I did it a couple of times in my history class. It was a big hit."

I saw that he wasn't convinced. "Walter's the one to talk to about this kind of thing," he said. "It's his shop."

"I was hoping you'd talk to him for me."

Will chuckled. "Really."

"The costume's the thing that catches people's attention first." I pulled a photo of myself in full regalia from the pocket of my parka to show him. "I worked two summers in Penetanguishene."

"What? At the loony bin there?"

"There's a historic site just across the road. An old British out-post."

"Walter's not much for razzle-dazzle," he said. "Maybe you haven't figured that out yet."

I jabbed the counter emphatically with my finger. "Give me a chance. I swear that I can get a shop full of kids so turned on by history that they'll want to know what's in at least a dozen of the books you've got languishing on your shelves back there."

Will smirked. "And you'd get what out of this?"

"Professional satisfaction."

"Oh, I see," he said dubiously. "Of course, the fact that Helen usually works on Saturdays would have nothing to do with it."

"We can help each other out here, Will."

"I'm sorry. I don't quite see what the payoff is for me."

"You make the proposal to Walter. You get the credit for bringing more business to the shop. He begins to recognize your true potential."

He sucked the stem of his reading glasses, cautiously reassess-ing me. He never would have taken me for a hustler until then. "And if it bombs?"

"It won't bomb," I said. "You have my word."

Even though I'd known Will for only a short time, I'd already figured out that he and I were alike in one very important respect: we both wanted to think the best of people.

"We can't pay you," he said.

"Understood," I said, beaming like an idiot.

If I'd learned anything from studying the exploits of the Europeans who'd mapped the New World — and Franklin's expedition, in particular — it was that the quickest way to an objective was not always a straight line. I had therefore decided that my initial efforts to win over Helen would be indirect but deliberate. In gaining Will's trust, I'd secured an important guide for my personal little expedition, someone who I hoped knew better than I how to negotiate the perilous waters that awaited me on the first leg of my journey. In fact, he proved himself a more enthusiastic ally than I could have imagined. Once he wore down Walter's resistance to my proposal, Will took the further step of shamelessly promoting my first appearance, reasoning, quite rightly, that our fortunes were now tied together.

"What do you think?" he asked, catching me in the school parking lot on my way home one day, two weeks before I was scheduled to make my first appearance. He passed me a promotional flyer that he'd made up and, he told me, already plastered all over town.

Exclusive to Donnelly's Books
Irving Cruickshank brings history's
heavyweights and lesser lights to life!
10:00–11:00 a.m., every second Saturday of the
month starting in April

*"Irving's in a class all his own. He'll take you
places you've never been."* —Farley Mowat

"It has punch, don't you think?" he said, admiring it over my shoulder as if it were some Impressionist masterpiece. "I especially like the testimonial."

"Did Mowat actually say that about me?" I asked nervously.

"More or less," he said, unconcerned. "You *are* a teacher, so being in a class all your own is hardly a stretch. And you did convince him to go to your school, a place he'd never been."

I didn't bother to remind him that it was Helen who actually got him there. I was more concerned that some indignant local friend of Mowat's would tear down one of the flyers and mail the fraudulent endorsement to him.

"Don't you think this is going a little overboard?" I asked.

"Hey, you're the one who talked me into this," he said, his hands on his hips. "Don't tell me you're getting stage fright."

I took a deep breath to steady my nerves. I couldn't afford to lose him now, not when I was so close to my objective. "You've done a great job," I said placatingly. "I suppose I'll just have to make sure I live up to the billing."

My early pangs of anxiety snowballed into unmitigated panic when, just two days before my appearance, the costume that I'd been counting on from my old boss in Penetang still hadn't arrived. Three desperate phone calls and twenty-four hours later, it finally came, complete with a split in the breeches that some fat-assed student had made the previous summer. And so I spent the night before my grand opening relying on my non-existent sewing skills to mend the damage and thus save me from making a public spectacle of myself.

Fortunately, when the big morning finally did arrive, my nerves eased considerably the instant I donned the uniform. I cut an impressive, if somewhat anachronistic, figure in my bathroom mirror, looking every bit the ambitious nineteenth-century Royal Navy lieutenant in my blue coat, brass buttons, and tall, arched hat. This was a role I'd played many times before, one I could wrap myself in. I was yesterday's man and proud of it.

I provoked many a stare as I ambled up Richmond Street that warm April morning. The last dregs of snow were gone; the grass in the park was reasserting its greenness after a long winter. I passed a florist who was doing a brisk business in tulips, daffodils, and Easter lilies. I tipped my hat to the patrons gawking at me as I went.

The bookshop was bustling with customers when I entered, no

doubt a result of Will's shameless publicity. Walter was standing on a wooden stepstool, retrieving a volume of Byron from a high shelf for a matronly looking woman who reminded me of my language arts teacher from grade five. His resting scowl slipped when he saw me, a fleeting, somewhat involuntary look of surprise taking its place. Although I was sure that Will had described the details of my proposed escapade, Walter clearly hadn't anticipated the impact my uniform would have.

I doffed my hat and tucked it under my arm. "Greetings, sir," I said to him, full of the audacity that comes from wearing such an outlandish yet imposing uniform. "Are you the proprietor of this establishment?" I was playing to the patrons, whose initial shock was now giving way to nervous smiles and tittering. Children whispered to their parents, asking them who the strange man in the blue coattails, short pants, and white stockings was.

For a moment, I thought Walter would refuse to play along. I'd heard through Will that his response to my Saturday morning show and tell had been lukewarm at best.

"We don't much take to sailors here," he said to me, his scowl reaffixed.

"I am no mere deckhand, sir," I said, recognizing that there was no turning back now. "My name is Bayfield, Henry. Lieutenant of His Majesty's Royal Navy. I am embarking on a hydrographic survey of the Great Lakes and am in need of able seamen to assist me."

"There's a tavern up the road," Walter said. "Maybe you'd have better luck there." There was a hint of mischief in his growl. He was enjoying the verbal sparring, I could tell.

"Why do you attempt to deceive me, sir?" I said, approaching a group of giggling primary-schoolers. "This shop is filled with sailors." I crouched down and smiled at a girl in pigtails. "Wouldn't you like to help me?" I asked her. She looked at me saucer-eyed, then glanced up at her mom for guidance. Mom nodded that it was okay. I wasn't a crazy man, just a silly one.

Within a minute, I'd assembled my recruits, a gaggle of children ranging in age from five to twelve. Some of the older kids in the crowd hung back, intrigued but not wanting to seem too eager. People passing by the store stopped and peered in through the front window, wondering what all the fuss was about. Some wandered in to investigate. Will squeezed his way through the throng and began ushering the newcomers in, making sure that younger children got a good view of the action. He gave me a thumbs-up as he nudged a nine-year-old forward to join my party of conscripts. Walter stood by the cash register, arms crossed, a bristly eyebrow cocked in grudging appreciation.

I explained to my recruits that the Royal Navy needed to have accurate charts of the eastern shoreline of Lake Huron in order to defend Upper Canada from the Americans, who only six years earlier had attempted to invade during the War of 1812. Wooden British warships could offer no defence if they wrecked against unseen jagged rocks and sank to the bottom of the lake. After verifying that there were no Yankee spies among my cadets, I let them each handle my surveying instruments and showed them early charts of the coastline we'd been charged to survey. I told them that I was confident they were all up to the task, that my previous crew had done quite well until they'd contracted scurvy and their teeth had turned black, and that if our provisions went bad (as they'd been known to do) we could always catch crows and gulls for food.

I used all the gimmicks from my days in Penetang to get onlookers involved. I mistook one of my recruits' fathers for a deserter from my old crew (I said I could spot his gap-toothed grin a mile away) and ordered his wife to hold him in custody. I saluted to a timid young boy hovering off to the side, pretending he was my mentor, Captain William FitzWilliam Owen, come to assess my progress and inspect my new crew. And when my hour was done, I cajoled those assembled, who were by then backed up to the front door of the tiny shop, to join me in a stirring rendition of "God Save the King."

Will clapped me on the back after I'd said farewell to my last recruit. "Inspired," he said.

Walter called to Will from the front counter, gesturing with a stern nod for him to take care of the customers who'd lingered to peruse the shelves.

"Who are you planning to do next month?" Will asked.

"I was thinking Galileo," I said. "Although my astronomy's a little rusty."

"Maybe you could get Walter to play the Grand Inquisitor," he said with a sly grin. He excused himself and began working his charms on some nearby browsers.

Helen was nowhere to be seen. Her red head wouldn't have been tough to spot, since she would have been among the tallest people in the throng. I made my way through the remnants of the crowd and past the front counter, still hoping to find her. Like any good performer, I was careful to hide my disappointment. I nodded my appreciation to a woman who complimented me on my uniform, and I smiled at a tot who, much to his father's amusement, saluted me as I passed. As much as I'd tried to convince Will that the aim of my performance was to capture the imagination of a new generation of readers, I had to acknowledge now that I'd failed to realize my true goal. I felt like a charlatan, a haplessly infatuated geek masquerading as a historic man of substance. I couldn't wait to get home and change out of my costume. After one last futile survey of the shop, I headed out the door.

From the sidewalk, I took one last look at my miserable reflection in the shop window. The uniform had lost its magic. I was simply a milquetoast history teacher dressed in a clown's outfit. I removed the magnificent, preposterous hat. My hair stood out at riotous angles as if a bully had rubbed his fist over my head. As I continued to lament my pathetic mirror self, another figure— a woman's—stepped out of the jumbled background of Richmond Street traffic and consolidated itself beside mine in the window. It was Helen.

"Why so glum?" she asked. "That was quite a performance."

I turned to face her, caught between emotions. I quickly wiped the hang-dog look off my face, but I wasn't sure what to replace it with. "You saw it, then," I said.

"From the back of the shop," she said. "I ducked out the side door just now so I could congratulate you." She smiled at me like she'd just found a valuable antique at a garage sale. "I hope you know that you've done something quite extraordinary: you've actually lived up to Will's hype."

I felt transformed from a forgery into an icon. "It's the clothes," I said, forcing back a bashful grin.

"Oh, I definitely think it's more than that," she said.

I was momentarily tongue-tied. I fell back into Bayfield's persona, hoping to borrow some of his bravado. "Would you care to take a walk with me, my lady?" I asked, boldly offering her my arm. I held my breath as she curled her arm snugly around mine.

We crossed Richmond Street to Victoria Park. My impressive hat helped to offset Helen's height advantage as we strolled along the paths that criss-crossed among the tall maples and oversized evergreens that the city lit up as Christmas trees in December. Just beyond the bandshell, the spires of St. Peter's Basilica kept watch over us like a chaperone. The silence between us was electric.

"When I first saw the uniform, I thought you'd come as Franklin," she said eventually.

"Guess I'm superstitious," I said. "I didn't want to play a doomed explorer my first time out." I took a handkerchief out of my pocket and dusted off a park bench, inviting her with a flourish to take a seat. "Actually, Franklin passed through Penetanguishene around the time Bayfield was using it as a base of operations for surveying the Great Lakes. Perhaps they even met." I sensed that I was babbling but couldn't help myself. "Franklin was on his way north, on one of his earlier overland Arctic expeditions. It's where he heard that his first wife, Eleanor, had died of TB back in England."

"You can't stop teaching, can you?" Helen said archly. "Not even for a moment."

I shrugged apologetically. "It's what I do."

"Well," she said, reaching up and straightening my stock, "you may find that I'm a rather unruly student."

"Will mentioned something about your being a writer," I said, taking the opportunity to turn the conversation towards her.

For the first time since I'd met her, I caught a tinge of embarrassment in her cheeks. Her lips drew tight, then re-formed into a stiff smile. "I used to dabble," she said. "You can't really call yourself a writer until you've published something."

"You should keep at it," I told her. "You're a good storyteller. That day in front of my class, you and Farley were terrific together."

She looked at me warily, uncomfortable with my praise. "Unfortunately, none of the editors I've sent my work to agree with you."

"James Michener didn't publish his first book until he was forty," I said. "It went on to become the musical *South Pacific* and won two Pulitzer Prizes."

She leaned back and gave me a sober second look-over. "You just have all sorts of trivia at your fingertips, don't you?" she said dryly. "I can see why you and Will get along."

"You known him long?" I asked.

She stared at me oddly. It was as if she'd just caught on to a practical joke I was pulling at her expense, one that was evidently so clever that I'd failed even to let myself in on it.

"What?" I said.

"So *that's* what all this is about," she said, shaking her head, miffed with herself for not figuring out my angle sooner. "He's already spoken for, you know."

"What are you talking about?"

"Will," she said. "He's already got a boyfriend."

"Will?"

Finally, she read the desperate confusion on my face. "Ah," she said, recognizing her mistake. "You didn't invite me here to talk about Will, then."

"No," I said, distressed that my sexuality could be so much in doubt to her.

"You really were making a pass at me."

"Well," I said reluctantly, "if that's what you'd call it."

"Right," she said, smiling at me contritely. "Well, continue then."

I stared at her, completely flummoxed.

"You were actually doing quite well up until that bit about Will," she said, sucking back a smile.

I sat there slack-jawed, hopelessly thrown off stride.

"I'm sorry," she said. "I've spoiled the mood, haven't I?" She crossed her leg over mine. "There. Does that help?"

"You're not just having fun with me, are you?"

She patted me on the chest. "Is fun such a bad thing to have?"

There was something very comfortable about the weight of her thigh. With her big frame, she could have easily played girls' volleyball in high school, but I guessed that team sports weren't her thing. While I relied on a borrowed uniform to give me confidence, she drew hers from the fit of her own skin.

"No," I said, letting the back of my hand run along the generous length of her thigh. "I suppose not."

She pressed the tip of my nose with her finger as if to reward me for a correct answer.

"I just thought that maybe you were already spoken for," I said.

Her finger pressed less gently. "No man ever speaks for me."

"What about that biology professor of yours?"

"Least of all him. Besides, we recently parted company." I sensed this was a recent development that perhaps might be news to him. "I used to think that older men had their advantages. Refined tastes. Experience. Maturity. Now I realize that they're just wilful little boys with wrinkles and bad habits that are that much harder to break. The last thing I need is another pompous ass who reminds me of my father." She slid her leg off mine and sat back, carefully inspecting me. She adjusted the hang of my coat and brushed one of her loose red hairs off my shoulder. "You have an honest face. Very transparent. I like that."

"Meaning I'm a sucker," I said. "I know that. Anything else?"

"You're not afraid of bossy women," she said, her eyebrows wiggling.

"A sure sign of bravery or stupidity." I could see the freckles at the base of her neck through the opening in her blouse and let myself imagine how far down they went.

She snatched my hat from my head. "Men always complain about women who keep them in line," she said, holding it out of my reach. "But without them they'd be stumbling around making a mess of their lives."

"Is that so?" I said. "Please enlighten me."

She tried on the hat. Much to my chagrin, it fitted her rather well. "The wise man, recognizing his limitations, defers to a woman's judgment in all things that are of any true consequence," she explained. "But he shouldn't be a doormat. No woman respects spinelessness. Acquiescence without obsequiousness, that's very important."

"I thought women only talked like that in plays by Oscar Wilde," I said.

"My father runs a bookstore. What do you expect?"

"Give me my hat back," I said.

"Make me," she said, daring me to manhandle her.

The melee that ensued attracted much attention from the people waiting in line at the nearby souvlaki stand. Helen and I wrestled for the hat, rolling in the muddy grass beside the statue of a copper green soldier in full Boer War regalia. I pinned her beneath me with one hand while groping for the hat, which had landed in a patch of daffodils, with the other. She could have sent me rolling ass over teakettle with one buck of her hips, but she didn't, which allowed me to retrieve the hat and perch it back on my head.

"I hope you know I let you win," she said, red-faced and panting, a wicked grin on her face. Her skin was flushed down past the base of her neck.

Streaks of mud and grass stains covered my uniform. My old boss back in Penetang would kill me if the dry cleaner couldn't get them out. But it was worth it. Helen pulled me closer. I hoped my button-up pants weren't giving away the boner I was developing.

"If we were on board my ship, I could have you flogged for such insubordination," I told her suggestively.

"You wish," she said.

A little girl in the souvlaki lineup looked at me, bewildered. I recognized her as one of my recruits. She whispered something to her mother, probably asking why the nice man in the funny suit from the bookshop was sitting on top of that woman. Her mother looked scandalized and steered her away. I'd besmirched Bayfield's reputation, violated the code of conduct for children's entertainers, shown myself to be a dissolute man just like any other.

"I should go home," I said to Helen. "Get changed."

"Take me with you," she said.

I'd imagined this moment with Helen many times while lying awake at night, but arriving at it so abruptly tipped me off balance. All I could think of was my dingy little apartment, the unwashed dishes in the sink, the dirty clothes on the floor, and the bedsheets I hadn't bothered to change in months. I was woefully unprepared.

"Well?" she said impatiently.

I must admit, I was more than a little intimidated. As eager as I was for action, I realized that I had about as much chance of surviving unscathed a sexual encounter with Helen as a novice First World War pilot had of surviving the chaos of his first dogfight.

I helped her up and brushed a flake of dry mud from her cheek. "My car's just across the street," I told her, determined to let valour be my guide. I took her by the hand and led the way, restraining myself from breaking into a trot. Dirty sheets or not, I wasn't going to pass up this opportunity.

Chapter 9

Marla wheezes beside me as I drive, her palm pressed against the fogged-up passenger window. More than once, I've had to make sure she's still breathing. I follow the cab up University Avenue, a snow-swept boulevard with four lanes in either direction and statues presiding over the major intersections from a wide, ostentatious median. At Dundas Street I recognize a tall, rectangular, modernistic sculpture that seems to be appealing to the gods for help. Smart-ass University of Toronto grads of my era refer to it as *Gumby Goes to Heaven*. I'd appreciate a little divine intervention right about now.

Within another few blocks, we enter a veritable canyon of hospitals—Mount Sinai, Sick Kids', Toronto General—their blockish battlements staring fiercely across the street at one another. I follow the taxi down a cross street into the semi-circular laneway of an emergency department. I'm not even sure which hospital we're at, and at this point I don't really care. The cabbie watches me in his rear-view mirror as I help Marla out of the car, then he pulls away, eager not to extend his role in our little drama, throwing up a rooster tail of snow from his back tires. Marla grabs my forearm as we shuffle towards the entrance. She stops partway and closes her eyes. Her grip tightens. Then she opens her eyes again and stares at the block letters on the sliding glass doors, realizing only now where I'm leading her. She balks.

"Come on," I say. An icy gust of wind whips my pant legs.

She draws a thin, laboured breath. "I just need fresh air." She gulps. "That's all." Her arm is as rigid as a stovepipe.

"Yeah, right," I say. "I'm not having you pass out in the car."

"What about Severn?" she says. "Avery?"

"Inside," I tell her. I pull her forward. She totters a little, and I put my arm around her shoulder to steady her. We proceed through the sliding glass doors.

The waiting area, half-filled with people forced to put their wretchedness on display, is as depressing as a downtown bus terminal. Near the door, a man in a denim shirt cradles his injured arm. His buddy, who's wearing a grease-stained ball cap advertising auto parts, alternates between distracting him with small talk and casting impatient glances about the room. One row of seats over, a frail elderly woman strokes the hand of her bleary-eyed husband, who sniffles oxygen from a portable tank through a tube clipped to his nose. Other nervous-looking people with less obvious ailments stare out the windows at the swirling snow, resigned to wait their turn to be poked and prodded and have their worst fears either confirmed or debunked. I've been in emergency departments before, with Helen. The waiting rooms all feel the same: a bubbling soup of pain and anxiety with the lid on tight. I swore I'd never step in one again.

I walk Marla up to the desk. The nurse asks us a series of matter-of-fact questions, turning to me whenever more than a few words are required in reply. She looks uncertainly, almost sceptically, at Marla, who's now leaning heavily on the counter.

"Can I see her health card?" she says.

I realize that I've left Marla's knapsack in the car with the doors unlocked. "It's outside," I say, hovering between propping up Marla and going to get it.

"Don't worry about it for now," the nurse says with long-suffering patience, as though we're not the first unprepared customers she's had to deal with today. She hands me a form to fill out and promptly disappears. I pat my jacket pockets for a pen but find that I'm not carrying one. Marla wheezes beside me like a visitor from another planet whose travel agent failed to inform her that earth's atmosphere was toxic to members of her species. The guy in the auto-parts cap is standing behind us now, agitating to get his friend some service. It's clear that he thinks we're holding up the line. I step out of his way and guide Marla back to the waiting area, the blank form clutched uselessly in my hand. I see a teenage girl with greasy hair sitting with her scuzzy-looking boyfriend, and I think of Severn. I wonder how many hours I'll spend in this place while her trail goes cold.

Before I get Marla to a seat, the nurse reappears. "Mr. Costello," she calls out. "Please bring your wife this way." She beckons for us to follow her down a corridor. The man in the auto-parts cap protests, but the nurse ignores him. He looks at Marla resentfully as we pass, offended that her wheezing should take precedence over his friend's busted arm.

"I'm not her husband," I tell the nurse as she shows us into a side room. "In fact, we hardly know each other."

The nurse takes Marla by the arm and helps her to an examination table surrounded by monitors and other dubious medical devices. I'm certain the next step will be to get Marla out of her street clothes and into one of those hospital gowns with the openings at the back. That's what they usually did with Helen.

"I'll go park the car," I say to the nurse, who's already tuned me out again. "They probably don't let you park out front like that, do they?" As I start backing out of the room, Marla looks at me wide-eyed as though I'm about to abandon her. I offer her a weak, placating smile, then duck out.

It's been no more than ten or fifteen minutes since I left the car, but already a rim of ice has crystallized on the base of the windshield. I chip the wipers free with my ice scraper, my bare hands stinging from the cold. Another car and a taxi pull in behind me, each discharging its walking wounded. A security guard appears to tell me to move along, I'm blocking access. I smile at him sourly and get behind the wheel.

As I start the engine and try to blow life back into my fingers, I realize that it's my chance to get away, to extricate myself from Marla. Not that I know where to look for Severn without her. Still, the temptation's to go it alone, just as I've been doing the whole of this past year. I've grown comfortable with my private failure; it's like the impression of my butt in a decrepit easy chair. I pull out to the street, telling myself to make for the Beaches and scour the neighbourhoods. Instead, I turn into a parking garage before I'm a block from the hospital and find a spot on the third level. I grab Marla's knapsack, climb down the garage's cold, damp concrete stairwell, and trudge back through the snowdrifts to the emergency department.

In the vestibule, I stomp my shoes on the mat, partly to dislodge the snow that's clinging to my pant cuffs and partly to shock some circulation back into my toes. There's a different nurse behind the desk now. This one's dressed in a burgundy uniform. In the old days, nurses all wore white. I wonder if they come colour-coded now. I plunk Marla's knapsack on the counter.

"The other nurse said she needed to see a health card," I say.

I open the bag and begin sorting through the contents in search of Marla's wallet. I pull out a sweater and an orange. Then I pull out a hardcover book. It's a copy of *Northwest Passage*.

"Is there something the matter, sir?" the burgundy nurse asks me. I realize that I've turned to granite in front of her, become as unintelligible as one of the statues on University Avenue. I think of all the sideways looks Marla has given me since we started out from London. Now I know the source of the intelligence she thinks she's gathered.

"You know what?" I tell the burgundy nurse. "I just remembered I have to be somewhere. Can I leave this bag with you?" I don't bother waiting for an answer. I leave the knapsack's contents, especially the book, lying on the counter and turn for the door.

Before I can take my first step, I feel a hand resting on my arm. It's the first nurse, the one who took Marla to the examination room. "Going somewhere?" she asks indulgently.

"Yeah, I have to meet my daughter," I tell her.

"Perhaps you can call your daughter and tell her where you are," she says. "I'm sure she'll understand."

"I may not be able to reach her," I say.

She exchanges a knowing look with her burgundy colleague, a look that says they see putzes like me all the time in their line of work. They're placing a silent bet on whether I'm a jerk or just plain dense, I can tell.

"When someone comes in with Marla's symptoms, we don't like to take chances," she explains, hoping I'll catch on that I should be treating this whole situation a little more seriously.

I feel like telling her I don't need a lecture on what serious is. I've been way past serious and back with Helen, and I don't particularly want to go there again.

"Does Marla have any family close by?" she asks.

I shrug. "Just an ex-husband who's out of town and a teenage son who's AWOL."

She starts repacking the knapsack. "I'll take this in to her," she says. "In the meantime, why don't you have a seat." She picks up the book and turns it over in her hands. "Here," she says, handing it to me, "a little reading material for you while you wait. I just finished this one at home. This guy's a great writer."

I'm left alone holding the book. I realize that it would be unseemly to chase after her to tell her she's a fan of a literary parasite, and so I reluctantly retreat to the waiting area and take a seat. From across the room, the old man with the oxygen tank tries to focus his watery eyes on me as if I am a rescue ship coming into view on the distant horizon. Then his face collapses in a spasm of phlegmy coughing. I look for somewhere less depressing to direct my gaze, without success. Before long, I have nowhere left to look but the cover of the book. The publisher's blurb on the inside leaf is revoltingly effusive, but I find myself reading it nonetheless, pulled along by my loathsome need to know what truths Severn may have seen in Jack Livingston's story.

> This eagerly anticipated new novel by Jack Livingston, the award-winning author of *Lover's Requiem* and *Path of the Prophet*, is a riveting tale of one girl's search for the truth about her bloodline and, ultimately, herself.
>
> Sally Campbell is sixteen when her mother, Grace, disappears, leaving a note signed, "Until you join me." Sally's father, a disillusioned high school teacher, insists his wife has simply taken an impromptu vacation. But when the police appear at the front door to report that Grace has gone missing near the Arctic settlement of Resolute Bay and is presumed dead, Sally's world is shattered.
>
> Sally flies North with her father, hoping against hope to reclaim her mother from the rolls of the dead. But once there, she realizes that there are things her father doesn't want her to know. Her mother has a hidden past involving a local outfitter who was the last man to see her alive.
>
> Set against the backdrop of Sir John Franklin's failed Arctic expedition, *Northwest Passage* is one of Jack Livingston's most haunting stories to date, a finely textured mystery with all the lyrical qualities we've come to expect from this acclaimed writer.

I half expect to find that Marla's scribbled notes directly on the book jacket: the comment "same initials" scrawled next to the name Sally Campbell; the words "disillusioned high school teacher" underlined; a double exclamation mark next to the phrase "things her father doesn't want her to know." But they're not there for me to see, although I'm sure Marla has made these notations in her mind. As has Severn.

The back of my neck is burning. The book suddenly feels heavy in my hands. I let it sink to my lap. No doubt Livingston sees himself as the enigmatic outfitter, the man with the secret to the lonely girl's past. All this time, I'd assumed that Severn was an inconsequential footnote in his life, a vague abstraction not worthy of a second thought. Yet here I find that he's devoted a considerable portion of his imagination to her—and once again inserted himself in the story.

Had his inspiration run so dry that he was reduced to looking back with self-indulgent wistfulness on a path not taken, packaging it all in a tidy little fiction that absolved him of his sins and, more important, kept the royalties coming in? I wonder if he'd even considered the possibility that Severn would read his book, much less seek him out, lured by the prospect of revelations about her mother's past just as her doppelgänger, Sally, was. I picture the scene at our local Imprint store on the day of his booksigning. Severn comes up to him, nervous, perhaps looking not all that different from the other fawning girls he routinely encounters who are too quick to see their own tales of teenage disillusionment in Sally Campbell's. But when she opens her mouth, he hears a strangely familiar timbre to her voice. Then he remembers that he's in London, the town where he met Helen, and he senses his imaginary world bleeding into reality. Severn hands him a copy of his book to sign. She appears poised to ask him an awkward question but can't find the words. His interest piqued, he asks her name. She shrinks under his gaze and loses her nerve. She mumbles to make the inscription out to her father, but this preserves her anonymity only briefly because his next question is to ask her father's name. She pauses awkwardly, sensing that she's at a point of no return. Irving, she tells him.

The picture turns fuzzy after that. Livingston had to have done something to spook her, to make her run from the store without paying for the book. Maybe after he signed his coy message to me, he scanned her face a little too closely for signs of himself. I imagine a look of leering curiosity, as though he were a debauched English professor who'd read *Lolita* far too many times. The fact that he didn't come to her rescue when the store manager accused her of shoplifting didn't surprise me. Severn would have been of much more interest to Livingston as a possibility rather than a reality, someone who wouldn't stray beyond his narrative. Real people generally demanded more concern than he was willing to give them. Their only value to him was as grist for his literary musings.

What troubles me now is why Severn is still pursuing Livingston even after the humiliation of their first encounter. Surely she's terrified by the prospect of throwing herself at his mercy again. I've pushed her to this, I realize. By keeping my memories of Helen at a distance, I've cut Severn off, left her out in the cold. Livingston has what she wants: the means to resurrect her mother as a younger, freer woman than she ever knew. He'll divulge the affair, perhaps even affect a show of melancholy. And then he'll mention to my daughter—just in passing, of course— that she was born six months after Helen came back to me.

I can't sit any more. I find a payphone and flip through the white pages. No Jack Livingston is listed, although there are several J. Livingstons. I'm not about to call them all. I try the department of English at the University of Toronto. He was teaching there when Helen met him. When I get through, a department secretary tells me that he hasn't been on faculty for years. I ask if she knows how I can get in touch with him. She says that they don't give out that sort of information. I explain that it's an emergency. She's afraid she still can't help me. That's as far as I get with her.

I could walk to the English department from the hospital, I realize. It's only a few blocks away. Perhaps some former colleague would be willing to tell me where he is. Then I wonder how many people have shown up asking for Jack Livingston's whereabouts before me—talentless wannabe writers; jilted lovers; irate husbands; disgruntled people who've found the details of their private lives scrambled in one of his books. I suspect that our welcome is long worn out by now.

Chapter 10

As I opened the door to my apartment, the dankness of my dingy little rooms stung my nostrils. I hesitated, afraid that Helen would turn and run the minute she saw how I lived.

"Well?" she said. "Are we going in or aren't we?"

I removed my officer's hat and took her by the hand. The inside seemed even darker than normal compared with the cheerful April sunshine outside. It took a moment for our eyes to adjust. When they did, my squalid bachelor's life emerged from the shadows in all its glory. I could see the flickers of doubt in Helen's mouth as she spotted the duct-taped laundry hamper, overflowing with dirty socks and underwear, propping open my bedroom door. Next to it on the floor was the empty Oreo cookie bag I'd raided for that morning's breakfast, along with a greased-stained pizza box from supper the night before. But as she warily scanned the apartment for more evidence of my slothfulness, she noticed the walls full of books. Her eyes brightened. I wasn't a complete Neanderthal after all.

"Can I get you something?" I asked, even though I knew that other than a bottle of flat ginger ale, I had very little to offer her.

She didn't hear me. She was busy checking out the spines of my books. *"Life on the Mississippi* by Mark Twain," she said, spotting my second-hand copy. Her gaze moved along the shelf. "Swift, Steinbeck, Shakespeare." She was duly impressed. "So you don't just collect history books." Her attention shifted to the next shelf down. It took her only a few seconds to detect the familiar pattern. "All alphabetized by author," she said with a tiny smile. "Such order amidst such chaos."

I made a belated effort to clean up some of my mess, gathering the piles of student papers that I'd left sitting on my sagging couch and relocating them to the top of the fridge. "I think I've got tea," I said, still playing the awkward host. "You want some tea?" I searched the kitchen cupboard in vain for a couple of clean mugs.

"I take it you don't have many women over," she said, watching me with amusement as I stumbled about the kitchen.

"How can you tell?" I asked, annoyed by the fool I was making of myself.

She edged up to me and combed my hat hair back into place with her fingers. "Relax, Irving," she said. "I'm not going anywhere." She kissed me softly on the mouth to prove it, immobilizing me as surely as if she'd doped me with curare. As she leaned back, she licked her lips, apparently musing on a description for how I tasted, perhaps classifying me alongside the many other specimens of male she'd catalogued.

It was clear from the way she cocked her head at me that I was expected to make the next move. I couldn't help feeling that I was about to be judged for technical and style points. I leaned forward and set my lips against hers, trying to find the right way to hold her without immediately impressing her with my all too palpable horniness. My hands searched for a suitable perch—my right one settling for the side of her face, my left oscillating between her shoulder blade and the small of her back like a drunken spider. She let me struggle on my own for a few seconds, seemingly intrigued by my clumsy efforts, then placed her hand around the cheek of my butt and firmly pulled my pelvis against hers. From that point, I merely tried to keep up. Pretty soon, I found myself pressed down on a rickety kitchen chair, my britches knotted around my ankles, with Helen peeling off her blouse on top of me. As hungry as I was after all my years in sexual purgatory, her appetite nearly overwhelmed me. She gorged herself on me, hauling me back whenever I threatened to come, only to torture me with a new set of gyrations. By the time she finally yelled out and collapsed on top of me, I was filled with an overwhelming sense of victory, even though I realized that I was about as responsible for her orgasm as a violin is for a finely played concerto.

After she returned from the bathroom, she resumed her inspection of my bookshelf in the nude as if our lovemaking had been a casual conversation. I was still sprawled on the kitchen chair, inhaling the lingering smells of sex and lavender. I glanced down at my sunken chest and my fat snake of a pecker sunning itself on my soft, pale belly, and tried not to wonder how my anatomy measured up to those who'd come before me.

"So," I said, trying to fill the awkward post-coital silence, "what does my book collection tell you about me?"

"That you were worth my while after all," she said. "I don't screw any man who has fewer than a hundred books, you know." Because her back was to me, I couldn't tell whether she meant to be ironic or not.

"What you're saying is that size matters," I said, opting for irony.

"It's only a minimum requirement," she said, still indecipherably deadpan. "The fact that you have a preference for the classics over supermarket thrillers is another point in your favour." She continued to scan the shelves. I noticed that her freckles went all the way down her spine.

I got up and wrapped my arms around her from behind, hoping she wouldn't find the gesture clingy. I knew I was being old-fashioned, but I felt I should show her that intimacy meant more to me than sex—not that I'd had a whole lot of experience with either. I was relieved to feel her bare body settle naturally into mine. At that moment, I first snatched at the hope that I might be more to her than a simple dalliance.

"Looking for anything in particular?" I asked, resting my chin on her shoulder.

"Ah, Dostoevsky," she said, isolating the D's on the shelves. "Not bad company, I suppose."

"Meaning?"

She reached back, rested her hand on my cheek, and whispered to me as if she were sharing a guilty secret, "I always like to see where my book would go."

And so it was, in the quiet moments after our repeated sexual encounters that week, as we lay tangled in my dirty sheets, that Helen revealed to me the origins of her aspiration to become a writer.

"Where it really started for me," she said, propped up on her elbow, carefully observing my reaction to her anecdote, "was when I read Alice Munro's *Lives of Girls and Women*. You can't imagine what an impression it made on a tall, gawky teenage girl who had boys at school sniggering behind her back. I mean, here was a writer—a woman who lived just an hour up the road—describing with such unassuming and startling clarity everything I was going through but couldn't put into words myself." Her right forefinger traced the line of my collarbone. "From that point on in my life, I began writing."

As the week proceeded, I wondered how many more visits I could expect from Helen before she tired of me, but for whatever reason, she kept coming back. Perhaps it was my attentiveness to her pillow talk, or maybe—although admittedly this was much less likely—it was my game, if not entirely successful, efforts to improve my sexual techniques under her tutelage. Whatever the reason, I had several more opportunities to hear her describe her childhood, including growing up in her father's bookshop. I sensed that by telling me these stories, she was hoping to unravel how she'd come to be the capricious malcontent she was now. Needless to say, the effect was to make me fall hopelessly in love with her.

"When Daddy saw that I was determined to become a writer," she said, "he indulged me at first. He figured I'd grow out of it once enough editors rejected me and I realized what an impossible task it was to get published. He still thinks that. That's why he let me have space upstairs at the shop to write. So I could get it out of my system. As if that were possible. The thing he can't make himself understand is that I'll never be happy simply peddling other people's words like he does."

I liked to think that even though she might have shared these private little glimpses into her past with other men before me, the version I was seeing was fuller, more candid, and given less conditionally. One evening, as we lay exhausted from our latest contortions, I asked her if she'd let me read one of her stories.

"Oh, I don't know that I'd have anything you'd be interested in," she said, her eyes skipping away self-consciously.

"I promise to be kind," I said.

She looked at me, momentarily offended, then rolled onto her back and frowned at a water stain on my bedroom ceiling. Apparently, sharing her written thoughts was a level of intimacy beyond sex and whispered confidences that she wasn't ready for. I thought I'd blown it right there, but after a few minutes of sulking, she was back on top of me, guiding my hand between her legs, coaxing me to go another round with her.

My marking fell behind that week. In the days that followed, we shifted our lovemaking to her apartment, with its crisp, clean sheets, mildew-free shower, and handy stash of condoms in every room. One night, as we lay spent on her living-room rug, I noticed a fresh bouquet of flowers, complete with card, sitting on her coffee table. I asked her about it, but she distracted me by licking my ear. Later, when she was getting us a drink from the kitchen, I checked out the message on the card. It was from her biology professor, a plaintive appeal to see her one last time.

For a woman who claimed to sleep exclusively with well-read men, Helen had surprisingly few books. She explained that she didn't believe in holding on to books once she'd finished them. It was only fair to their authors that she recirculate them as soon as possible by selling them to second-hand stores or donating them to the library so more people could enjoy them. I didn't doubt that this practice of hers extended beyond books.

I began searching for a way to avoid being recycled, to find a more permanent foothold in Helen's life. One night as she was sleeping naked beside me, I eased myself out of bed and padded into her living room. There, in the bookcase by the TV, wedged between the *Joy of Cooking* and Italo Calvino's *Invisible Cities*, I found a stash of exercise books that I'd spotted earlier, like the ones I'd taken notes in when I was a high school student. From Helen's accounts, I knew that she'd typically done her writing in notebooks like these. I settled into a corner of her living-room couch, pulling an afghan over my bare body, and began reading. The writing was mostly in fragments— ideas for stories or characters or opening passages—but every once in a while, I'd run across a page or two of overly earnest prose peppered with painful, brilliant flashes of adolescent angst. I could tell by the deliberate, wide loops of the handwriting that these were early efforts, probably written by Helen in her years at high school.

Before I could get to the second notebook, I noticed Helen standing over me, still completely naked, her hands pointedly on her hips.

I smiled up at her sheepishly. "Do you have anything more recent than this?"

She plucked the notebook from my hands, then yanked the afghan off me. "Out," she said menacingly. When I was slow to move, she began to hurl articles of clothing at me from the trail that I'd left on the floor from our clutch-and-grab journey to the bedroom—my balled-up dress shirt, a stray sock that fluttered short of its mark, a shoe that bounced off the wall behind my head.

Once again, I thought I'd blown it—for good, this time. As I drove home through the deserted late-night streets of London, I mockingly congratulated myself for lasting as long as I had. But as it turned out, my exile was only temporary. Helen and I were back at it in her shower the following night.

I returned to the bookshop that Saturday, fancying myself the proverbial conquering hero. Helen had told me to meet her at noon so that we could go for lunch at the café across the street. I imagined lunch leading smoothly to another roll between the sheets in her apartment.

By summer standards, the day would have been bone-chilling, but it was still only April, and for a city full of people tired of five months of winter coats, it was downright balmy. Everyone was eager to chase the memories of winter away. Children and parents promenaded with their first ice-cream cones of the year. Bare-legged university students soaked up the sun, ignoring, for the moment at least, their next final exam.

I braced myself for Walter's glare as I entered the shop, but he wasn't at the till. The place was humming with customers. A mother with a young son recognized me from two weeks before and asked me impishly why I was out of uniform. I bantered with her and her son for a while, cultivating the modesty of a minor celebrity.

Will breezed by me on his way to ring in a purchase for a teenage girl he'd been helping at the back of the shop. "Howdy, skipper," he said on his way past.

"Where's Helen?" I asked.

Will's eyes pointed at the ceiling as he slipped behind the front counter. A line of impatient-looking patrons, books in hand, had formed by the cash register. He asked which one of them had been waiting the longest.

I heard the faint scuffling of footsteps above us. They seemed to belong to more than one person.

"She up there with anyone?" I said, trying to make it sound like a quip to camouflage my jealousy.

Will snapped open a plastic bag and slid a couple of just-bought books inside. "Walter, as a matter of fact," he said, too busy to conceal his annoyance.

I drifted to the back of the shop to wait for Helen. There, I met a couple of my students who'd heard about my acting debut. They promised to come to my next show and bring a couple of their friends along. Careful to show them I hadn't completely succumbed to their flattery, I wished them luck on my test the coming Tuesday and reminded them to study hard.

As I began to browse the travel section, I heard two muffled voices coming from upstairs. The voices were arguing, although I couldn't make out the words. The stern one definitely belonged to Walter. The argument stopped abruptly at the top of the stairs. The next thing I heard was the sound of a pair of feet descending the steep steps. Helen emerged from behind the closet curtain, her cheeks flushed, a canvas bag slung over her shoulder.

"Trouble?" I asked.

Helen ignored my question. "Ready to go?" she asked. "I'm hungry."

As we made our way to the side exit, Walter stepped out of the closet, stiff from his awkward climb down the stairs. He smote us both with a reproving stare.

"When can I expect you back?" He spoke to Helen as if she were sixteen. "We're going to be busy here this afternoon."

"I don't know, Daddy," she said impatiently. "Anyway, I'm sure you and Will can manage just fine without me."

She took me by the hand and pulled me out the door behind

her. Walter's evil eye lingered on me, the shiftless boy who dared steal away his daughter.

"You're sure this is okay?" I asked Helen once we were out on the sidewalk. "I mean, we can always go for lunch another time."

Helen pulled up short, and I nearly stumbled into her. "What's the matter?" she said, turning on me. "You don't want to keep our date?"

"No, no," I assured her. "It's not that. I'm just saying that if this is a bad time—"

"The time is fine."

"You're sure? Because your father didn't seem too pleased just now."

"You think I should skip lunch and work the rest of the afternoon?"

"No," I said. "I'm simply saying that you don't have to piss off your dad on my account."

"Don't flatter yourself, Irving. This isn't about you. I've been pissing Daddy off since way before you came along."

I gave up. I could see there was no point in arguing. "Fine," I said, starting towards Richmond Street. "Let's go to lunch."

She glowered at me. "Now you're pissed off."

"What do you want from me?" I asked. "I'm acquiescing. Acquiescence without obsequiousness, remember?"

"Daddy expected me to work last Saturday afternoon too," she said. "I didn't hear you complaining when we went to your apartment instead."

"You're right," I said, unequivocally admitting defeat so long as it meant an end to our skirmish. "I know nothing about your family, and from now on, I promise to withhold comment on same."

"I'm glad to hear it," she said, still eyeing me suspiciously. "Now let's eat."

She took me by the hand again and dragged me out into the middle of Richmond Street in front of a pickup truck, secure in her assumption that the driver would brake to let her cross, which fortunately he did. Ditto for the city bus coming the opposite direction. She waved to both drivers as they stopped. They even waved back, hoping perhaps that she would ditch me and hitch a ride with them.

The café waitress had only just brought our menus when Helen reached into her canvas bag and presented me with a small sheaf of papers.

"What's this?" I asked.

"You wanted to read one of my stories," she said in a subdued tone.

I fingered the pages gingerly, recognizing the angst she'd overcome to surrender them to me. I made sure not to show any of the glee I felt over graduating to this next level of intimacy in our relationship. "Thank you," I said.

She folded her hands like a prisoner awaiting sentence. Apparently she expected me to read her story and offer my appraisal right there. It struck me then that Walter hadn't simply been arguing with her about her predilection for long lunches. He'd discovered that she was intending to show me one of her manuscripts, and that I was attempting to revive her selfish dream of becoming a writer.

The minestrone soup I ordered turned cold as I read. Helen watched me intently, registering my every twitch and murmur, interpreting them as coded criticisms of her work.

"I like it," I said when I got to the end.

Helen frowned, construing my reaction as faint praise.

"It reminds me of *The Tempest*," I said, trying to show her that I'd given my critique some thought. "The bookworm father raising his beautiful but wayward daughter alone in the country. The young man appearing on their doorstep in the snowstorm when his car gets stuck. The jealousy of the father when the young man shows an interest in his daughter." I refrained from pointing out the obvious parallels with her own life. She'd written the story before she met me, so I assumed the young man was a representation of a past lover.

"You don't think it's very original, then," she said, apparently determined to put a negative spin on my comments.

"Didn't someone say once that there are only a handful of truly original stories that date back thousands of years? The task of the writer is to tell them in new and interesting ways."

She pointed a french fry at me argumentatively. "I've sent that manuscript to at least twenty different publications," she said. "It was rejected twenty times."

I shrugged. "I'm not an editor. All I'm saying is that you've got a talent that's worth developing."

She dropped the uneaten french fry on her plate, leaned back and looked at me with hooded eyes. "Ah, I see. 'Worth developing.' Meaning it's underdeveloped now. Weak. Scrawny. Stunted."

I plunked the manuscript on the table in frustration. "Helen, I'm trying to tell you that you shouldn't give up writing. One day, if you just keep at it, I know you'll get published."

A self-conscious smile cracked through her scowl. She was finally allowing herself to believe me. "You're just saying that because you're still hoping to get laid this afternoon," she said.

Helen let me finish my lunch after that, cold as it was. She watched me swallow each spoonful with a love in her eyes I hadn't seen until then.

She didn't go back to work that afternoon.

Chapter 11

It's 1:54 p.m. by the time Marla walks out to the waiting room. She has her street clothes back on and her knapsack slung over her shoulder. She seems embarrassed to have kept me waiting so long.

"So," I say, "they're letting you go."

"Yeah," she replies, clearly not wanting to go into it.

"What was the problem?" I ask.

"Nothing," she says. "I'm fine."

The tight-lipped routine that she's been sticking to since we left London is beginning to grate on me. "I wouldn't call nearly passing out on the road nothing."

"I'm fine," she insists, her eyes avoiding mine. The emergency department has got busier since we arrived. Her gaze falls on an old woman who's wrapped in a blanket and strapped to a stretcher. An ambulance crew has just brought her in.

"Come on, Marla. If you expect to get back in that car with me, you've got to do better than that."

She heaves a sulky sigh. "It's happened to me once or twice before. It's no big deal. They gave me some pills. I'm good to go."

"So what is it? Asthma? Some kind of heart condition?"

She thrusts her jaw forward, annoyed that I won't let her brush

87

me off. She looks me squarely in the eye. "It was a panic attack, all right?"

I look back at her impassively, not wanting to tip her off to all the doubts now racing through my head about her state of mind. My gaze drifts towards the old woman on the stretcher, who's now being wheeled into one of the examining rooms. She seems confused by her restraints and the conversations going on around her.

"What set it off?" I ask guardedly.

Marla knows what I'm thinking. My shifty eyes have given me away. "Look," she says, "I've had two, maybe three attacks in the past twenty years. It's not like I'm going to have another this afternoon."

"So they just happen," I say sceptically. "On their own. At random."

Her eyes harden. "I was sixteen when I had my first one," she says. "A few months after my mother died."

And then I feel it from her, just as surely as I feel it so frequently from Severn: the unfettered resentment of the victim whose pain I can't possibly understand. Its sharpness stuns me. Time obviously hasn't dulled its edge for Marla. She's merely found a way to keep it sheathed under normal circumstances.

"Can we go now?" she says, impatiently shifting her knapsack on her shoulder. "Hospitals give me the creeps."

I reach down to the seat where I've laid her copy of *Northwest Passage*. I hand it to her. "You don't want to forget this," I say curtly.

She hesitates, then takes it from me.

"Interesting choice of light reading," I say. "Worried you might get bored on the trip?"

She stuffs it back in her knapsack. "It's paid for, in case you're wondering," she replies sarcastically.

She heads for the exit and marches off into the snowy afternoon, not bothering to wait for me. I trail after her grudgingly. The wind has subsided. The snow is drifting down as fat, lazy flakes, muffling the noise of the traffic on University Avenue.

"The car's this way," I tell her.

"Don't worry about me," she calls over her shoulder. "I'll take the subway."

"Hey!" I scurry after her. She still hasn't given me the address to her ex's condo. It takes me half a block to catch up with her, my shoes skidding on patches of ice hiding beneath the freshly fallen snow. "You're not just leaving me here," I tell her, nearly out of breath.

"Why not?" she says, still walking. "I'm obviously cramping your style."

I grab her by the arm and pull her to a stop. "I waited for you in that stupid emergency department for three hours."

"Fine," she says frostily. "Thank you. Now let me go."

"What the hell is the matter with you, anyway?"

A bitter little laugh escapes her lips in a puff of steam on the cold February air. She lets the strap of her knapsack slide off her shoulder and all the way down her arm. It hangs from her fingers for a moment before she lets the bag fall to the snow at her feet. She looks at me, defying me to show any empathy. "You don't get it, do you?"

Now I realize that she isn't just some annoying woman with a feckless son. She's a Dickensian apparition, the ghost of Severn's future, the quietly tormented soul my daughter might one day become.

"All right, listen," I say. "Whatever kind of jerk you take me for, I'm here because I'm worried about Severn. I didn't come two hundred kilometres in the middle of a snowstorm just for my own amusement, okay? And although I may not be able to demonstrate an adequate understanding—to your satisfaction, anyway—of what you've been through in your life, and how that may or may not be similar to Severn's experience, I'd nonetheless appreciate your help in finding my daughter." I pick her knapsack up from the snow, dust it off, and hand it back to her. "Are you ready now? The car's back this way."

Marla takes the knapsack and slings it back onto her shoulder. I can see that my diatribe has shamed her back into being an adult. It's just as well. There's snow in my shoes again, and I'm not dressed for arguments in these kinds of temperatures.

Chapter 12

It was said that Franklin's final expedition was the best equipped of its day. His two ships, which together had previously braved Antarctic waters under the command of James Clark Ross, had hulls that had been specially reinforced to withstand the grip of polar sea ice. Both were fitted out with sails of triple-strength canvas and steam engines that powered single-screw propellers. Enough provisions were stowed on board to last the two crews at least three years—seven if wisely supplemented by fish and game caught in the Arctic—far more time than anyone thought they'd need to safely complete the voyage. Due attention had also been paid to the emotional and spiritual needs of the crews, who would be enduring months on end without daylight or even the faintest promise of spring. An organ made the trip with them for Sunday services. They were also accompanied by an extensive library. The Admiralty had spared no expense.

I thought of this library, doomed to perish in the Arctic along with both crews, as I waited at the front of the bookshop for Walter to finish with a customer. I wondered whether many of the classics on the shelves surrounding me had been on board Franklin's ships, and whether they had provided any comfort to the men in their misery. After all, no one knew how many of them had actually been able to read.

Walter was taking an extra long time with his customer, making me wait even though I'd arrived promptly at the hour he'd specified in his summons. It had come through Will, who'd called me at home earlier in the week. "The old man wants to have a talk with you," he'd told me ominously. When I'd asked what "the old man" wanted to talk about, Will couldn't say, or maybe just wouldn't say—I wasn't sure which. I got the impression from Will's uncharacteristic brusqueness on the phone that he'd worked his way into Walter's doghouse as a direct result of his association with me.

Finally, Walter bade his customer good day and made his way to the till, not bothering to look at me. He reached under the front counter and pulled out a clipboard, checking a piece of business on it that was obviously more important to him than I was. I stood there waiting for him to look up, vacillating between a posture of patient respect and one of determined nonchalance. As I began to wonder how long he intended to carry on this game of quiet intimidation, he broke the silence with his headmaster's voice.

"Do you realize how long I've owned this shop?" he asked me, still not looking up from his clipboard.

I felt as if I were being quizzed on homework I hadn't done. I knew I could probably find the answer painted on the front window next to his name, but I wasn't about to let him catch me cheating. "Quite a while, I suppose," I said, trying to sound unashamed of my ignorance.

He scrutinized me with the disdain one might reserve for an impudent street urchin. "It's been my life since soon after I returned from the war," he said articulating his words precisely. He waited for me to show signs that I appreciated how long that truly was in one man's lifetime.

"You must still have been a young man," I said.

He tipped his head in reluctant agreement. "About your age," he said, placing the clipboard back under the counter. "Nearly forty years. Since before I was married and had children. Businesses have come and gone on this street, but this shop has been here the whole time." He gazed out through the display window at the pedestrians passing by. I could tell that he was picturing men in grey flannel suits and homburgs escorting ladies with sensible dresses, horn-rimmed glasses, and little white gloves. "It takes perseverance to keep a shop like this going. Long hours sometimes, without much reward. Before she died, my wife told me that I spent too much time here. My doctor still does. But no one will ever understand how much this place is in my blood. How I'd feel incomplete without it."

I could hear the hard edge to his voice gradually softening, until the faint strains of melancholy became unmistakable.

"Books have been a constant in my life," he went on. "I grow attached to them, like children, even though I'm not the one who creates them. Whenever a new one arrives, I make sure I get to know it, discover what makes it unique. I've always considered this place a kind of adoption agency. I try to find good homes, good matches for each of them. To act as their guardian for as long as they're here. To me, this line of work is as much a calling as it is a business."

He'd begun to sound less like a schoolmaster and more like an abbot presiding over the illumination of ancient manuscripts. But just as I was imagining him with a tonsure and vestments, his severe, intractable demeanour unexpectedly reasserted itself.

"I called it Donnelly's Books," he declared, "because from the beginning, it's always been a family business. Helen's spent her whole life here. It's in her blood too. I still hold out hope that one day, before I'm too old and feeble, she'll realize that for herself."

"I know I'm new here," I said, trying not to sound too impertinent, "but that seems like a pretty slim hope."

He responded with a dismissive grunt. "I don't expect you to understand," he said.

"What about Will?" I suggested helpfully. "He may not be family, but he certainly seems to have the same love of books that you do."

He stared down his nose at me. "Please. You think I don't realize that the two of you are in cahoots?"

I smiled uneasily in an effort to project my innocence. "Will was just helping me out. It's not like I'm plotting with him or anything."

"I'm well aware of his ambitions." He raised his chin and proceeded with his pronouncement. "I thank you for your fine performance the other Saturday, but I'm afraid it was your last here."

"Wait a minute," I said, flabbergasted. "It brought all sorts of extra business to this store."

"That may be. But this is a bookshop, not a performance hall."

"That's silly. How can you do this?"

"I own this establishment, that's how."

"Didn't you see the look in those kids' faces?" I said, still staggered by his stubbornness. "All of a sudden, history meant something to them. As someone who's so concerned with tradition and continuity, you can surely appreciate that."

Walter remained impervious to my appeal. The matter was already decided. "Of course," he said, tucking his reading glasses into his shirt pocket to signify that our conversation was coming to a close, "I realize I have no influence over my daughter's choice in boyfriends, but I'm under no obligation to accommodate you here in this shop."

And with that, he picked up the phone and called to check on an overdue order. It took me a moment to make myself believe what had just happened. I'd been banished from his shop.

Chapter 13

Marla's ex-husband's condo is part of a cluster of units perched above an eclectic row of narrow storefronts—an upscale convenience store, a walk-in pet hospital, a tea/chai shop, and a tiny real-estate office whose window features photos of hot properties throughout the Beaches. Streetcars rumble along the tracks on Queen Street East as Marla peers up at the condo. Its blinds are drawn. There's no hint of life inside.

We follow an alleyway that leads us to the parking lot and main entrance at the rear. Marla pushes the buzzer on the downstairs intercom several times, but no one answers.

"Don't you have a key?" I ask.

Marla is annoyed by my question. Surely I should understand that women do not generally hold keys to their ex-husbands' apartments. The reasons should be obvious. She buzzes one more time, holding the button down for a full five seconds. It doesn't help.

"Is there a neighbour who'd be willing to let you in?" I ask.

Obviously another stupid question. She doesn't even bother to acknowledge it. She heads back outside and takes one last look up at the windows that overlook the parking lot.

"Come on," she says.

We retrace our steps out to Queen Street. After a few blocks, we arrive at a funky little bistro. Through the window, I can see a row of booths down one wall, a clue that this was once a diner, and that the new owners aren't so snobbish that they want to deny the restaurant's humble past. I follow Marla inside. She doesn't wait to be seated as the sign by the door requests, but instead walks to the back, where a waiter is picking up an order from the window to the kitchen.

"I'm looking for anyone who was working yesterday evening," she tells the waiter.

"That's me," he says, loading up his tray with soups and salads.

"I'm wondering if you served my son," she says.

He looks at her apprehensively. "Why? He's not sick or anything, is he? We run a clean kitchen here, you know."

"No, it's nothing like that," she says.

The waiter still doesn't know what to make of Marla, I can tell. "I've got this order to deliver," he says. "Why don't you have a seat in one of the booths at the front?"

I sit in the booth with my back to the window, fiddling with the cutlery. Marla leaves her jacket on. She keeps turning to check on the waiter. He's been flagged down by a couple who want to order.

"So," I ask her, "does Avery visit his father a lot?"

"Every other weekend," she says distractedly. "Jay takes him to ball games, buys him video games, lets him stay up all night. Acts like his best buddy."

"I can see how that might make things difficult for you," I say.

Marla looks at me askance, wondering whether I'm being sympathetic or patronizing.

"I see it a lot," I explain, "with the kids I teach. The ones whose moms and dads have broken up. The parent they spend the most time with gets stuck playing the bad cop all the time."

She's uncertain how to react to me now. My apparent sympathy for her predicament has temporarily befuddled her. "Yeah, well . . ." She slumps back in the booth, her eyes trailing away. "That waiter's sure taking his time."

I sense a slackening of her defences and cautiously lean forward. "What did Severn say to you?" I ask.

"Not all that much, really," she says coolly. "She didn't have to."

"Meaning?"

"There's something about that book, isn't there? Something you're not telling me."

"I don't know what you're talking about."

Marla can see that I'm lying.

I wearily let my hands drop on the table. "Forget it," I say, trying to stuff the genie back in the bottle. "Forget I ever mentioned it."

"You bastard," she says. "You're not going to tell me what it is, are you?"

The waiter clears his throat. He's been standing there, waiting for us to notice him, for I don't know how long. He hands us a couple of menus and asks us if we'd like some coffee to start with. I tell him I'm not interested, even though the only thing I've eaten all day is a Timbit. Marla describes Avery and Severn to him. She asks if he remembers either of them from last night. He says they have a lot of people come through the bistro. He asks us whether we're sure we don't want to order anything.

Before I can tell Marla that there's no point in hanging around, I feel an icy draft from the front entrance spill past my ankles. Marla's eyes shift from the waiter and lock on the person who's just walked in. I recognize the flash of anger in her cheeks before the parental reflexes take over, coiling her muscles tight to propel her out of the booth. I track her stare and see Avery in his baggy pants and jacket. He scans the bistro uneasily, still unaware of us. He's already started to back out the door when he sees me with his mother and freezes like a startled rabbit.

Mother and son wait for each other to make the first move. Marla wriggles out of the booth and stands, ready to chase after

Avery but hoping she won't have to suffer the indignity. The waiter sees that he's become irrelevant, shrugs, and moves to another table. Avery's calculating the consequences of bolting out the door, I can tell. In the end, he shuffles towards us, careful not to look at me, feeling the heat of my gaze.

"Hi, Mom," he says, pretending this is some happy chance encounter. I wonder what lies his brain is frantically trying to concoct.

Marla doesn't reply. She waits for an explanation, an apology, a sign of remorse.

"You guys having lunch?" he says, continuing to play it cool. "They have great burgers here."

I get to my feet. "Where's Severn?" I ask, not bothering to conceal the threat implied by my question.

"Oh hi, Mr. Cruickshank," he says, as if he's just noticed me.

Marla steers Avery away. This is her son, and if there's any interrogating to be done, she'll be the one doing it. "Do you know how worried I've been about you?" she says, struggling to keep her voice from quavering.

"I figured you'd know where I was," he says, shrugging off his guilt with practised indifference. "Besides, the battery on my cell was dead." He sneaks a peek at me over his mother's shoulder, the hint of a smirk on his face. He thinks that I can't touch him, that he's safe with his mother between us.

Marla deepens her voice in a clumsy effort to assert her authority. "Did you bring Severn with you?"

He contemplates the slush-encrusted tops of his running shoes.

"Well?" I say menacingly.

He looks up at his mother. "She asked me to drive her," he tells her, as if it were no big deal. Despite his off-handedness, I can see the splotches on his face turning crimson.

Marla shakes her head incredulously. "So you didn't think I'd have a problem with your skipping a day of school?" she asks.

"Not to mention spending the night alone with a girl in your father's condo?"

"Dad said I could use the place anytime I wanted to," he shoots back.

"I'm sure he did," she says bitterly.

This little mother–son shuffle is getting us nowhere. Severn could be wandering the streets alone, searching for Livingston. She'd be easy prey for any pervert who took a fancy to her. The longer we stand here listening to Avery's half-assed excuses, the less chance I have of finding her in time and getting her home safely.

I brush past Marla and take a step towards Avery. "Where is she?" I ask.

He stuffs his hands in his pockets, still trying to look unconcerned. "Hey, she wanted a lift, I gave her a lift. She's probably shopping or something."

"When did you see her last?" I ask, continuing to press him.

He hesitates before he answers, as if he's still working out his alibi. "Last night," he says, clearly not wanting to elaborate.

"And what happened last night?"

His stoop deepens. "Nothing," he says, no longer able to look me in the eye.

"Why don't I believe you?"

"She was looking for a place to stay," he says, as if that justified whatever he wasn't telling me.

I've had enough. I grab a handful of his jacket and yank him towards me. "Where is she?" I ask again.

Avery staggers, barely staying on his feet. He looks at me as if I'm some kind of lunatic off his meds, inexplicably bent on his destruction. Marla shrieks like a mother bird defending a hatchling. She tries to pull me away, but loses her grip as I shove Avery towards our booth.

"Tell me what happened," I say. My rage is burlesque. I fling him to the bench. He flails, clawing at the vinyl, nearly sliding under the table. I stand over him, shaking, wanting to blame him for turning Severn against me, but it's useless. I know that she ran away because of me. It's all my fault. I deserve her contempt. I've lied to her since the day she was born. My anger begins to collapse in on itself. Suddenly there's nothing left to hold me up. I grab blindly for a chair at an adjoining table and sink into it, a quivering, gelatinous lump.

The whole bistro has stopped to gawk at the incredible imploding man. I can feel it. The annoying waiter, who's poised to call the cops. The couple a few tables away, who nervously slide to the edge of their seats, ready to break for the rear exit. Marla, who hovers over me, not sure whether to console me or restrain me. But it's Avery's look of fear mixed with revulsion that makes me shrivel even further, until I'm just a stain in the chair.

Chapter 14

Helen asked me to tell her more about Lady Jane Franklin. I conducted most of our private lessons on the subject in her bed, where we now spent most of our time. I taught her about Lady Jane's success at enlisting Charles Dickens to refute scandalous (but accurate) claims that the valiant men of her husband's expedition had resorted to cannibalism in a final, futile attempt to save themselves from starvation. She learned about Lady Jane's infamous, although perhaps unfairly portrayed, role in precipitating the dismissal of Sir John as the governor of Van Dieman's Land (present-day Tasmania), and her subsequent efforts to secure for him the Arctic command that ultimately regained his reputation and took his life. I told Helen about an alleged incident when Lady Jane, concerned that her husband not catch cold on the eve of his fateful voyage, covered him as he lay dozing in their parlour with the Union Jack she was sewing for the expedition. Sir John was reported to have woken up in alarm and exclaimed: "Good God, woman! Don't you know that they drape flags over men at sea when they're dead?"

Often when I woke up in the middle of the night, I'd find Helen sitting cross-legged at the end of the bed, her bare, freckled back towards me, scribbling in a spiral-bound notebook. I knew that she was using my lessons about Lady Jane to write a new story. Sometimes I'd slip in behind her, kissing the back of her neck or sliding my hand up her naked thigh, trying to get a peek at what she'd written so far. "Not now," she'd say, flicking me away and pressing the notebook against her breasts. "You can read it when it's finished."

One morning, as she was hunched over her notebook, I brought her a bowl of cereal. She'd been writing most of the night while I'd slept the smug sleep of the sated. I knew that once I left for school, she'd crawl back under the sheets and probably not rise again till noon. I was already dressed, having picked out a shirt and tie from the small collection I now kept hanging in her closet.

"I had a relative on that expedition, you know," I said in an attempt to pique her curiosity.

"Really," she replied, looking up at me doubtfully. She closed her notebook and tucked it firmly under her leg before accepting the bowl and spoon from me.

"It's one of the reasons I got interested in the whole Franklin story to begin with." I sat down beside her on the bed and reached for the notebook. "How's it coming?" I asked.

She slapped my wrist and yanked the notebook out of my reach, spilling a splodge of her cereal on the bedspread in the process. "Now look what you made me do," she said, eyeing the mess in disgust.

I grabbed a fistful of Kleenex from the bedside table and handed them to her. "Meet you at the café on Richmond Street after you get off work?"

"Sure," she said, preoccupied with mopping up the spill.

"What time? Five-thirty?"

"Fine." She fluttered her hand at me, impatient for me to go and let her get back to her writing.

I kissed her on the top of the head and let myself out, checking to make sure I had everything before I left. I hadn't yet graduated to the status that granted me a key to Helen's apartment, and I could imagine the annoyed look on her face if I made her answer the door because I'd forgotten my wallet on her dresser.

I waited for her at the café until six-fifteen. The place had pretty well cleared out by then. The only people remaining were those lonely few who apparently didn't have anyone to go home to. I wandered across the street to the bookshop and pressed my face against the front window, but the place was shut tight from what I could see. I backed up to the curb. The sun had sunk behind the building just enough that I could make out a faint glow in the window upstairs.

I tried calling Helen at home that night, but there was no answer. I lay alone in my own bed, unable to sleep, the image of her flush-cheeked biology prof emerging from the closet stairway replaying itself in my head. By dawn, the image had multiplied into a parade of middle-aged men descending the stairs from the garret one after the other, each wearing a uniformly supercilious grin.

I called her one last time before I headed off to school the next morning. She answered but was none too pleased that I'd woken her up.

"Where were you last night?" I asked.

"What do you mean?" she said groggily.

"The café. Five-thirty."

"Were we supposed to meet?" Her tone implied that I was making it up, and even if I wasn't, that she could hardly be expected to remember every little date she made with me.

"I called last night, but you didn't answer."

"I got writing," she said dismissively. I could tell that she didn't much care for my self-righteous tone. "That's what an aspiring writer's supposed to do, isn't it?"

I looked at the clock in my apartment and saw that I was running late. I regretted calling her and starting this fight. There was no time for a graceful resolution. I knew it would fester with both of us for the rest of the day. "Listen," I said, switching hurriedly to damage control, "why don't I take you out to supper tonight? Someplace special."

She hummed and hawed, wanting me to show some contrition by grovelling. By the time I was done, I had completely prostrated myself and was in serious danger of arriving late for homeroom. Nonetheless, I had a date.

It would have been simplest if I'd met her at the bookshop; however, I didn't feel like waiting outside just so Walter could glower at me through the window like I was a tomcat on the prowl. Helen thought I was silly for taking her father's order of banishment so seriously. She accused me of cowardice unbecoming a man hoping to win her favour. I assured her that Walter didn't scare me; I had no delusions about a dungeon filled with failed suitors in the shop's basement. The truth of the matter was that I simply respected his right to hold sovereignty over his own domain, as anyone who taught the history of kings and feudal lords would.

I called on her instead at her apartment a half an hour before our seven-thirty reservation. She wasn't home. I waited in the parking lot until a quarter to eight, but she never showed up. Reasoning that she had got off work late and decided to go directly to the restaurant, I drove downtown. The maître d' informed me that Ms Donnelly had not yet arrived. Would I care to wait for her at our table? After fifteen minutes of sitting with the menu unopened in front of me, I got up and tried her number on the payphone by the coat check. No answer.

I drove home via Richmond Street, trying to invent excuses on Helen's behalf. When I passed the bookshop, I saw the light on upstairs.

A fine rain had begun to fall by the time I circled the block and parked the car. Maple keys from the trees in Victoria Park had twirled to the ground on the balmy spring breeze, searching for a soft patch of earth to impregnate with their seeds. They crunched under my feet as I walked towards the shop. The headlights of approaching cars reflected off the glistening pavement, making it difficult for me to see in the shop's front window. I could just barely make out a faint light at the back of the store. It took me a moment to recognize that it was coming from the closet that led upstairs.

I walked around the corner and looked in through the glass of the side door. I could see the light more clearly now, spilling out from under the floral curtain that veiled the doorway to the garret. The fabric fluttered, seemingly from a breeze wafting down the stairs. I tried the door. It was unlocked.

I hesitated, imagining Walter's satisfaction when I was arrested for breaking into his shop after hours. Then I wondered if the door had been left purposely unlocked for someone without a key to the shop. I stepped inside.

The wooden floor creaked beneath my shoes. I paused to see whether my entrance had been heard. No one stirred overhead. I brushed the curtain back and stepped inside the closet. The steps ascended sharply to an opening that was dimly defined by the half light of the room above. I climbed up, my hands feeling their way along the nosing of the higher steps.

I emerged like a gopher from its hole into the attic. A lone hurricane lamp held vigil, illuminating the rough-hewn walls that sloped with the pitch of the roof. The floorboards smelled of rope and sawdust and kerosene. A wooden jib and pulley that had once hauled goods from horse-drawn carts in the street below stood sulking by a boarded-up window. As I crawled up on the deck of the floor, I sensed I was in a kind of anteroom, a weigh station between a past century and my own. Down a galleyway and through a low doorway, I could see movement.

I crept along the galleyway, cringing at the sound of each squeaky floorboard. As I drew closer, I could see that the room was lined with flickering candles. A chair sat empty at an antique writing desk. Vague shadows swept across the walls; I imagined the obscene dance of bodies that was casting them. But still I moved forward, drawn inexorably to the humiliation that I was certain awaited me.

I stepped into the doorway. Helen looked up at me from the settee, startled.

"Jesus Christ!" she said, her hand to her heart.

In her surprise, she let the manuscript she'd been flipping through fall to the floor. She was completely alone.

"What the hell were you thinking, sneaking up on me like that?" she said. "A woman alone in an attic. Jesus, I thought you were some wacko rapist."

"You shouldn't have left the side door unlocked," I said, admonishing her to hide my embarrassment.

She frowned as if preparing to contradict me, but then thought better of it. My sudden presence in her garret was a rather annoying fact that she seemed ill-prepared to explain away. She began gathering up her papers from the floor.

"I waited for you," I told her. "First at your apartment building, then at the restaurant."

She kept collecting her papers from the floor.

I crossed my arms and leaned against the door frame. "Is there something you're trying to tell me?"

"What do you mean?" she said, reaching for a page that had strayed under the settee.

"That I'm suddenly past my best-before date or something. That our time is up, but I'm too dense to take the hint."

"Hint?" she said, as if I were talking piffle.

"Two nights in a row you've stood me up. Some might call that a hint. Although not a very subtle one."

"Ah," she said, blithely arranging the pages into their proper order. "Our restaurant reservation. What time is it now?"

"Nearly nine o'clock."

She peered under her desk. "I'm missing page eight. Help me find page eight."

"Come on, Helen," I said, my hands dropping to my sides in frustration. "You can't just pretend I'm not here. At least make a tiny, little effort." I could tell I wasn't getting through to her. I flopped down on the settee, disconsolate. "I thought we had something. Not just the sex—which, don't get me wrong, is pretty incredible—but a special . . . I don't know . . . connection. Something that might last beyond a few weeks in the sack."

She blinked at me. "Are you finished?"

"Why?" I said, bracing myself to be dumped.

She handed me the manuscript.

"What's this?" I asked, caught off guard.

"I wanted you to be the first person to read it."

"Your story?" I said, taking it from her uncertainly.

She leaned over and kissed me long and slow. "Thank you, teacher," she said as our lips finally parted. "For being so awfully patient with me."

I'd been granted another reprieve. I pulled her down on the settee beside me and held her close, content to sniff her sweet lavender scent and watch the candlelight flicker on the ceiling. "I suppose you want me to read it now," I said after a few minutes.

She sat up, smiling. "What I want you to do is take me to supper first. I'm starving."

I nearly lost my footing on the steep steps following Helen down into the shop with the manuscript tucked under my arm. She kissed me again when I stepped through the floral curtain, whispering seductively that she'd be with me as soon as she collected her purse from under the cash register. I dawdled along a few steps behind her as she moved into the front of the shop. The light from a car driving down Richmond Street slid up the shelves of the classics section and across the pressed-tin ceiling, elongating the shadows in the room. Before the light slipped away, I saw an incongruous look of horror on Helen's face. At her feet, one shadow was slanted differently from the rest. It took me a moment to realize that it was a leg.

Helen froze in panic as she stood over Walter. He was crumpled behind the cash register, his other leg folded underneath him, his back against the base of the counter. When I got to him, I could tell he'd wet his pants by the dank smell of urine. His eyelids flickered as I shook him for signs of life. He laid a shaky hand on my arm. I told Helen to call an ambulance, praying his weak grip on me wouldn't slip.

Chapter 15

I wake up in somebody else's bed with my clothes on, my knees tucked to my chest. I'm drenched with sweat as if I'm breaking a fever. The sheets smell vaguely of men's cologne. The room is dark, lit only by streetlight from the window. I slowly take in my shadowy surroundings—a computer on a desk in the corner, an oversized bottle of aftershave on the dresser across the room, and a set of suit jackets and pants in dry-cleaner's bags hanging from the back of the closed door. I roll to my other side. The glowing numbers of the bedside clock radio read 7:12 p.m.

The liquor of sleep still fills my veins. It tries to take me under again. I know that all I have to do is close my eyes, and I'll be gone. The thought is seductive, but I fight it. I claw my way to the edge of the bed. I can't summon the energy to sit up, so I lie on my belly and let my legs slide off the bed until I'm kneeling on the floor, my face still planted on the mattress. Slowly I push myself up. I feel like a little kid saying his bedtime prayers.

I have a fuzzy recollection of Avery fumbling with the key to his father's condo, of Marla making up the bed and insisting I get some rest. My meltdown at the bistro now seems ridiculously theatrical. I shouldn't have let a little low blood sugar and a few nights' lack of sleep overwhelm me so. Of course I know it was more than that. For the first time since Severn was born, I suddenly doubt I'm the man I've always held myself out to be: the steadfast father, the understanding husband. I've spun fictions no less devious than Livingston's, except that he makes his deceptions plain by binding them between two covers, while I pass mine off as fact in the guise of normal family life. No wonder my legs have been knocked from under me now that all my years of prevarication are starting to fall apart. I can feel my tenuous grip on Severn slipping. If I lose her, I know it will be like losing Helen all over again.

It's several minutes before I gather enough confidence to wobble to my feet. As I steady myself against the bedside table, I consider the seam of light at the bottom of the bedroom door. I wonder what awaits me on the other side. I set the doorknob as my target and slowly make my way towards it through the shadows, testing my footing with each step. I achieve my objective unscathed. I turn the knob.

The light on the other side of the door hurts my eyes. I totter awkwardly on the threshold until I adjust to the glare. The smell of toast and coffee greets me. For a moment, I panic that it's breakfast time and I've slept through the night after all. I stagger forward into the living room, stopping after only a few steps to lean against the back of a leather reclining chair that's pointed at an oversized TV screen. The Weather Network is on, the sound muted. More snow forecast. Wind chill overnight. The time stamp at the bottom of the screen reassures me.

Marla's heard me and emerges from the kitchen to investigate, a slice of toast in her hand. She prudently keeps her distance. "You're up," she says uncertainly.

"Barely," I say, surveying the leather-and-chrome decor, which I obviously failed to notice in my stupor when I first arrived.

"You want some toast?" she asks. "The pickings are pretty slim, I'm afraid. Jay hardly has any food in the place."

"That's okay," I say, waving her off.

"For Christ's sake," she says, "you need to eat something. I think I saw a can of stew. I'll heat it up for you."

"Why are you doing this?" I ask her.

"What?"

"Trying to take care of me," I say. "Didn't I just about throttle your son?"

"Maybe I should have let you finish the job," she says, casting a disgruntled glance at the closed door beside the one I exited. She and Avery must have had a tête-à-tête while I was out of it, I realize, and now he's sulking in the spare bedroom.

"I had no right to go apeshit like that," I say. "I'm a teacher. People are supposed to be able to trust me with their kids. You should have called the cops."

"You're welcome," she says acerbically and heads back into the kitchen.

She makes me sit at the dining-room table and watches to make sure I eat. Once the food hits my tongue, my hunger awakens, making even the preformed meat chunks delectable. The bowl is empty before I know it. She refills it for me.

"Apparently, Severn was gone when Avery got up this morning," she says. "He's been looking for her most of the day." She judges my mood carefully before continuing. "I asked him what happened last night."

I stop eating. "And?"

"He was vague on the details," she says.

I push my bowl away. I've lost my appetite again.

"Avery's always been a loner," she confesses. "When he first brought Severn home, I wasn't sure what was going on between them. He didn't have any experience with girls, and I didn't want him getting in over his head. Of course, when I asked him about Severn, he just shrugged and answered in monosyllables." She meets my distrustful gaze, feeling obliged to defend her vigilance as a mother. "I kept my eye on them, just in case you're wondering."

"When you were at home," I say.

I hear a key in the front door. Marla turns in her chair, then curses under her breath. A moment later, a wide-shouldered man carrying a suitcase and a garment bag enters the living room. He does a double take when he sees us looking back at him from the dining room and slowly removes his fogged-up glasses.

"Hello," he says, waiting for Marla to explain. It's not hard for me to figure out from his territorial air that this is her ex-husband.

She smiles at him stiffly. "Avery said you weren't supposed to be back for another couple of days."

"I got called back early," he says. "Crisis at the office." He holds out his hand to me. "Jay Costello. And you are . . . ?"

I get up unsteadily. "Irving Cruickshank."

We shake. He keeps a firm grip on my hand as he studies my bleary eyes and dishevelled hair. "Looks like you're not long out of bed, Irving," he says, slipping a cynical sideways glance at Marla.

Marla resents the innuendo. "We came here looking for Avery," she tells Jay.

"Oh yes?" he says sceptically.

"He brought a girl here last night without telling me," she says. "Irving is the girl's father."

"I see," he says. He tosses his overcoat on the back of the leather chair in the living room and squeezes past us with his bags.

Marla follows him into his bedroom while I hover outside in the living room. I see him plonk his bags on the bed, but not before he takes note of the rumpled sheets.

"Where's the girl?" he asks Marla.

"She's gone missing," she tells him.

"Ah." He starts unpacking. "I take it you don't approve of Avery's behaviour."

"He didn't come home last night," she says. "What was I supposed to think?"

"That he's seventeen," he says, tossing some socks in his laundry hamper.

"Meaning?"

"Honestly, Marla. How long did you expect him to stay a virgin?"

"He had no right to worry me like that."

"So what was he supposed to do? Ask you for permission to spend a night with this girl?"

I don't much care for the direction this conversation is taking. "Excuse me," I protest.

Jay looks at me as though he's annoyed to find me still hanging around. He removes all the suits from his garment bag together and hangs them in his closet. "Where's Avery now?"

"In the spare room," Marla says.

Jay brushes past me and knocks on the door of the spare room. "Avery," he says to the door. "It's Dad. Can you come out here, please?" He wanders into the living room, unclips his cellphone from his belt, and sets it on the coffee table. He picks up the TV remote and flicks through the channels, finally settling on a business newscast.

The door opens slowly. Avery sees me and immediately averts his gaze. He shuffles into the living room, giving me a wide berth, his hands in his pockets.

Jay turns to look at him. "Avery," he says, "your mother seems to think you had a girl here last night. Is that true?"

"It's not what you think," Avery says, weary from his mother's interrogation.

"Calm down," Jay says. "I don't have a problem if you did. So long as you were safe about it."

Avery casts a wary glance my way. "Severn asked me to drive her to Toronto. She needed a place to crash. We're friends, okay? I wanted to help."

Jay loosens his tie and begins polishing his glasses. "Didn't you think her father would worry when she didn't come home last night?"

"She asked me not to tell anyone," Avery says.

Even in her grief, Severn has this boy wrapped around her little finger, a skill she inherited from her mother. He seems too prone to embarrassment to have taken advantage of her.

"Where is she?" I ask.

"I wish I knew," he mutters. I can see him reconsidering his defence. "When I woke up this morning, she was gone."

Despite his hangdog expression, I wonder whether he's covering for her still. I can hardly blame him, considering my blow-up at the bistro.

"Look," I say, "I just want to know that she's safe."

He falls silent. Marla directs an I-told-you-so look my way. She begins clearing the dishes from the dining room table. Jay, weary from travel, massages his eyes, clearly not in the mood for a prolonged question and answer session. I'm about to write off my chances of discovering anything useful from Avery, when he clears his throat.

"I drove her to some apartment yesterday," he volunteers. "I was going to check there next."

"Apartment?" I ask.

He looks at me circumspectly. "In the West End," he says. "She made me wait in the car."

Marla pauses, surprised, and perhaps a little annoyed, that Avery is offering this information to me instead of her.

"Do you remember the address?" I ask.

He gives me the cross streets. Marla finds me a pen and paper so I can write them down. He says the building looked like an old factory.

"I think she went to see that writer guy," he says.

Now it's my turn to fall silent.

"What writer guy?" Marla asks. I can feel her staring at me.

"The guy at the bookstore," Avery says impatiently, loath to revisit the whole shoplifting incident with his mother. "The guy Severn got all weird over."

"How long was she inside?" I ask curtly.

Avery considers this for a moment. "I don't know. Ten, maybe fifteen minutes?"

Jay has grown bored with the conversation. He's started to flip through the channels again.

"Did she say anything when she got back to the car?" I ask Avery, not entirely sure I'm ready for the answer.

Avery shakes his head. "But I saw someone looking down at us from one of the windows. An apartment on the third floor. The end of the building closest to the park."

Despite all his evasions, I can see that he cares what happens to Severn in his own inept, self-absorbed, adolescent way. I begin to sense the loyalty he feels he owes her, and his remorse at having betrayed it. What's more, I realize that in the past year, he's seen more of her then I have, and as a consequence, he probably understands the girl she's become far better.

I fold the address and stuff it in my shirt pocket. "I think it's time I was going."

I feel Avery's eyes following me as I head to the front hall to collect my jacket. For an instant, I almost believe he's about to offer to join me.

Jay follows me to the front door, making sure that I'm well and truly on my way. "Nice meeting you, Irving," he says with about as much sincerity as a pitch man on the Shopping Channel.

I slide my feet into my shoes. The insoles are still cold and wet.

Marla pushes past me to get her anorak. "You're not going out there on your own," she says. "You're barely back on your feet."

"I'm fine," I say.

She looks back at Avery as though she feels she owes him a partial apology but doesn't know how to word it. There's a moment's sticky silence between them.

"Wait here until I get back," is all she tells him in the end. I can see that she's not thrilled leaving him with Jay, but for whatever reason, her priorities are finding Severn and keeping me out of trouble in the process. I'm not sure that I like the idea of becoming her latest lost cause, but I have too little energy to protest with any effectiveness. I let her hustle me out the door.

Chapter 16

After the ambulance came for Walter, I drove Helen to the emergency department. The paramedics had already rushed him in on a stretcher by the time we arrived. As I hurried through the sliding doors, I quickly realized that Helen was no longer by my side. I looked back to see her standing motionless on the sidewalk. I circled back, squeezed her hand, and blathered on at her reassuringly—not that I really understood what to say that would soothe her frayed nerves. After all, she'd just found her father sprawled on the floor of his own shop and immediately come to the realization that while he'd been gasping for life, she'd been working her feminine wiles on me directly overhead. After a few seconds of my prattling, she pulled herself together with a deep, if slightly ragged, breath and let her hand slip out of mine, as though I'd offered it like some garish gift at an inopportune moment. She proceeded to corral her unruly hair with a clip, wipe her puffy eyes with the back of her hand, then stubbornly will herself through the doors.

We caught up with Walter near the triage desk. Despite Helen's efforts to put up a brave front, she almost immediately shrank back from him, horrified by his gaunt, vacant face. There was no denying it: her lion-hearted father had been reduced to a withered carcass. Before she could summon the courage to step forward again, he was whisked away, leaving her to field a nurse's questions about his medical history, most of which she couldn't answer.

We spent the night waiting outside the cardiac care unit, and Helen continued to shun my efforts to comfort her. She sat as rigid as a cenotaph, staring into space, her eyes shifting, apparently replaying on an invisible screen in front of her each moment of grief she'd inflicted on her father since she was a teenager. I got the distinct impression that as she tallied the transgressions, I was included among them.

I gave Helen some space, convinced that her guilt-ridden reaction was to be expected under the circumstances, and that my best strategy was to wait her out. Not knowing what else to do, I phoned in reinforcements in the form of Will, who appeared on the scene a scant fifteen minutes later. Helen fell blubbering into his arms the moment he arrived as if he were the caring older brother she'd never had. It made me shamefully jealous, even though I realized that Will posed no threat to me. I comforted myself with the notion that that was why Helen accepted his sympathy over mine—it was safe, devoid of sexual baggage. I wondered if she realized how much he quietly resented her for frittering away the faith that Walter had placed in her but withheld from him.

As Helen and Will commiserated, I retired to a quiet seat at the end of the row and pulled Helen's manuscript from my jacket pocket.

"What the hell do you think you're doing?" she snapped when she noticed.

Will turned to look at me, curious to see what I'd done to set Helen off.

"Sorry," I said, quickly putting the manuscript back in my pocket. I realized too late that it reminded her of the argument she'd had with her father in the garret only a few days before, which she'd probably concluded had been the offence that had pushed him over the edge. "I'll read it later."

When Helen got up a few minutes later to find a washroom, Will shifted to the seat next to me. "So," he said softly, "that must have been quite a shock for you, finding Walter like that."

"You could say that."

He studied me for a moment. "You've done well," he said. "Sticking with Helen this long. What's it been? Three weeks? I think you're approaching some kind of longevity record."

"Are you telling me you keep statistics?"

Will chuckled. "Not exactly." He scanned the coastline to check that Helen wasn't returning prematurely from the washroom, then leaned in towards me conspiratorially. "Still, you seem more intent than most of her boyfriends."

"Yeah, well, bully for me, I guess."

"I hope you haven't made the mistake of actually falling in love with her."

I smiled perversely. "History owes a great deal to men too naive or too stubborn to recognize the folly of their quests."

"I see," he said, nodding his condolences.

"I can't help it, Will. I see something in her—brilliant flashes of this warm, thoughtful woman waiting to be discovered. And then the very next moment, she shuts me out, and I feel that I'm about to be sloughed off like every other man she's ever slept with."

"You're sure you're not just chasing an illusion?" he asked.

I fell silent. It was a question that I'd tried hard not to ask myself.

Not long after Helen returned from the washroom, a male nurse came out to tell her that she could see her father. She hesitated, then looked at Will nervously, completely ignoring me. Will stood resolutely and extended his hand to her. The nurse interjected, advising them that only immediate family were allowed inside. Helen said that wasn't a problem, since Will was her brother. The nurse nodded, seeing no obvious reason to disbelieve her, and escorted them through the imposing doors of the cardiac unit.

Rather than sit like a boob on my own, staring at the walls and ceiling tiles, I decided to go downstairs to look for a coffee machine. I found the nearest bank of elevators and pushed the call button. After a while, one set of doors dinged open, but the elevator was going up. A guy whose jacket and pants were too big for him stepped off. His cheeks were sunken, and he wore a ball cap to cover the translucent veins of his bald head. He seemed to recognize me.

"Lieutenant Bayfield," he said, finally placing me. "Donnelly's Books." His voice was painfully young and hopeful, tipping me off that he'd probably been out of high school for only a couple of years.

I smiled at him politely, still waiting for my elevator to arrive.

"You must be here for Walter," he said, undaunted by my sub-dued response.

"You know Walter?" I asked uncertainly.

"I know Will Graham," he said eagerly. "Is he here?"

"He's in the unit, visiting," I said. "With Walter's daughter." If it hadn't been for his street clothes, I would have assumed he was a patient wandering the halls with a case of late-night insomnia. As it was, I doubted that he was simply a casual friend of Will's paying his respects, given that the rest of the city was fast asleep.

"How's Walter doing anyway?" he asked, lowering his voice as if he'd just remembered the gravity of the situation.

"Not good," I said.

He nodded gravely, but within a few seconds, a smile returned to his emaciated face. "You're Helen's boyfriend, right? Will talks a lot about you."

"You don't say."

"Maybe even a little too much," he said with a laugh. "Made me wonder whether I shouldn't be getting jealous ." He wagged his finger at me. "I'm Kevin," he said significantly.

"Ah," I said, pretending his name meant something to me.

His smile began to slip. "Will never mentioned me, I take it."

"Sorry," I said.

He shrank like a leaky balloon. There was hardly enough of him left to keep his clothes standing. "I guess that shouldn't surprise me," he said.

"Will and I don't really know each other all that well," I said awkwardly, feeling obliged to lessen the blow.

"Which way to the waiting area?" Kevin asked, trying to overcome his disappointment.

I showed him the way. As he took a seat, I saw a spot on the back of his neck and another on his wrist like the ones I'd seen described in magazine articles over the past two years. Most scientists were quoted as saying that the disease could be passed on only through bodily fluids, that you couldn't catch it like a cold. Just the same, when he coughed, I held my breath.

"Who are you doing next?" he asked, oblivious to my cowardice.

"Excuse me?" I said.

"At the bookshop," he said. "What figure from history are you going to be next?"

"Unfortunately, I had to cut my run short."

"Too bad. You could have been an actor."

I smiled at him civilly.

"*I'm* an actor, you know," he said, almost shyly. His need to engage me in conversation seemed a little desperate.

"No kidding."

"Commercials, mostly," he said so I wouldn't get the idea he was trying to puff himself up. "I mean, I haven't actually done any yet, but I have an agent in Toronto."

"Huh," I said, trying to sound impressed.

"I wish I'd had you as a history teacher," he said. "The guy who taught me in grade ten was a living fossil."

"I'm sorry to hear you had a bad experience."

He contemplated the depressing green walls for a moment. I wondered how many times he'd already seen the inside of this place, and how many more times he'd see it in the days to come.

"Those old surveying instruments you were showing the kids at the bookshop," he said with unrelenting, boyish curiosity. "Do you actually know how to work those things?"

Before long, he had me explaining navigation by the sun and the stars. I couldn't help myself. He seemed so eager to make up for what he'd missed out on in high school. In exchange, he told me how much he enjoyed lying on his parents' dock on Georgian Bay and watching the northern lights spill across the summer sky. Then he went on to share with me his favourite "Star Trek" episodes.

He was still chattering away when Will and Helen finally emerged from the cardiac care unit. Helen looked paler than when she'd gone in.

"Is everything okay?" I asked her. When she didn't respond, I looked to Will, but his attention was fixed on Kevin. He seemed startled, even a little alarmed, to see him.

Kevin smiled anxiously at him. "I thought I'd come by to . . . you know, see if there was anything I could do," he said, pressured by Will's dubious greeting into justifying his presence. "I know how much Walter means to you."

I ignored the scene unfolding between them and kept my focus on Helen. She sank into one of the waiting-room chairs and rubbed her arms as if she'd caught a chill. I approached her and tentatively laid my hand on her knee. She didn't wiggle away this time, just gnawed at her bottom lip.

"They say the next few hours will tell the story," Will said sombrely, looking away from Kevin just long enough to answer my question, then taking him firmly by the arm and hustling him aside. He began hissing at his young boyfriend below the threshold of my hearing, likely admonishing him for coming to a building filled with sick people and vicious, opportunistic bugs in his condition. I couldn't help thinking that Will might also have been a tad irked at having his cover blown, at having a side of his life revealed that I wasn't meant to see.

I leaned closer to Helen, still trying to get her to make eye contact with me. "You want me to get you something to eat?" I asked her. "You never got any supper."

She shook her head.

"How 'bout a coffee?" I asked.

She finally looked at me, her eyes hollow. "Don't you have your first class in a few hours?" she asked, offering me an excuse to leave her alone.

"I thought I'd stay," I said.

She shrugged.

Having completed his dressing-down of Kevin, Will interrupted our awkward little exchange. "Look," he said apologetically to Helen, "I should leave now if I'm going to open the shop this morning."

She nodded, knowing that Walter wouldn't want to hear that the shop had failed to continue on without him.

Will steered Kevin towards the elevators. "I enjoyed our conversation," Kevin called back to me, determined not to let Will's bad mood put a damper on his enthusiasm, at least not in my presence.

I stuck by Helen for a few more prickly hours, until a doctor came out to tell her that her father was in no immediate danger, that they'd continue to monitor him closely, and that the hospital would call her if there was any change in his condition.

I drove her home, reminding her that if there was anything she needed, she had only to let me know.

She never called. In fact, she didn't answer any of my calls after that.

Chapter 17

"Well?" Marla asks once I park across the street from the apartment building. "Are you going to tell me why Severn is so interested in Jack Livingston?"

The building is one of those old West End warehouses that's been converted into lofts. I look up at the windows on the third floor. The lights are on in the apartment at the end closest to the park.

Marla sees me peering at the window. "You think she's up there, don't you?" she says. "With him."

"Jack Livingston is an old friend of the family," I say blandly, trying to quell her vivid imagination.

"Really." She swings the passenger door open. "Then you won't mind me tagging along."

She's already out of the car before I can object. I consider staying buckled in my seat, refusing to indulge her nosiness any further, but I realize what a hopelessly petulant act that would be. I'm also forced to concede that as much as I resent having Marla as an escort, I wouldn't have made it this far without her.

A doughy man with a red face is shovelling the snow from in front of the main entrance, looking like he's about to have a heart attack. He leans on his shovel and wheezes softly as we pass, giving us the once-over with bloodshot eyes. I ignore him and hold the door open for Marla. He resumes shovelling, casting a suspicious glance through the glass doors as we scan the listing of tenants on the callboard in the vestibule.

"Doesn't look like he's listed," she says.

"Celebrities like their privacy," I say.

"I've never met a famous author before," she says coyly. "What's he like?"

I shrug indifferently.

Marla sees that I still haven't figured out how I'm going to get in the building. "I guess he can't be a very close friend of the family if you don't have his phone number to tell him we're here."

Our predicament is solved when a man wheeling a double bass in a huge black case steps off the elevator and struggles to get it through the security door. I quickly step in to help him, giving us the chance to slip into the lobby once he's clear. The red-faced man outside has been watching, however, and marches towards us, shovel in hand. I guide Marla into the open elevator by the elbow. Fortunately, the doors close behind us before the man and his shovel can cross the lobby.

"So how did Severn get this address?" she asks.

I frown at her, annoyed by the perceptiveness of her question.

"Come on," she says. "Don't try to tell me you knew it before Avery gave it to you."

It's a disturbingly good question. I want to assume that Livingston slipped it to Severn at the bookstore before she bolted, except that doesn't seem to make a whole lot of sense within the scenario I've sketched for myself to explain what happened that day. Why would she blithely accept the address from him one moment, then turn and run out of the store with his book under her arm the next? I silently watch the floor numbers count up as I consider the unsettling possibility that she got it some other way at some other time.

When the elevator opens on the third floor, my nose is

assaulted by the smell of cooked cabbage. We make our way to the end of the corridor until I'm pretty certain we're outside the proper apartment. I wipe my sweaty palms on my pants and knock on the door. I realize too late that I haven't thought of what I'm going to say if I find Severn here.

After a moment, the door opens a crack. A woman who's thirty-five going on sixty-five, dressed in a knee-length T-shirt and fuzzy slippers, scrutinizes me from inside. She keeps the chain on the door.

"Is this where Jack Livingston lives?" I ask.

She replies by slamming the door in my face.

Marla looks at me with a smirk. "Definitely not a close friend of the family."

I knock again, this time louder. I know this might be the wrong apartment, but until I can get confirmation either way, I'm not about to give up. "Just tell me if a girl visited you yesterday," I shout. "Her name's Severn. She's my daughter. I'm looking for her."

"She's not here," the woman yells back from the other side of the door. Her voice sounds of whisky and cigarettes.

"Did she come here?" I shout back, certain that every tenant on the third floor can hear me now. "Just tell me if you've seen her."

No response.

"Listen," I say, "I'm worried. I haven't heard from her in two days. I'd really appreciate your help."

Still no answer. After several moment's silence, I figure that she's decided to ignore me completely. A bald guy with hairy legs in a floral bathrobe glares from the other end of the hall, his arms akimbo. Just then, the door in front of us cracks open again.

The gravel-voiced woman on the other side inspects me once more, studying my face for signs of treachery. "What kind of name is Severn, anyway?" she asks gruffly.

"Could we come in for a minute?" I ask, noticing that her hawk-ish face has softened just a little.

The woman reluctantly unchains the door. Marla and I step

inside. The place reeks of turpentine, linseed oil, and old cigarette smoke. The bones of the old warehouse are evident here— the worn brick walls, the exposed pipes, the dented metal hoods of the light fixtures hanging from the girdered ceiling two storeys up. Stacks of huge canvases—some violently splashed with colour, others swathed in muted tones—lean against the walls. Paint-spattered easels stand like sentries in the middle of the floor. Various sticks of furniture are scattered about the space as an afterthought—a battered wingback chair, a stained velour loveseat, overturned crates passing as tables. A tiny galley kitchen apologetically occupies one corner of the apartment. A set of stairs leads up to the sleeping area. Old sweatshirts and bras hang from the upstairs railing.

The woman reclaims a burning cigarette from the edge of a saucer that's previously served as a paint palette. "She's not the first kid who's ever come looking for Jack, you know."

Marla glances idly at the canvases in their various stages of completion, pretending not to hear anything, even though I know she's hanging on every word.

"Do you have any idea where I might find her?" I ask the woman.

"I imagine she's still looking for Jack," she says.

"He doesn't live here?"

The woman laughs bitterly. "Not any more. Cleared out two months ago."

"You know where he is now?"

The woman blows out a twin stream of smoke through her nostrils, regarding me as though I'm either terribly slow or terribly insensitive. "He didn't leave a forwarding address."

Marla can't resist any more. She looks up from an unfinished painting of an Arctic landscape that's lying on the floor. "What does that mean? 'She's not the first kid who's ever come looking for Jack'?"

The woman turns to me. "This your girlfriend?" she asks with a cynical smile.

"Just a friend," I say.

She nods at me as if I'm lying. "She doesn't know about Jack and your wife, I take it."

Marla clears her throat, waiting for me to finally explain what's going on. I'm not about to oblige, preoccupied as I am with what the woman might have told Severn.

"Oh, don't worry," the woman says, reading my mind. "I didn't spill the beans to your daughter. Not that it mattered. Seems she already figured things out for herself."

I feel my legs buckle again. I knew all along that the only explanation for Severn's coming to Toronto was that she knew, but hearing it from this wreck of a woman makes it undeniably real to me.

She takes another drag from her cigarette. "So you're Helen's husband."

I look at her, my head spinning. "You knew her?"

"Never met her," she says. "But then, I didn't really have to."

She can see from my punch-drunk expression that I'm not up for riddles, so she starts rummaging through a mound of torn magazines, dog-eared phone bills, and what appear to be cast-off manuscripts that's taken up residence in one corner of the loveseat. From the pile, she shakes loose a single spiral-bound notebook and hands it to me. I accept it hesitantly and stare at the wrinkled cardboard cover, afraid to open it. When I finally work up the nerve to look inside, I'm confronted with Helen's handwriting, with story notes she scrawled while she sat on the end of our bed as I lay sleeping all those years ago. In the margins, someone else's writing intrudes, a man's editorial comments, suggestions on how to make her story work better.

I'd always assumed that Helen was fascinated with Lady Jane Franklin because she saw in her a kindred spirit, a restless, nomadic woman who bent men to her will with her considerable, albeit frequently disingenuous, charm. But now, as I pore through Helen's notes, I see that it was the maddening puzzle of Lady

Jane's devotion to Sir John that cropped up again and again in her writing. I imagined her reconciling it with another familiar story, the one about the bookseller's irrepressible daughter who went on to marry a lapdog husband.

"Jack's been through a lot of women in his life," the woman says. "Once he turns a page and moves on, that's it. He generally doesn't look back. That's what happened to me last month. Our story didn't interest him any more. But Helen . . . seems he never really managed to forget her."

As I continue to flip through the pages, a newspaper clipping slips out and flutters to the floor. I pick it up. It's Helen's obituary. "Do you have any more of these notebooks?" I ask, my throat constricted. I slide the obituary back between the pages like it's a pressed flower.

"Scads of them," the woman says, her voice crackling with phlegm. "Take them if you like. You'd be doing me a favour."

She throws a dropcloth back from a workbench, revealing another snowdrift of paper. I begin sifting through it, rescuing Helen's notebooks from the debris as if they're precious artefacts from an old, unexplained shipwreck. The woman stands back and watches me with artistic detachment.

"Jack used them when he was working on his last novel," she says.

I open up another one. Page after page of Helen's prose, a part of herself that she'd kept private from me, covered with another man's handwriting. "Did you show these to Severn?"

"Hey, I wasn't about to encourage her. Besides, the last thing I needed was some teenage girl blubbering all over my canvases."

I offer her a weak smile of thanks and catch a glint of acknowledgment in her eyes. She recognizes me now as a fellow victim of Livingston's wandering attentions, someone who speaks the same dialect of pain.

"He moved in with a wannabe poet barely out of university," she says, anticipating my next question. "Tight buns, perky tits. A modicum of talent. I don't know where they're living, and I don't care to."

"Is there anywhere else I might find him?" I ask. "A class he's teaching? The library? A favourite bar?"

She studies me, her chin cupped in her hand, the cigarette still protruding from between her fingers. "Your wife. What did she look like?" she asks, as if trying to compose a portrait of Helen and me in her mind.

"Tall," I say, wishing she'd answer my question. "Red hair."

She nods enigmatically. "I thought so."

"I really need to find him," I say, trying to get her back on topic.

She stubs out her cigarette and hoists a canvas onto one of her easels. It's a night-time scene of a rustic churchyard cemetery in early winter. A stone cairn amidst a field of crumbling grave markers dominates the foreground. Its inscription is just beyond deciphering. Light spills out from the open church door across the yard. An arguing couple are captured in the doorway in silhouette, their towering, inverted shadows warring with each other on the snow-dusted sod.

"I finished this just before Jack moved out," she says. "It's some of my best work. He brought it out in me." She sinks back into the wingback chair and gazes at it. "Since then, everything I've done is garbage." She draws up her legs and hugs them to her chest, exposing her threadbare panties. Her hair looks like it hasn't been washed in a week. She gropes between the seat cushion and the arm of the chair, pulls out a mashed pack of cigarettes, and lights up again. Her hand trembles ever so slightly as she tries to hold the lighter steady. "It's what a lover does, I guess: rubs up against you until he wears away a perfect notch that only he can fill. And then once he's gone, all you can feel is the ugly hole he left." She stares intently at her painting. Eventually, she averts her eyes in disgust. "I told your daughter to go home, to get as far away from Jack Livingston as she could. Not that she was about to take advice from a bitter old witch like me."

I stand there staring at her uncertainly, with Helen's notebooks held tight to my chest. She looks up at me, all irony receding from her eyes.

"You've got your stupid notebooks," she says. "It's time you were going."

I feel Marla's hand on my arm. She leads me quietly towards the door like she's an usher at a funeral. I take one last look over my shoulder at the woman, who remains curled up in her chair, rocking herself gently into a state of catatonia.

Chapter 18

I received reliable intelligence from Will that Helen had immersed herself in taking care of her father during the two months since his heart attack. By Will's account, she seemed bound and determined to make up for all the grief she'd given Walter with double measures of devotion—taking up residence in his spare bedroom, cooking his meals, helping him bathe, doing his laundry, and in all other respects acting as his nursemaid.

I called Walter's number and caught her answering the phone one day, but she sidestepped my renewed offer to help. Perhaps she felt that this was her penance to pay on her own, or that Walter wouldn't appreciate my company. Whatever the case, I couldn't compete with the lush guilt she'd wrapped herself in.

Walter's convalescence dragged on, and thus so did Helen's cloister. Even after his strength returned, she continued to fuss over him. Without her, I found the cheeriness of the mid-summer afternoons oppressive. Sometimes I wandered alone through Victoria Park and saw young couples lying on blankets in the warm sun, many pressed together in sweaty clinches, unconcerned by the looks of passers-by. Once I found a girl from one of my history classes lying on top of a boy with a scraggly moustache in the very spot where Helen and I had rolled among the daffodils. Their lips were locked together. The girl's pelvis ground against the boy's crotch. I stared at them, simultaneously repulsed and envious.

Helen had little time for the bookshop while she was looking after her father. Ironic, considering it was the thing closest to his heart. Will was left to run the place on his own. Rather than wallow in my loneliness, I quietly offered to help him while school was out for the summer, still somewhat mindful of my banishment by Walter.

Will didn't talk much about Kevin during our days together in the shop, but I could tell by the sagging corners of his mouth that things weren't going well. During the last week in July, he asked me to close up for him three days in a row. I found out later, through polite but persistent questioning, that he'd been visiting Kevin in hospital.

"Is it serious?" I asked.

"Double pneumonia," Will admitted, his wavering voice undermining his attempt to sound matter-of-fact. "They're beginning to worry about his kidneys as well."

I asked him why he was at work; it sounded like Kevin needed him. He said that someone had to be in charge of the shop while Helen was preoccupied with Walter. Despite his attempts to suck it up, I could hear the resentment in his voice.

"You need to come into the shop," I told Helen on the phone that night.

"What are you talking about?" she said.

I explained what was going on with Kevin. "There's no way you can expect Will to manage the place right now," I said.

"I can't leave Daddy yet," she said.

"Helen, it's been over two months since his heart attack. I'm sure he can manage on his own for a few hours each day."

There was annoyed silence on the other end of the line. I was in no position to be making such pronouncements, as far as she was concerned. I hadn't been caring for him day in and day out like she had.

"He's still not quite right," she insisted.

"Fine," I said. "Then I guess you're going to have to let me run the shop."

"You?"

"You need to be with your dad. Will needs to be with Kevin. You can't afford to close the shop for the summer. What other choice do you have?"

"Daddy would have another heart attack if he ever found out."

"Well, think what his reaction will be if you let the shop fail."

She fell silent again, resenting me for forcing the issue. As hard as she'd tried to avoid taking responsibility for the shop, she knew that she couldn't dodge it any more.

"Call Will," I said to her. "Tell him that his place is with Kevin right now. He won't leave the shop unless you make the decision for him."

I shouldn't admit that I was surprised that Helen made the call, but I was. Perhaps my confidence in my powers of persuasion wasn't what it should have been. Or perhaps, if I'd really been honest with myself, my faith in her ability to see beyond her own troubles was what had been lacking. Still, I was glad to find myself proved wrong. Will spent the following day making sure that I was ready to take over from him, that I understood all the shop's procedures, from handling orders to repairing the leaky plumbing in the washroom at the back of the shop. When he wasn't tutoring me, he was on the phone making arrangements for Kevin's return home from the hospital. He talked with nurses and doctors and pharmacists and medical-equipment supply stores. Before he left, he wrote down his home number and told me to call if something came up that he hadn't explained to me.

My first day in charge was a slow one. Only a handful of customers came into the shop, all browsers. People were out of the city on summer vacation, and for those still around, the thought of coming downtown on a hot, sticky day wasn't very appealing. To keep myself from going crazy with boredom, I passed the time reading a newsmagazine at the front counter. The cover story had caught my eye. A team of anthropologists from the University of Alberta had begun exhuming the only bodies ever found from the Franklin expedition. I gawked at a picture of a frozen corpse so well preserved by the Arctic permafrost that the man's skin and clothes were intact after more than 130 years. There was still a grimace on his face. His fogged-over eyes glistened.

Just then, out of the corner of my eye, I caught a flicker of movement. I looked up to find Helen standing just a few feet in front of me. "Jesus!" I said, nearly jumping out of my skin. She must have slipped in the side door without my noticing.

"Well," she said, "I can see that you're hard at work."

She'd cut her hair short for the summer, leaving the graceful lines of her neck uncovered. Sweat glittered on the sun-flushed skin at the base of her throat. My eyes wanted to go farther south, revisit the intimate places they'd once frequented, but I wouldn't let them.

"So," I said, "you were able to leave Walter on his own?"

"An old friend of his dropped by to see him," she said coolly. Her eyes drifted to the photo of the corpse in the magazine that was still lying open in front of me. "Relative of yours?"

"Not him." I said. I folded back the pages and showed her a picture of another grave on the same gravel beach, this one only partially excavated. A wooden coffin lay at the bottom, its lid exposed, the rest of it still sealed in ice. "This guy. John Hartnell, able seaman. My great-great-great uncle."

She seemed unimpressed by my discovery and glanced around the shop, apparently surprised that I hadn't run the place into the ground during the one morning I'd been in charge.

"You've been avoiding me," I said.

"I've been busy with Daddy," she replied, as if I were being obtuse.

"I told you I was willing to help out any way I could."

"And here you are," she said, not sounding particularly thankful.

"You don't want me here?"

She sighed impatiently. "I didn't say that."

"Then tell me what I did to deserve such a cold shoulder from you."

She looked away, annoyed by the sudden blush of embarrassment colouring her cheeks. "Nothing."

"Well then . . . ?"

She pulled a folded, official-looking sheet of paper out of her purse and handed it to me.

"What's this?" I asked.

"I applied to the creative-writing program at the University of British Columbia before Daddy got sick," she said. "It's my acceptance letter."

I stared at the words on the paper.

"I applied because of you," she said with a misshapen smile. "You got me writing again. It's only the best program in Canada."

It was as if she was thanking and blaming me at the same time. "Congratulations," I said, slowly handing her back the letter. "Sounds like the opportunity of a lifetime."

She could see the disapproval in my eyes. "You don't want me to go."

Once again she'd succeeded in turning a reason for her to feel remorse into an occasion for me to be defensive. "Of course you should go," I said, forcing myself to sound grown-up about it. "If that's what you want."

She carefully refolded the letter but didn't tuck it back in her purse right away. "I haven't told Daddy yet," she said.

I wondered whether she was waiting for me to tell her that she shouldn't worry, that her penance was paid. I said nothing.

"Did I ever tell you I used to hide under this counter?" she asked, running her hand along its burnished, wood-grained surface, a melancholy smile on her lips. "When I was little. Right by Daddy's feet when he was at the cash register. I'd curl up with a book he'd give me. No one could see me except him. It was my secret place. Mine and his. Sometimes I'd untie his shoelaces when he was talking to a customer just to annoy him. He'd always keep talking, never letting on that I was down there." Her smile faded.

I realized that it was this impish little girl I'd fallen in love with, the one who still craved the approval of the men in her life despite trying to wrap each of them tightly around her little finger. It helped to explain why I'd so often found Helen's selfishness endearing, and why even now I was so eager to forgive her for dashing my heart against the rocks. I was convinced that if I could just hang in long enough, she'd eventually emerge from her hiding place and reveal her true self to me, free of conceit and obfuscation.

"Who knows," I said, finally capitulating. "Your dad may be well enough to run the place himself by the time you have to go."

She shook her head dejectedly. "I'm not sure he'll ever be ready."

I wanted to reach out and rest her head against my shoulder, but I was worried that she'd interpret any attempt at physical contact as one last desperate come-on. Her lavender scent kept tormenting me, pulling me back to my kitchen chair and the moment we first made love.

"Don't worry," I said from behind the counter. "We'll work something out while you're gone."

"I'll have to leave in just a few weeks," she said. "Will may not be back at work. You'll be going back to teach."

I could tell what she was thinking. The fate of the shop depended on her. If Kevin's illness was protracted, Will might not be available for several more months. There would be no one to run the place. Unless Helen stayed at home, the shop would have to be closed or, almost as appalling, turned over to strangers. It pained me to recognize that I was still only a minor variable in her equations, cheap but temporary labour. Even though I reminded myself not to take it personally, I could feel my heart slowly mummifying to the leathery texture of my great-great-great uncle's corpse.

Chapter 19

I find the nearest police station and report Severn missing. An officer takes down all the details. I give him her school photo, which I carry around in my wallet. He asks me whether Severn knows anyone in Toronto other than the boy who drove her here. I tell him about Jack Livingston, although I try to portray her obsession with him as nothing more than teenage idol worship. The officer can see that I'm not telling him the whole story, but he doesn't probe any further. He tells me that he'll enter the information I've given him into their database. Someone will contact me as soon as there's any news.

Marla and I find a coffee shop down the street from the police station. The moon-faced woman behind the counter looks as scuffed as the tired linoleum floors. It appears the shop is a refuge for people with nowhere else to go. Most sit alone, ignoring the signs that tell patrons not to loiter. There's a definite down-on-your-luck flavour to the place. We retire with our coffees to a table by the front window. I begin reading through the notebooks that Livingston's ex-girlfriend gave me.

"That officer was nice," Marla says.

"I felt like I was accusing Severn of a crime," I say, not lifting my eyes from the pages. "Like she'd stolen something from me."

"You did the right thing," she says.

I'm still not so sure. I picture the cops catching Severn on Livingston's doorstep, then taking her by the arm and delivering her to me in the back of a cruiser.

Marla stares down at the notebooks. "Tell me about Helen," she says.

My eyes snap up. "You mean, did Jack Livingston knock her up?"

Marla grimaces.

"Why should it matter if he did?" I say. "I'm still her father. In all the ways that matter, anyway."

She stays quiet for a moment, waiting for my anger to subside. "Have you decided what you're going to say to Severn when you find her?" she asks softly.

I let my head settle in my hands. "No."

"Maybe you should be honest with her."

"You mean admit that I'm a fraud?" I say with a cynical laugh. "Yes, I'm sure that would set everything right."

"You must have had reasons for not telling her. Reasons you thought were important at the time."

I stare across the coffee shop at a girl, just fourteen or fifteen years old, sitting alone. She's hunched over a donut like a mongrel over a scavenged piece of meat, tearing it into strips with her teeth. Her nose and ears are studded. She watches the other customers warily with eyes much too old for her age. Her army-surplus coat is unzipped, revealing a pink Hello Kitty T-shirt underneath.

"Livingston never cared that Severn even existed," I tell Marla.

"Maybe his book suggests that isn't entirely true," she says.

"Just because he wrote a fictional story about a teenage girl who lost her mother doesn't mean he's basing it on Severn."

"You think it's just a coincidence, then?"

She can see that I don't, really. There are too many other similarities in character and situation, details that he's stolen from our lives and from Helen's writing. I know this without ever reading more than the jacket copy. *Northwest Passage.* I doubt that Livingston knew the first thing about Franklin's expedition until he went through Helen's notebooks. He took her ideas, twisted them slightly, and passed them off as his own. I always assumed that he'd finished using her when she came back to me. Apparently, I was wrong.

Severn wouldn't understand this about Livingston. She'd see him as a man with remarkable, poetic insight into her situation. Someone much better qualified to be her father than I could ever hope to be.

I don't explain the significance of the notebooks to Marla, although I'm certain that she's already figured out who the handwriting belongs to. My eyes trace the loops of Helen's ascending and descending penstrokes. I feel the indentations that her ballpoint pressed in the paper. I let myself believe that they were made only a few days ago, and that Helen is still substance, made of flesh and breath and living emotion. The paper is a membrane that connects her past with my present. I want to whisper to the pages, tell her that Severn will be all right, that I'm looking after things. But I know she won't believe me. I was always transparent to her.

We finish our coffees and head out to the car, which is parked just in front of the coffee shop. I fumble with my car keys, trying not to let any of the notebooks slide out from under my arm to the slushy sidewalk. "Where do you want me to drop you off?" I ask Marla.

"What do you mean?" she says.

"Listen, you've been a big help. But I'll probably be driving around town all night. Is there someplace you want me to take you? Back to Jay's? A friend's place? A hotel, maybe?" The keys slip from my hand as I try to unlock the driver's-side door. I curse under my breath. "Honestly," I tell her, reaching down towards the pavement, the notebooks balanced precariously on my hip, "you've already done more than enough."

She crouches beside me and plucks the keys from the snow. "I think you stand a better chance of finding her with me along."

As Marla unlocks my door, I hear the sounds of a scuffle coming from behind me. I turn to see the girl in the army-surplus coat struggling to get away from some low-life who's followed her from the coffee shop. I holler at him to leave her alone, but he ignores me. I yell again, taking a few steps towards them, hoping that my implied threat to intervene will make him back off. This time he swings around to look at me, a bad-ass grin on his face.

"Leave her alone," I shout.

She scurries free of him, but he's already cramming money he's taken from her into his own pocket. I hear Marla in the background, frantically telling me to get in the car, but I don't listen.

"Give it back to her," I say.

Without warning, someone shoves me from behind, ramming me face first against the cold wall of the coffee shop. Oh shit, I realize too late. He has a friend. Helen's notebooks slide to the sidewalk, splatting in the slush. I feel my wallet being plucked out of my back pocket as a shoulder presses hard into my back, squashing my cheek against the rough brick. Out of the corner of my eye, I see the slimeball who mugged the girl extract all my cash and drop the wallet to the ground. His friend runs his knee into my kidney and lets me slide down the wall.

As I lie in a heap, I watch them kick at Helen's notebooks before running off. Within a few seconds, Marla is crouching over me. She helps me sit up, asks if I'm badly hurt. I stare hopelessly at the mangled notebooks. She begins retrieving them from the slush for me.

Chapter 20

Will had been away from the bookshop barely two weeks when Kevin died. He phoned me at the shop a few hours after they'd taken the body away. In a halting voice, he thanked me for filling his shoes at work and allowing him to be with Kevin in his final days. He said it was a very generous gift that I'd given him. Then he broke down. I let him cry uninterrupted, knowing that nothing I could have said would have been of any genuine comfort.

When I'd dropped by their apartment the week before, I'd simply intended to pay Will a visit. I'd brought along a bag of takeout, figuring that he probably didn't have the time or the energy to feed himself. My plan had been to offer him a few words of support and then be on my way. But when he invited me in to say hello to Kevin, I realized that he'd see through any excuses I might invent for not staying.

Will had escorted me into the bedroom. The bed that they'd shared had been replaced by a steel-framed monstrosity with side rails. Kevin was propped up, an IV threaded into the back of his hand, his cheeks sunken. The pneumonia had taken a firm hold by then, filling his lungs and slowly, relentlessly pulling him under. I stood there uselessly, staring at Kevin's ravaged body, selfishly wishing I hadn't come. He was a husk of the ill but still shining young man I'd met at the hospital only months before. A weak smile wrinkled his lips when Will leaned down to tell him who'd come to visit, but he was too exhausted to open his eyes. I was glad that Will didn't make me stay more than a couple of minutes.

The funeral reception was held in their living room. A disproportionate number of young men in dark suits milled about, eating from paper plates and drinking from plastic cups. I heard one mention that it was the third funeral he'd been to in three months. The fellow standing across from him nodded gravely and looked about the room. At that moment, I was overcome by an image of the last surviving men of Franklin's expedition, their bodies racked by scurvy and starvation, shuffling across the frozen wasteland of King William Island in their hopeless attempt to reach a Hudson's Bay Company outpost hundreds of miles to the south. I imagined them looking at one another just as Will and Kevin's friends were doing now, watching for signs of wasting, wondering who would be the next to fall.

Helen had taken care of all the food and drink. She'd skipped the interment to rush back to the apartment and greet early guests, letting herself in with Kevin's old key, which Will had given to her. She continued to act as hostess, serving people tea and coffee, wiping up spills, and shooing Will away whenever he offered to help. She offered no excuse for her father's absence, and none was requested. Apparently, he still wasn't sufficiently recovered from his heart attack.

Will and I stood at the edge of the crowd with glasses of punch in our hands. There was a look of lost purpose in his eyes, as if, having directed all his energy towards easing Kevin's pain—massaging his withered limbs, bathing him, wiping his ass—he no longer knew what to do with himself.

"I got a call from Toronto this morning," he told me, flashing a painful smile. "They wanted Kevin to audition for a TV commercial. It was the call he'd been waiting for ever since I met him."

I offered to get Will more punch, but he politely declined. My gaze shifted to a couple in their mid-fifties sitting alone on the couch in the living room, dourly surveying the proceedings. They'd abstained from any refreshments. At the funeral service, I'd seen them sitting in the front pew, well away from Will. When one of Kevin's friends had introduced himself to them afterwards, they'd avoided shaking his hand. I realized that they were Kevin's parents. Will was careful not to look their way.

A stocky woman moved in to hug Will and offer her condolences. I took the opportunity to wander into the kitchen. Helen was there, busy scooping discarded plates and cups into a plastic garbage bag. She suggested that I stop stuffing my face and make myself useful. I was given an empty bag and dispatched to the living room. As I cleared the coffee table of debris, Kevin's father, now sitting alone, eyed me with disdain from the couch. I quickly moved on.

After making my way around the living room I did a survey of the perimeter. That's when I noticed that the door to the room where Kevin had died was yawning open. I went to close it but stopped when I saw Kevin's mother inside, standing by the monstrous hospital bed, her back towards me. I could tell by the way her shoulders were shaking that she was crying. I tried to back away undetected, but she turned and saw me. She was clutching a photo to her chest, the one I'd seen on Kevin's bedside table during my visit. I recognized the frame. I remembered the picture too— Kevin, maybe twelve years old, bare-chested, beaming for the camera on a dock by a cottage, triumphantly holding a glistening lake trout aloft. The summer sun cast a Grecian glow on his skin.

"I'm sorry," I said. "I was just doing a little clean-up."

She looked at me as if I'd spoken to her in some incomprehensible foreign tongue. Her hand searched for the side table as she wobbled slightly. Her mascara had begun to run.

"You want me to close the door?" I asked, trying to sound sympathetic but really looking for a way out.

She patted the picture next to her breast. "He was so normal as a child. Happy. Rambunctious. Just like other boys." Her eyes dipped towards the mattress. "He was furious with us for not understanding."

"Will took very good care of him," I said, trying to offer her some consolation.

She stared at me icily. "Kevin didn't belong here."

I felt like a first-class dick standing there with the garbage bag in my hand. "I'm sorry I interrupted," I said. "I'll give you some time to yourself."

She gently ran her hand over the pillow where Kevin's head had lain. Then she straightened, her spine growing stiff.

I closed the door behind me and returned to the less emotionally demanding task of trolling for garbage, working my way back towards the heart of the gathering. A guy with a buzz cut the texture of peach fuzz was saying goodbye to Will and bestowing well-meaning advice upon him. Others in the living room were taking their cue, finishing off their butter tarts and Nanaimo bars, carefully planning their exits to avoid the appearance of a stampede for the door. I continued to do my best to blend into the background, until Helen intercepted me and told me to help her take the bags that we'd filled out to the garbage chute.

As we dragged our loads past the elevators, I caught her sneaking glances at me. It was as though she wanted to tell me something but kept thinking better of it. "This is going to sound awful," she said finally. "But the fact that Kevin died so quickly certainly makes my life a lot easier."

I yanked open the steel-jawed door and jammed a bag into the chute. "You're right," I said. "It sounds awful." Since the day she'd come to the shop to show me her acceptance letter, I'd been waiting for something more from her, something to acknowledge that we'd become close enough to throw off the workings of each other's emotional clockwork.

"At least now I know that Will can look after the shop while I'm at UBC," she said.

"He may not want to go right back to work," I warned her. I didn't much like the temporary role she'd placed me in: confidant without concomitant privileges.

"I know that," she said, annoyed by my inference that she didn't understand the delicacy of the situation.

"Have you told your dad?" I asked.

Her lips shrivelled to a thin, crooked line. Clearly she hadn't. By my estimation, she had a little over a week, two at the outside, before she'd have to leave.

"You got your plane ticket yet?" I asked. An embarrassing wrinkle crept into my voice, betraying my secret hope that perhaps she was having second thoughts.

She looked at me irritably. "Of course I do."

"And you've got a place to stay lined up in Vancouver?"

"No, I thought I'd sleep on the street."

"Ha, ha." The stench of years of fetid kitchen scrapings was wafting out at me from the garbage chute. It was stupid of me to expect her to change her plans now, to set aside her dream of becoming a writer for me. I let the steel door snap shut. "Is that the last bag?"

She looked at me as if she'd caught me in a lie. "You don't think I should go."

I let my arms fall to my sides. "Why should that make any difference?"

"You're right," she said, lowering her eyes. "It shouldn't."

I tried to figure out whether it was remorse or resentment colouring her words. "You'll need a ride to the airport," I said, wanting the offer to sound matter-of-fact, as though she couldn't crush me even flatter by turning me down.

She tugged on the sides of her sleeveless, olive green dress to smooth out its lines. It set off her red hair perfectly. Even in mourning, she had an unrelenting sense of style. "I suppose you'll want me to phone you once I get to Vancouver," she said. "Even call you after that."

"Is that unreasonable?" I asked.

She considered this for a moment. "No, I suppose not."

I felt a hopeful churning in my belly. I was like a distraught gambler determined to regain his winnings from a fizzled hot streak.

"What day are you flying out?" I asked, trying to maintain my poker face.

She hesitated, then gave me the time and the date, matching my impassive tone. It occurred to me then that perhaps she was looking for the same thing from me as I was from her: a last-minute plea; a bitter brush-off; anything but this bloodless parting of the ways that we seemed determined to play out. No matter how much I felt my tenuous hold on Helen slipping, however, I wasn't about to have a naked expression of heartache greeted with embarrassed silence. And so it was that we made our way back down the corridor without another word spoken.

Helen made for the kitchen once we were back in the apartment, leaving me to hover on the fringes of the assembled masses. During my meanderings, I spied Kevin's mother leaving the bedroom, carrying the framed photo and several other mementos with her. Will saw her too from his perpetual post in the front hall. For a moment, I thought he was about to intercept her, but then he turned away to accept the condolences of another departing guest. Kevin's mother motioned to her husband that it was time to leave. They slipped out without saying goodbye.

It wasn't long before everyone had cleared out. Helen and I stayed behind to clean up, exchanging only perfunctory remarks as we worked. When we were done, we sat with Will, drinking coffee at his dining-room table. I volunteered to drop by later in the week and help him return the rented hospital equipment in the bedroom. Helen promised to take him out for supper the next few nights so he wouldn't have to eat alone. It felt like a contest to see who could promise him the most support.

"Don't feel like you have to rush back to work," she told him, flicking an eyebrow at me on the side. "Take a week or two if you need it."

Will didn't seem to be listening. He was staring blankly at a weighty second-hand copy of *Anna Karenina* that he'd picked off a stack on the sideboard. "I used to think books were everything," he said, his voice thin and cracked. "Well, they never prepared me for the past two weeks."

"I imagine nothing really could," Helen murmured consolingly.

"I haven't even picked any of these up in the past two weeks." He laid down the Tolstoy and began inspecting a biography of Mary Pickford, whose black-and-white face smiled out from the back cover at her adoring, long-expired public. "Suddenly they seem so trivial."

Helen patted him on the back of the hand. The strain of being so considerate and understanding for an entire afternoon was beginning to wear a pair of tense little brackets around the corners of her mouth. "You'll be back to reading soon enough."

Will met her solicitous gaze with the full-bore sincerity of a man who'd survived a plane crash. "Actually, these past two weeks have brought a lot of things into focus for me."

"Oh?" she said, a tense strand threading its way into her voice.

"I think of all those moments with Kevin that I never had because my head was stuck in a book." He dropped the biography on the parquet floor, letting it land with an emphatic *thwap*. He drew back his shoulders. "I've decided not to come back to the shop."

Helen forced a smile. "Stop talking drivel."

"There's no future for me there," he said.

"Of course there is," she said, no longer bothering to sound calm and reasonable.

Will looked at Helen wearily. "Walter will never treat me as anything more than a hired hand."

"You know that's not true," she said, leaping to her father's defence. "You're like family to us."

"Then why isn't he here?"

Helen found herself without a comeback. She started fidgeting with her placemat. "He's not feeling well today," she said lamely. "He wanted to be here—"

"Oh, come off it, Helen," he said, sagging back in his chair. "The truth is that he couldn't stand the thought of being in the same room with any of my friends. God, even Kevin's parents were here, and they've never wanted to acknowledge my existence."

Helen's neck turned a splotchy red, but she said nothing more. I felt oddly annoyed with her for not doing a better job of sticking up for her father.

"Will," I said, "there's something you should know."

He turned towards me, his forehead furrowed.

"Walter may not be able to run the shop any more," I said.

Helen shot me through with a look of betrayal.

Will's glance shifted uncertainly between us. "What are you talking about?"

Helen looked away, refusing to answer.

"You're the only man who can fill his shoes," I told him.

I could see him rolling over what I'd said in his brain, wanting to believe it. For a moment, I even thought he was about to recant, but then the corners of his face tightened. "I'm sorry," he said to us flatly. "I can't help you."

His fatalistic tone alarmed me. I suddenly wondered if he'd begun to see Kevin's early symptoms reflected back at him in the bathroom mirror. Beside me, Helen sat with her hands covering her face, oblivious to this ominous possibility, contemplating instead the ice jam that Will had just created in her own life.

Chapter 21

Marla returns from the hotel reception desk with access cards for two rooms. "Here," she says, dropping mine in my lap. I'm coiled up in a wingback chair in a quiet part of the lobby. I don't want anyone to see the scrape down the side of my face from the bricks of the coffee-shop wall.

I struggle to my feet. Marla takes my elbow as I straighten up. In her other arm, she cradles the remains of Helen's notebooks. She guides me to the elevator. I shuffle like an old man in a nursing home.

I get Marla to pass me one of the notebooks as we ride up in the elevator. She's tried to smooth out the pages, but most are beyond salvation. The cover is limp with moisture, the pages gritty and mashed. Those words of Helen's that remain are smeared and bleeding. I feel my throat ache but manage to suppress the tears that threaten to ambush me.

Marla helps me off with my jacket when we get to my room. I immediately stagger over to the phone at the side of the bed and try Severn's cellphone number again. I get the same automated message telling me that the mobile customer I'm trying to reach is currently unavailable. Next, I call home and check the answering machine, just in case Severn has unexpectedly doubled back on me. Nothing there either. Marla plumps up the pillows and forces me to lie back while she cleans my scrape with a face cloth from the bathroom.

"We should call your ex-husband," I say. "In case Severn showed up back at his place."

"Not until we get you looked after," she insists, holding me down by the shoulder. She pulls some antiseptic ointment out of her knapsack and dabs it on the wound. "That was a very noble and stupid thing you did."

"I try." I wince as she touches a raw spot on my face.

"Did Helen always have to rescue you like this?"

"Hardly ever," I say. "Besides, she didn't carry around a first-aid kit in a knapsack like you do."

"Scrapes and cuts I can handle," she says. "Avery had enough of them when he was growing up. But the next time you decide to pick a fight with a street punk, you're on your own."

"Understood," I say, suitably contrite.

Marla wipes the ointment off her fingers with the face cloth, then calls Jay. I can tell from her insincere apologies on the phone that she's woken him. Their conversation doesn't get any more cordial. She asks whether Severn's there, but the answer is no. When she goes on to ask after Avery, a prickly exchange ensues. She quickly reaches the end of her patience and cuts the call short by tersely reminding Jay to phone her on her cell if there's any word from Severn.

While Marla is on the phone, I gingerly pick one of the notebooks from the pile at the foot of the bed. The cover comes away in my hands. The moisture is still eating away at Helen's words. I can see her dissolving before my eyes. I take the face cloth that Marla has discarded and begin blotting the pages, but it does no good.

"Let me spread those out," Marla offers once she gets off the phone. She begins arranging them by the heater so the warm air can dry them out. By the time she's done, over a dozen notebooks in various states of decay are lined up on the floor like fatalities from a bus crash awaiting identification. She comes to retrieve the final one, which I'm still holding in my lap.

"A few of them aren't too badly damaged," she says, trying to cheer me up with false optimism. "Maybe we could go back to the loft and see if that woman has any others."

I gently run my fingers over the disintegrating ink.

Marla leans against the edge of the bedside table, looming over me like a well-meaning but overbearing nurse. "It's hard to know how to remember someone you've lost when you refuse to talk about her."

"I remember her just fine," I say.

"Do you?" she says sceptically. "It seems to me that you're awfully interested in protecting her memory. Regardless of what she did to you."

"Severn doesn't deserve to have her image of her mother spoiled."

"Pretending she was a saint is just as bad."

I smile crookedly. "Don't worry. I'll never confuse Helen with a saint."

Marla wrinkles her nose as though I'm giving off an insidious, mildly offensive odour. "My father never talked about my mom after she died. He packed everything of hers in boxes, pretended she never existed." I look at her dully, wondering whether she actually expects me to draw a moral from her tale of woe. "I felt completely alone," she says, not letting my unenthusiastic response keep her from elaborating. "The person I was closest to all my life had left me forever, and somehow I was expected just to get on with things."

I sag against the headboard in exasperation. "Look, I've tried. She's just so . . . angry."

Marla sits beside me on the edge of the bed. "She's not just angry at you, you know. She's angry at Helen as well. For dying. For abandoning her."

I roll my eyes dismissively. But I know the anger she's talking about. Better than I want to.

"She wants Helen to be this wonderful memory," she says. "Just as you do. But she can't pull it off. It makes her feel like a traitor."

"Are you through?" I ask.

She saddles me with a ponderous look of disappointment. She takes the ink-stained face cloth from my hand, reluctantly gets to her feet, and returns it to the bathroom. I pick up the phone and check back in with the police to see who's following up on Severn's case. While I'm on hold, Marla collects her anorak from the back of the desk chair.

"If you need me, I'm just across the hall," she says testily.

I wave to her vaguely and watch as she lets herself out. Not long after, a police officer whom I've never spoken to before comes on the line to tell me that he and his colleagues are pursuing Severn's case but have nothing to report yet. As I hang up the phone, I notice that my hand is shaking.

I try watching TV, but I only come across late-night news stories about missing children, overflowing homeless shelters, drug busts, sexual assaults, and homicides. I end up clicking off the remote and staring at what's left of the lone notebook still splayed out on the bed beside me. When Severn was little, she used to fill the same type of notebooks, provided to her by Helen, with stories of clever princesses and witty woodland creatures. It was all part of Helen's grand scheme to fulfil her thwarted dreams through Severn. At first, the encouragement was gentle—bedtimes spent inventing new endings to favourite fairy tales, Sundays whiled away playing word games at the kitchen table—but as Severn's promise grew, so did Helen's resolve. When other girls Severn's age were reading Nancy Drew mysteries, Helen assigned her the works of Margaret Laurence, Gabrielle Roy, and of course, Alice Munro. When Severn's friends went camping in the summer, Helen enrolled her in creative-writing courses taught in stuffy classrooms. Each day, two hours were set aside for Severn to practise her craft with the devotion of a piano prodigy. Her eleventh birthday present was a laptop computer and a printer. By the time she reached the eighth grade, she used the laptop only for video games. Her notebooks were shoved to the back of her closet. Her preferred works of literature were *Seventeen* and *Teen People*.

I wish Severn was here with me now, no matter how surly her mood, just so I can be certain she's safe. Almost as an afterthought, I wonder what feelings this roomful of mangled notebooks would evoke in her. The joy of nestling in her mother's lap and elaborating on the rhymes of Dr. Seuss? Or the guilt Helen wrought for her abandoning the writer's path? Perhaps Marla was right. She had no way of reconciling one with the other.

Chapter 22

After the funeral, Helen started coming by the shop more frequently, glumly preparing for the day when I went back to school and she began running the place on her own. She helped me sort through the fall shipments from publishers, which threatened to overrun what little storage space we had, and return the unsold deadwood from the spring and summer, which I'd left cluttering the shelves. As we unpacked boxes together, I suggested that she might want to talk to Will again. Perhaps the initial shock of Kevin's death was beginning to fade and he was willing to reconsider. She dismissed my idea, saying that he'd made his position very clear. She wasn't about to go to him with cap in hand.

I might have quietly celebrated the prospect of having Helen tied to London had it not been for her impenetrable funk. I knew that all she could see was her golden opportunity passing her by while she languished in the backwater of her father's shop. I certainly gained no benefit from seeing her more often. We never met outside of work. It was as if she'd walled me off along with her writerly ambitions. After all, I was the one who'd encouraged her, and intentionally or not, I was the one who would always remind her of the freedom she'd failed to achieve.

If Helen wouldn't coax Will back to the shop, then it was up to me. It seemed to me that like Helen, he'd isolated himself in his grief, and also like her, he'd turned away from the one true passion of his life out of a confused sense of guilt. I had the feeling that his declaration of independence from Donnelly's was less about finding his own path and more about surrendering himself to the undertow of Kevin's death.

I chose an afternoon when I knew Helen was taking Walter to the doctor's to phone Will. I told him that I was on my own without backup and didn't have anyone else to turn to. The toilet at the back of the shop was overflowing, and I was overrun with customers. He said he'd be right there, even though he clearly suspected me of subterfuge. He wasn't really in a position to refuse me, though, given that I'd backed him up when Kevin was sick.

When he arrived, he found me mopping up the water I'd sloshed on the bathroom floor to simulate the disaster I'd described to him over the phone.

"It's not going to work," was the first thing he said to me.

"I'm sorry?" I said.

"Getting me in here," he said. "Hoping that the smell of the books will bring me back."

"What are you talking about?" I said, feigning innocence.

He grabbed the mop from me. "Here, let me do that. You go up front and serve customers."

As I stepped out of the washroom, a chubby woman in a tank top and cut-off jeans intercepted me with a copy of *On the Road* in hand. She wanted to know whether it was true that Jack Kerouac was French Canadian by birth. Out of the corner of my eye, I could see Will eavesdropping, waiting to hear what answer I'd give. I told her I wasn't sure; beatniks weren't my specialty. I heard a little huff from Will in the background. She turned the book over in her hands, apparently still trying to decide whether to buy it. I glanced back at Will, who'd stubbornly returned to mopping, determined not to let his bookseller's impulses take over. It wasn't until she was about to replace the book on the shelf that he finally let the mop handle clatter against the bathroom wall.

"You're right," he told the woman, emerging from the bathroom like some kind of guerrilla bibliophile. "His full name was Jean-Louis Lebris de Kerouac. Ti Jean to his family. His parents were French-Canadian immigrants who settled in New England. He actually didn't speak any English until he was six years old. He originally submitted the manuscript for *On the Road* as one unbroken roll of paper. It was rejected, and he carried it around the country in a rucksack until it was finally published years later."

By the time the woman left the store, Will had convinced her to buy an audiotape of the poetry of Allen Ginsberg as well.

"What are you smiling at?" he said to me after she'd gone.

"Nothing," I said.

"You set that up, didn't you? That woman was a friend of yours."

I rearranged a book that some customer had put back on the fiction shelves out of alphabetical order. "So what have you been doing with yourself?" I asked him.

He shrugged evasively. "Nothing special."

"Been getting out of the apartment, I hope."

"To tell you the truth, I consider getting up in the morning an accomplishment right now."

"Be patient with yourself," I said.

He fixed me with a moody gaze. "'T is all men's office to speak patience / To those that wring under the load of sorrow, / But no man's virtue nor sufficiency / To be so moral when he shall endure / The like himself."

"Shakespeare?"

"*Much Ado about Nothing*, actually."

"Just goes to show you what wisdom sometimes lies in words written long ago."

"Helen put you up to this, didn't she?"

"Actually, she'd probably blow a gasket if she knew I was talking to you."

"Then why are you doing this for her after how she's turned her back on you?"

"Patience again," I said. "It's what any teacher worth his salt has plenty of."

Will glanced around the shop. Only a couple of customers remained. "Looks like you don't need me here any more."

"Admit it, Will. This place is in your blood."

"How can that be?" he said. "My last name's not Donnelly."

As he turned to leave, an old man walked in the door. It took us both a moment to recognize the bristly eyebrows, greyer than we remembered. He gazed up at the bookshelves and the pressed-tin ceiling like a pilgrim entering a cathedral.

"Just as I left it," he said, allowing himself a little grin.

"We're only staying a minute, Dad," said Helen, hard on her father's heels.

"The doctor said I was ready to come back," he insisted, chafed by her fussing.

Helen stopped in her tracks and scowled when she saw Will. Walter, on the other hand, flashed him an uncharacteristic smile.

"Save me from her, Will," Walter pleaded. "Ever since my heart attack, she's been treating me like a feeble old man. She took away my car keys, if you can believe it. Wouldn't even drive me here, no matter how many times I asked her to. Damned if I was going to take a cab or a city bus to my own shop." He rested his hand on Will's shoulder. "My only consolation was that I knew you were looking after the place."

Will was stunned by Walter's sudden display of fatherly affection. The reaction made Walter self-conscious. I noticed a slight tremor in his fingers as he slowly removed his hand from Will's shoulder. To hide his embarrassment, Walter shifted his gaze to me.

"Who's this?" he asked. "Some new recruit?"

For a moment, I thought he was being sarcastic. But then I

realized that he really had no clue who I was. Walter read my face and saw that he'd inadvertently made a fool of himself. He sneaked a quick peek at Helen, then wandered off to continue with his inspection, eager to gloss over his slip-up. I watched him make his way up the steps to the back of the shop, his shaky hand creeping up the wall to steady his climb.

"He didn't come to Kevin's funeral because I never told him about it," Helen said.

Will stared at the steps. "I didn't realize how much he . . ." His voice trailed off apologetically.

"The doctor said his brain went without oxygen a long time." She let the weight of months of worry settle on her face. "I couldn't keep him away from here forever."

Will looked at Helen, realizing now that her concern for Walter wasn't overblown after all.

"I was thinking of having him start back a couple of afternoons a week," she said wearily. "His long-term memory's okay, but I wouldn't want him working the cash register."

Will simply nodded. "This place wouldn't be the same without him."

Will started back at the shop two days later, giving me a few unexpected days of vacation before I had to return to school. At Helen's request, I dropped by the following Monday to help her pack the items from the garret that she'd need in Vancouver. Walter was at his post that afternoon, perched on the stool behind the front counter, a volume of Tennyson open before him. He cast his customary stare at me as I entered, but it no longer had the same intimidating effect. His silver-grey eyebrows now made him look more like a startled elf than a stern sorcerer.

"When I told him about my offer from UBC, he just nodded and asked me how much I'd paid for my airline ticket," Helen said as we strolled through Victoria Park after we'd finished her packing. "Like he couldn't wait to be rid of me and my nagging." It clearly irked her that the allegations of betrayal she'd anticipated from Walter, and for which she'd so firmly braced herself, had not materialized.

"That's probably a good sign," I said, sensing her last-minute doubts. "He'll be fine, Helen. Will and I will keep an eye on him."

We sat down on the same bench that we'd occupied the day of my performance as Bayfield.

"You must think I'm very self-absorbed," she said.

I tentatively laid my hand on top of hers. "You almost lost your dad. It's only natural for you to get a little protective of him."

"But I didn't have to shut you out at the same time." She looked at me, searching for the answer to a puzzle in the lines of my face. "Why you've stuck with me, I'll never understand."

Perhaps I was letting her off too easily, given the grief she'd put me through. But at that moment, I believed I was talking to the authentic, unaffected woman she'd always wanted to be with me. "Maybe it's because I knew you wouldn't disappoint me in the end," I said.

Her eyes widened as if I'd just paid her a ridiculously extravagant compliment, then she laced her fingers through mine and snuggled up against me.

Chapter 23

As I lie on the hotel bed in the dark, the shadows play tricks on me. At the edge of my vision I see movement, but when I turn to look, it's the curtains fluttering in the warm draught from the electric heater or the tiny red light of the smoke detector blinking on the ceiling. I know that if I'm patient, if I don't wish for it too hard, Helen will appear. It sometimes happens when I slip into that pocket between sleep and consciousness, a bittersweet land of delirium where life and death are no longer opposite points on the compass. The place is elusive. I chase it through the foggy channels in my mind.

I've just drifted off to sleep when the sensation of her sitting beside me on the bed pulls me back. I'm careful not to turn too quickly and break the spell. I let the scent of lavender envelop me. She pulls the bedspread over my shoulders. It feels coarse against my cheek. As I lay my hand on hers, I notice she's wearing a lacy cuff. My gaze trails slowly up her arm, and I make out a shawl around her shoulders. Her hair is pulled back, old-fashioned.

"You looked cold," she says, her eyebrow cocked.

It's then I realize that the woman's not Helen. I quickly shift my hand off hers and onto the bedspread, which now feels strangely stiff. My fingers trace the diagonal ridges that have materialized on its surface. I look down and see that I'm touching the cross of St. Andrew. The woman has draped me with the Union Jack.

"I've been looking for you for so long," she says.

I know this apparition is Lady Jane Franklin, even though her features keep shifting. My mind lends familiar fragments to her face: Helen's penetrating eyes, Severn's haughty chin, and Marla's ghostly complexion.

"They told me that you were dead," she says. "That your crew consumed one another's flesh."

I fold back the Union Jack and sit up in bed. Despite the weight of my movements, the apparition holds its shape.

"I knew you'd find the passage, my love," she says, resting her hand on my cheek. "Many doubted, but I always knew."

I shrink from her icy touch. I can see that she's convinced herself that I am Sir John. She will not be dissuaded. I am to be the vindication of her enduring faith, my appearance made to fit the myth of the man she worked so hard to create. She clutches me by the wrist.

"Let me go," I say hoarsely.

"You don't know how hard I tried to find you," she says. "How I fought against all those who said you'd failed."

Her fingers are like manacles now. The room has turned cold. I think I can hear the rush of rising water, the cracking of wooden bulkheads.

She lays me back. The rush of water is growing louder. I hear waves lapping up against the side of the bed.

"You will be remembered as a great man," she whispers as she tucks the Union Jack around me. "I made sure of that."

She kisses me lightly and then pulls the flag over my face. I can't breathe. My arms are bundled at my sides, my legs bound together. Suddenly I feel my body tumbling, committed to the sea before its time. I struggle frantically to break free, but the more I fight, the more tightly trussed I become.

I wake up in a tortured knot of sheets, my heart racing. The window curtains still flutter over the louvres of the electric heater. The floor is dry. Helen's mangled notebooks remain where I left them. I am completely alone.

I sit up on the edge of the bed, trying to catch my breath. My wrist aches mysteriously where Lady Jane gripped me in my dream.

I wonder whether Helen ever felt this trapped, held hostage by my expectations for her.

Chapter 24

When the day arrived for Helen to fly west to UBC, I imagined how Lady Jane Franklin had felt as she saw her husband sail off on his own voyage of discovery. She'd worked tirelessly to ensure that Sir John was given the chance to make the trip. She knew that above all else, he was an explorer, and that it was only as an explorer that he'd be able to claim his rightful place in history. Yet she hated to be separated from him. Any time he set sail, she understood there was the chance that she'd never see him again. But the risk was especially palpable this time.

So it was, with similar mixed emotions, that I waved goodbye to Helen as she disappeared through airport security. In the few days remaining to us, we'd made love in every room of her apartment. Now she was off to the Pacific coast, and I faced the agonizing prospect of being separated from her just when we'd drawn closer than ever before. I knew that as all-consuming as our last week together had been, time and distance threatened to blunt Helen's memories of me. The same couldn't be said for me. I'd be counting the days to Christmas break, when she'd be coming back home. Until then, I'd have to absorb myself in the prosaic details of a high school teacher's life to fill the empty expanse in the calendar.

While Lady Jane had no way of contacting her husband, I at least had the telephone. I called Helen every other day throughout the first month she was in Vancouver. It allowed me to pretend that she wasn't that far away after all. Our conversations lasted for hours. When we ran out of news to share, we simply rubbed our voices up against each other, substituting timbre for touch. It invariably took us many attempts before we finally managed to say goodbye. Given the three-hour time difference, I often found myself getting off the phone at two in the morning.

By mid-October, Helen was in her student digs less often when I called. Course work was heating up, she explained to me when we did connect. She lamented about spending long hours at the library. A plaintive strain had begun to creep into her voice, which I attributed to mounting exhaustion. Our conversations grew shorter. She had less time for intimate babble. Sometimes she'd say that she had to get back to a writing assignment with a looming deadline after we'd been talking for less than half an hour. I always professed my understanding and extracted a promise that she'd send me a copy of the final product. Secretly, though, I worried that as the demands of her new life pressed in on her, I was becoming an inconvenient distraction.

By November, I was having trouble reaching her at all. Whenever I did catch her in, she seemed to be on her way out the door. One time, I heard a male voice in the background.

"Who's that with you?" I asked, embarrassed by how suspicious I sounded.

"A starving poet," she said wryly. "I'm taking him out to supper. Is that a problem?"

"Should it be?"

"Listen," she said, trying hard to be patient with me, "we're meeting some people. I've got to go."

"Give me a call when you get back, then."

"It won't be until late," she warned. "Probably the wee hours for you."

"That's okay. You can wake me up."

There was a moment's silence on the other end of the line. I thought of how clingy I'd begun to sound, like my first girlfriend right before I dumped her.

Not surprisingly, Helen didn't call that night. In a way, I couldn't blame her. I resolved to play it cool, to let her take her time getting back to me. To show her—and perhaps more importantly, myself—that my world didn't revolve around her completely. As part of my self-imposed probation, I invited myself along to Friday night happy hour with some of the other young, unattached teachers from school. I bought my share of rounds and even flirted with my share of female colleagues. Nevertheless, I couldn't help feeling that it was just another performance. Instead of pretending to be Lieutenant Henry Bayfield, though, I was acting the part of the spoken-for-but-still-decidedly-fun-loving single man. When I returned to my bachelor's hovel and learned from my answering machine that Helen still hadn't called, my heart sank.

Two weeks passed without a word from her, then three. Christmas break was fast approaching, and she still hadn't told me what day she'd be getting back to town. My self-pity gave way to resentment. I tried calling again, but she was never there, and I was damned if I was going to leave some sad-sack message on her machine. One morning in early December, in sheer frustration, I phoned before I headed off for school, knowing full well that it was still four-thirty in the morning on the West Coast, and that I'd catch her in bed. There was no answer.

I didn't go into work that morning. I spent the day slumped on my couch with the blinds drawn, wearing nothing but my underwear and a grungy T-shirt. When I wasn't seething over how Helen had left me to dangle from the fraying memories of our last week together, I was inventing alibis for her, scripting the belated call that would put everything right between us again.

That call never came. With just a week to go until Christmas, I didn't even know whether she was back in town. To find out, I was reduced to spying on the bookshop from the other side of Richmond Street through a lacy cascade of heavy snowflakes. Sure enough, she was behind the counter, helping out with the Christmas rush. She was wearing the same Icelandic sweater she'd had on the day we met.

I decided to wait for business to die down, but it never did. I considered coming back later—another day maybe, when things weren't so hectic—but I knew that was just the coward in me. I set my jaw and crossed the street.

She was too busy at the till to notice me when I first entered the shop. Walter was helping her by bagging purchases as she rang them in. He handled each book reverently, passing the filled plastic bag across the counter to the buyer as if it contained robes of investiture. He frowned when he spotted me but said nothing to Helen. I'd been coming into the shop every week since she'd left, fulfilling my pledge to keep an eye on him even after she'd stopped calling, and so he'd come to recognize me again. From his reaction, I wondered whether he also at last remembered my ill-advised infatuation with his daughter.

I picked up a glossy volume of paintings by Georgia O'Keeffe from a nearby display and got in line. Helen finally noticed me as she was imprinting the credit card of the woman in front of me. She nearly fractured it in the process of slashing it in the machine. Even though the collar of her sweater covered the base of her neck, I could tell that it had turned an uneven pink.

"When did you get back in town?" I asked matter-of-factly when it was my turn to step up to the counter.

"A few days ago," she said, trying to camouflage her embarrassment with haughtiness.

"You didn't call."

She gestured to the mayhem in the shop. "I've been busy."

"Maybe you could take a break. We could talk."

She stared at the space over my head, unable to bring herself to look me in the eye. "Unfortunately, I'm not sure I'll have time for a break today."

Walter grumbled beside her. "Go," he said.

She gave him a dirty look.

"I've done without you for three months," he said. "I can survive another fifteen minutes." Before she could raise a protest, he added gruffly, "Don't worry, I'll get Will to handle the cash."

We stepped out the side door to find a bit of privacy. She didn't bother to bring a coat with her. Snowflakes began alighting in her hair and eyelashes like fleeting fairies. She tucked her hands under her armpits to keep them warm and waited for the interrogation to start.

"How was Vancouver?" I asked.

"It rained a lot," she said.

"You make lots of friends?"

A tic tugged at the corner of her mouth. "Look, I'm sorry I didn't call."

"Hey," I said with a shrug, "I should be used to it by now."

I wouldn't have blamed her for rolling her eyes at me, set as I was on playing the wounded martyr, but she just hugged herself a little tighter. She seemed surprisingly prepared to bear my sarcasm. "Maybe you expect too much from me," she said. I couldn't tell whether she meant it as a criticism of me or of herself.

"Who is it?" I asked. "The starving poet?"

She tipped her head skyward, blinking as a snowflake landed in one of her eyes. "I'm sorry I disappointed you." Little beads of water started to creep down her cheeks. I didn't know whether they were tears or snowmelt.

I stood there, stupidly prolonging the moment as my organs mummified inside me all over again. Although the distance between us had shrunk from thousands of miles to a few feet, Helen was now more out of my reach than ever. I might as well have been a corpse listening to his lover treading on his grave with her new boyfriend.

Helen was beginning to shiver, but rather than step out of the cold, she left the next move to me. There was nothing for me to do but turn and walk away, and wish that the falling snow would swallow me whole.

I spent Christmas in Ottawa with my parents, enduring my mother's queries about "that girl I seemed so serious about." Since I was a teenager, Mom had worried about my shyness around members of the opposite sex. I got the distinct impression that she would have been thrilled to find a condom in my wallet or to catch me with a girl in my room. I was a bit too well behaved, in her estimation. The fact that I had anyone who could come close to fitting the definition of a girlfriend was progress for me.

Of course, I wasn't about to tell her that I'd broken up with Helen. Mom would have had me explain everything in agonizing detail. I would have been forced to reassure her that I was fine and there was indeed still hope for me when I knew I was lying on both counts.

I was almost relieved to get back to my depressing little apartment in London. I began teaching again, intent on insulating myself from what promised to be an especially bleak January.

I'd been back at school for three weeks when I got a call from Will. "I have a book you might be interested in," he said over the phone. "Something to add to your Franklin collection."

"Thanks, but I've stopped collecting," I told him.

"Yeah, right. How's Saturday? You can come by the shop."

"I don't know, Will. I'm behind with my marking."

"You could come in and say hi at least," he said. In the end, he wouldn't take no for an answer. I didn't really want to step inside that shop again, but I didn't feel right about giving Will the brush-off either. After all, he'd lost his lover too, under far more traumatic circumstances. We needed to stand by each other. Besides,

Helen would be back out west, so there was no chance I'd run into her again.

Will was reading *Shakespeare's Dog* at the front counter when I dropped by the shop that Saturday. He glanced up from the book and smiled at me. "Cold out?" he asked, as if my twenty-two layers and frost-burnt face weren't enough of a clue.

"Actually, I was thinking of having a barbecue in Springbank Park later," I said, struggling to peel my gloves off my frozen fingers. "Want to come?"

He smirked and went back to reading.

"So," I said, "where's this book you thought was so interesting that it was worth me losing all my toes to frostbite?"

He reached under the counter and brought out an old, green hardcover.

"What?" I remarked. "You're stocking antiques now?"

"I came across it at a second-hand bookstore just down the street. Paid all of two bucks for it."

"I didn't know shopping at the competition was allowed."

"Don't worry. I wore a disguise."

I opened it to the title page. "This is a biography of Lady Jane," I said.

"Published in '51. Seen it before?"

I shook my head and started leafing through it.

"Interesting reading," he said, "if a little stultifying in its detail at times. She was quite the formidable woman."

I hunched over the counter, skipping over the accounts of Lady Jane's childhood, looking for the description of her first encounter with Sir John. I was intrigued to see what explanation the biographer gave for her attraction to him. As I read, I heard the steps to the back of the shop creak. I glanced up, expecting to see Walter or a lonely customer. Instead, I saw Helen, frozen in mid-step, staring back at me.

I turned to Will sharply.

He looked at me unapologetically over the rim of his reading glasses. "I seem to recall someone luring *me* to this shop not that long ago," he said.

Helen edged past me and proceeded to rearrange books in the front window, giving them far more attention than they deserved.

"Well," said Will, "I'll leave you two to catch up, then."

With his withdrawal to the back of the shop, the room fell ominously silent. I could hear the wind howling outside, but already I'd begun to sweat under all my layers. Melted snow was puddling around my boots. I unwrapped my scarf from around my neck and slid my parka back on my shoulders in an effort to vent my suddenly overactive boiler. "I thought you'd be back at UBC," I said to her at last.

"Yeah, well . . ." she said irritably, refusing to look at me.

I really didn't feel like playing twenty questions with her, but things suddenly didn't add up. "It's not Walter, is it?" I said, worried that he'd taken a turn for the worse.

She put her hands on her hips and hung her head like a weary runner after a foot race. "No." She finally looked my way, radiating equal parts of grief and exasperation.

"Fine," I said. "Don't tell me." I pulled my gloves back out of my coat pocket and started for the door.

"They told me not to come back, if you must know."

I stopped.

"I failed to complete my writing assignments on time," she said with a bitter smile.

I could see the pain in her eyes now. Her lifelong dream had been turned to compost. I stepped back from the door.

"I tried, Irving," she said, sounding like a little girl defending a poor report card. "I really tried. I hardly slept. Sometimes I'd be at it till three or four in the morning, but the words just wouldn't come."

"You were never at home when I called," I said, not about to be duped.

"You know I never answer the phone when I'm trying to write."

"So what are you saying? That there weren't other men?"

She sat down on the windowsill with a jagged sigh, carelessly disturbing the display that she'd just worked so hard to make presentable. "One of my profs took a special interest in me," she admitted in a small voice.

I let out a sad, little, unsurprised laugh.

"He offered me private tutoring," she said.

I reached for the doorknob again, making a mental note to thank Will for arranging this humiliating instant replay with Helen.

"I turned him down."

I looked back at her. She returned my gaze with the trademark wounded eyes of the falsely accused.

"That's right," she said. "Even though he probably would have found a way for me to pass if I'd said yes."

I stood there, looking like a Michelin Man who'd lost his way after following one of his own maps. "Why didn't you tell me this before?"

"You seemed so certain of what I'd done."

"Only because you kept distancing yourself from me," I said, managing to retrieve a morsel of my indignation.

"I stopped calling because I didn't want you to find out what a fraud I was."

"What are you talking about?"

She tipped over one of the books balanced beside her and stared at its fallen carcass dejectedly. "All my big talk about becoming a writer."

"Why should that matter?"

"Because you always believed that I could do it. Because I would never have been able to go to Vancouver if you hadn't convinced Will to come back to the shop."

And then I understood. That's why she'd told me I expected too much of her, why she'd said she was sorry for disappointing me.

"Do you understand what it's like for me?" she said, tears of resentment brimming in her eyes. "To find myself caring so desperately about what one man thinks of me? To be miserable because I can't be the person he wants me to be?"

I sat down beside her like a penitent on a church pew, my hands between my legs. She wiped her eyes with the cuff of her sweater.

"Want a Kleenex?" I asked, producing a flattened piece of pulp from the folds of my parka. Her eyes widened when she saw it. I shrugged and returned it to my pocket. "For the record," I said, "I didn't fall in love with you because you wanted to be a writer."

She smiled at me with a wobbly chin. I swung my arm back, inviting her to settle in against me and all my winter padding.

Chapter 25

I hear Marla calling my name from the other side of the hotel room door. She's concerned that I haven't answered yet. I stumble to my feet, my eyes still sticky. Morning light has seeped around the edges of the curtains and tinted the hotel room bluish-grey like a watercolour wash. I've slept in my clothes again; they're rumpled and rank.

I must be a horrifying sight because when I open the door, Marla looks at me as though I've just crawled out of some back alley. She asks me if I realize what time it is, but of course I don't have a clue. She tells me it's almost ten o'clock, and she's already had breakfast. She elbows past me and yanks back the curtains. I shield my eyes like a vampire caught outside his coffin.

Marla orders me to take a shower. I let the hot water rain down on my head for nearly half an hour. When I dry myself off, I realize that she's sneaked into the bathroom and scooped up my pile of dirty clothes, except for my underwear. I poke my head out the bathroom door, holding a towel around my waist. She hands me a pair of sweatpants and a T-shirt, spares she'd packed for herself, she explains. Cast-offs from Avery. Before I can close the bathroom door, she hands me a toothbrush and a tube of toothpaste that she had the concierge deliver when I was in the shower. She tells me that they didn't have any razors.

When I emerge from the bathroom, she's on the phone with Jay, asking him what Avery's up to and telling him that she'll call again when she's ready to pick up the car and drive Avery back to London. As she hangs up, she tosses me an orange from her knapsack. She says that room service should be up any minute with my breakfast. She hopes I like my eggs scrambled.

I pull on the pair of socks she's left for me on the bed. "You don't need to do this any more," I tell her.

"What?"

"You should take Avery home," I say, gesturing towards the phone. "You don't need to tag along with me."

"He's fine with Jay," she says unconvincingly.

"Honestly, I can find Severn on my own."

"You don't even know where to look for her," she says.

"I'll figure something out," I insist.

She smirks.

"Look," I say, "I'm not trying to sound ungrateful here."

She thrusts a printout from a web page at me.

"What's this?" I ask.

"On my way back from breakfast, I told the guy at the front desk that I'd heard Jack Livingston was doing a book-signing somewhere in town. I batted my eyelashes and asked him if he could check on his fancy-dancy computer for me." She points to the bottom of the page. "Jack's scheduled to appear downtown at two this afternoon."

I stare at the printout, dumbfounded by her tenacity. Livingston isn't the only one on the bill. Fellow literary heavyweights Roddy Doyle and Peter Carey are to follow him on stage. I note that Imprint Books is one of the big sponsors of the event. The venue is the dance theatre at Harbourfront Centre.

"Quite frankly," Marla says, "I don't think it's a good idea for you to attend unescorted."

"What's that supposed to mean?"

"Let's just say that your reactions have been a tad unpredictable lately," she says. "I don't want you showing up as the lead story on the evening news. 'Crazed teacher assaults famous author.'"

I'm not about to confirm her doubts about my state of mind by describing my nocturnal visit from Lady Franklin.

We drive down to Harbourfront early to buy our tickets. The box office isn't open yet, so we kill time by strolling along the water's edge, past the vacant moorings of the summer tour boats. The skies have cleared and the nearby outdoor rink is crowded with Saturday skaters. The fresh snow on the frozen harbour gleams so brightly that it makes me squint.

"How do you know Jack is Severn's father?" Marla asks me out of the blue.

The question sounds remarkably naive to me. For as long as I can remember, I've lived under Livingston's shadow, resigned myself to the profanity of his and Helen's genes continuing their slow dance through Severn's veins. "Believe me, I know."

"Figuring out paternity isn't always straightforward," she says. She doesn't understand that I've long ago given up dreaming that some blood test is going to prove what I've always wished were true.

"Helen was with him long enough," I say curtly. "I did the math."

I hope she'll take the hint and drop the subject, but she's not through yet. "So why did you decide to raise her if you were so sure she wasn't yours?"

I shut my eyes and tip my head back, wondering how she can possibly expect me to explain sixteen years of earnest self-delusion in the space of an idle conversation on a frozen quay. The sun offers my cheeks no warmth, but its glare is so intense that it penetrates my eyelids as a fuzzy, bloodshot glow. "I should tell you that I was doing it for all the right reasons," I say, drawing in a sharp, cold breath that makes my nostrils shrivel. "But the thing was, after Livingston dumped her, Helen was desperate. I was just happy that she needed me again." I open my eyes and flash a broken grin at Marla. "Makes me sound kind of pathetic, doesn't it?"

Marla shrugs and peers out beyond the painful blue horizon. "I'm hardly one to talk. Jay screwed his legal assistant for three years, but I didn't want to know."

I wonder whether she thinks that by telling me this, she's made us soul buddies, members in our own private little club of emotional doormats. I let her words condense and drift away on the cold air without comment.

She nudges a chunk of ice into the harbour with her foot. "You must have realized that Severn would find out sometime."

She makes it sound as though it was an inevitability. But the truth is that until Severn ran away, I'd begun to let myself believe that maybe, just maybe, I'd go on being her only father. When I lost Helen, the secret became mine alone, and quite frankly, I thought that sharing it with Severn would have only made her more confused and angry than she was already.

Marla diverts her attention to the skaters. "That looks like fun," she says, trying to lighten the mood. "You want to rent some skates?"

I raise my eyebrows as if she's made a bad joke.

"We've got time," she insists. "My treat."

"I don't skate," I say.

Her look says I must be lying simply to put her off.

"Really," I say. "Weak ankles."

"And you call yourself a Canadian?" she says.

I give a little shrug. Undeterred, she takes me by the hand and drags me down the steps to the indoor rental counter.

"We're supposed to be looking for Severn," I say.

"How do you know we won't find her here?" she says.

"You're not getting me in a pair of skates."

"Fine. Then you can watch me."

That's what I used to do with Severn when she was small—

stand at the edge of the little rink by the bandshell in Victoria Park and watch her wobble along. Helen would be out there, gliding slowly beside her, holding her hand. When Severn slipped, she'd dangle from Helen's arm like a helpless doll, the collar of her coat riding up around her chin. Helen didn't like letting her fall, even though she knew it was all part of learning how to skate.

When they came off the ice, I'd be waiting for them with hot chocolate in Styrofoam cups. Severn would squint up at me and ask whether I'd remembered to get marshmallows in hers this time. She'd sit down on a park bench, and I'd start to unlace her white skates, careful not to cut myself on the little teeth jutting out from the front of her blades.

Marla puts on her rented skates and heads out to the crowded ice. I pull out my cellphone and go through my now familiar drill—calling Severn's cell, the answering machine at home, and the Toronto police—with the same disappointing results. As I watch Marla out on the ice, I catch a glimpse of Severn when she was twelve, still with dreams of becoming a figure skater. I hear the familiar scrape of the blades as Marla bobs towards the middle of the rink, carefully avoiding the tottering novices and breakneck boys in hockey jerseys. She carves an arc on the ice and begins a wonky spin. After a few revolutions, she digs her edge in and nearly topples over. She catches her balance, then smiles at me with the glee of someone who's just averted disaster.

I check my watch. The box office still won't open for another half hour. I hoist up Marla's knapsack, which she's left with me for safekeeping, and wander up the steps to Lakeside Eats. Their hot chocolate machine is broken, so I buy two coffees and take them back rinkside. There's a spot free on the end of a bench next to a snotty-faced boy whose parents have made him wear a snowsuit. As I sit and gently lay the two cups beside my feet, Marla's knapsack slides down my arm, nearly knocking them over. I yank it back up to my lap, feeling the dead weight of the hardcover inside. I look out at the rink. Marla's doing laps now. I open up her bag, dig through my dirty clothes, and pull out Livingston's book.

The top corner of one of the pages is bent over. I open to it and begin reading. The girl, Sally Campbell, has just approached the outfitter who last saw her mother alive. He's sitting in the cafeteria of a local inn. It's a place favoured by Southerners who use Resolute as a staging point for summertime expeditions in the High Arctic.

> He squinted up at her reproachfully, as if a white girl of six-teen wearing nail polish had no business being this far north.
>
> "You know my mother," she said to him, careful to continue referring to her in the present tense.
>
> He said nothing, choosing instead to contemplate the clocks above the steam tables, each of which was set to a different time zone. Sally was beginning to understand that time didn't follow the same rules here. This close to the top of the world, time zones were just thin wedges, traversable so quickly that they no longer had meaning except for homesick Southerners. Here, days couldn't even be defined by the rising and setting of the sun. A man on the plane had told her that night wouldn't return for another month. Meanwhile, the incessant grey sky and cold rain made July feel more like March.
>
> "My father says you're the one who reported her missing," she said.
>
> "Is that so?" he said with tempered disdain. "I'm not sure he'd want you talking to me."
>
> "What happened to her?"
>
> "Hasn't your father already told you?"
>
> She was tired of deciphering her father's sullen silences. "I wanted to ask you myself," she said.
>
> He studied her face for a moment. "What makes you think I'll give you a different answer?"

She thought of her mother's note, the one that read, "Until you join me." She chose her words carefully. "Everyone thinks she's dead. But nobody can say for certain. They just keep telling me she's missing."

He swirled his coffee in his mug. He was clearly annoyed that the task of teaching her about the realities of life in the High Arctic had been left to him. "The British named a lot of the places up here," he said, breaking it to her slowly. "Rather presumptuous on their part, considering that the Inuit had already been here for thousands of years. More often than not, they'd choose a name to commemorate another one of their failed attempts to find a way through the ice to Asia in their wooden boats. For instance, this place, Resolute, was named after HMS *Resolute*, abandoned in the ice—as were four other British naval vessels—during the search for that dunderhead Franklin one summer. More than a year later, an American whaler found the *Resolute* floating intact a thousand miles from here. The ice and the currents had carried her all that way without a crew to steer her. Of course, the other four ships were crushed like paper cups. The British never understood the Arctic. They thought they could outwit it, overcome it with equal parts of pluck and pig-headedness. And they invariably paid the price. Hundreds of them, including Franklin and his men, went missing, never to be heard from again." He looked up at her with eyes that had seen many brutal winters without a sun. "Your mother could be just as pig-headed when she wanted to be."

I'm suddenly conscious that Marla is standing over me, still in her skates. I snap the book shut instinctively.

"What part were you reading?" she asks.

I feel silly for acting like a guilty schoolboy. Just the same, I stuff the book back in the knapsack. I hand her one of the coffees. "You done?" I ask.

She half smiles at me. "Sure," she says, letting me off the hook this time.

We make our way back to the change area so she can return the skates.

Chapter 26

After Helen and I got back together, she lavished me with attention, clearing a permanent place for me in her life. On days when
she wasn't working at the shop, she brought a special lunch to
school for the two of us and ate with me in the teachers' lounge.
I basked in the envy of my male colleagues as they watched
Helen wipe stray bits of couscous or flakes of baklava off my chin
while they chewed on their egg-salad sandwiches. After school,
she often took me clothes shopping, insisting that any man she
was going to commit to had to look stylish in public, even if he
had no sense of style himself. Early in the spring, she helped me
haul my old furniture to the dump and moved me in with her for
good. She even made room for all my books, buying extra cases
to put them in and intermingling our collections. My patience
had finally been rewarded.

We picked a date in September to get married, nine months after
Helen's ignominious return from the West Coast. We told Walter
about our plans in May. It was one of his afternoons at the bookshop. He was sitting on the stool behind the front counter, reading
Voltaire. I'd noticed that since his heart attack, he'd sometimes
stare at a book without turning a page for fifteen minutes, his mind
straining to squeeze meaning from the text. At first he blinked at us

when we sprung the news on him, as if he'd missed what Helen had just told him. Then, as I started talking about our thoughts on where to hold the reception, the fog cleared from his eyes.

"Congratulations," he said, offering up a frail smile.

Helen joked that he could heave a sigh of relief now that she'd be the bane of another man's existence, but she failed to get the rise out of him that she was clearly hoping for. I nervously leapt in and began explaining that we wanted to keep the celebration small, just family and close friends. When we ran out of things to say, he murmured his congratulations one last time and resumed reading his book.

I could see that his meek response had deflated Helen, although she tried not to show it. His approval had always been so hard to win, but now it was being given to her like a cheap trinket.

Will helped us plan the reception. He seemed to know half the caterers and restaurateurs in town on a first-name basis. Helen even took him along to pick out her wedding dress. It was then I recognized a fact that I'd managed to ignore up to that point— Helen had no girlfriends to offer her frivolous advice. She clearly and consistently favoured the company of men.

Having seen how much faith Helen put in Will's fashion advice, I took him along with me to the tailor's. He told me that it was a myth that all gay men had a sense of style. The world was littered with more queer slobs than I'd care to know about. But because I was such a good friend he'd agreed to help me out, despite the risk he ran of reinforcing the stereotype.

Will convinced me to order a tailor-made suit rather than buy one off the rack, as I'd originally intended to do. When I objected to the price, he advised me that this was probably the only time in my life that I'd rate a suit so fine, and that I shouldn't diminish the importance of the occasion by being cheap.

"Besides," he said, "I know what Helen's wearing. We don't want you looking like an organ grinder's monkey beside her."

Next, he tried to talk me into getting lifts for my shoes. I resisted, insisting that I wasn't embarrassed to be a few inches shorter than Helen. He reminded me that my bride would be in heels; fashion dictated no less. I should be glad that he'd managed to steer her away from a billowing veil that would have only exaggerated the height differential between us.

"Jesus, Will. If you thought Helen and I were such a mismatch, why the hell did you scheme to get us back together?"

Will smacked me lightly on the cheek. "You, my dear Mr. Cruickshank, should not look a gift horse in the mouth."

For a moment, a flash of candour illuminated his face. The message was clear: he cared who Helen ended up with, notwithstanding his frequent barbs about her capriciousness. If I had irked him by failing to pay her homage over the past year and a half, we would not be picking out a wedding suit. His consent, tacit though it was, was no less important than Walter's. My ongoing performance had been evaluated; my worthiness measured and found sufficient. Right then, he might as well have truly been Helen's older brother.

Will helped me decide whether to have my pants cuffed. He picked out three Italian silk ties—one for the wedding and two for what he wryly referred to as my trousseau. The shoes he had me buy were Italian too, but without lifts.

As we left the tailor's, Will peered dolefully at the wispy summer clouds overhead. He told me that he'd taken the HIV test that had just become available, and that it had come back negative. He said it matter-of-factly, as if he were commenting on the weather. I told him that was great news.

He flashed an ambivalent smile. "I don't know," he said. "I almost feel like I'm cheating on Kevin."

The fire happened one week before the wedding. It started in the garret. Helen hadn't been up there in months, presumably because her experience at UBC had turned her off writing. Perhaps she went there to rekindle her writing spirit, or maybe to lay it to rest. She never explained the reasons for her visit to me.

I was at home in our apartment watching "Masterpiece Theatre" when she called in a panic. I knew that she'd gone to visit her father that night, and when she began sobbing on the phone, I thought for sure that he had had another heart attack. But then, between the sobs, I began picking out words that told me otherwise—something about candles, a curtain, the flames spreading too fast.

When I arrived, the firemen were already rolling up their hoses. The frame of one of the upstairs windows had turned to charcoal. The bricks were scorched tar black up to the eaves. Helen was rocking anxiously on the hood of her car with her arms wrapped tightly around her knees. I sat next to her, put my arm around her, and asked if she was all right. She kept rocking, telling me that this was an omen. That I shouldn't be marrying someone so careless, so stupid.

Will was there as well, trying unsuccessfully to convince one of the firemen to let him into the shop so he could rescue the books from the water that was leaking down through the ceiling. I watched as he stood in the ankle-deep puddles in the street, staring helplessly at the front window, which was already fogging up with condensation. First Kevin, I thought as I saw him kick a puddle in frustration, now this.

The wedding went ahead on schedule the next week. It was a civil ceremony downtown, and we were careful not to drive past the burned-out shop on Richmond Street on our way. My parents were there from Ottawa, my mother beaming from ear to ear. Walter was more subdued. He smiled obligingly as we exchanged rings, but there was a lost look in his eyes. He hardly spoke to anyone during the reception, spending most of the time staring into his glass of Scotch. When he failed to rise and toast the happy couple, Will tactfully stepped in, speaking of his affection for both of us and joking about what a brave man I was, for which he received many hearty seconders. To Will's credit, he somehow managed to rise above his heartache for the shop. The rest of our guests eagerly followed his lead. Everyone was intent on having a good time, on making sure that our special day wasn't diminished by the fire. If anything, they tried a little too hard, as if they felt obliged to compensate for Walter's quiet despair.

Helen was desperate in her lovemaking that night—perhaps hoping that extreme passion would purge her memories of the fire. But no matter how hard I tried, I couldn't fill her desire enough to completely force the demon out.

Chapter 27

Marla and I are waiting by the theatre box office when it opens, only to be told by the woman at the wicket that the afternoon's readings are sold out. I plead with her to squeeze us in, let us stand at the back or take the seats of no-shows. She is very apologetic. Fire regulations require that the aisles remain clear, she says, and there's already a long list of people waiting for unclaimed tickets.

I grumble to Marla, insinuating that we should have called ahead instead of hanging around the skating rink. Rather than take offence, she wades into the crowd of assembling ticket holders and, within ten minutes, buys a pair of seats from a couple by offering them four times what they paid for them.

"You can pay me back later," she says, folding my fingers around the tickets.

We comb the lobby for Severn without success. The theatre doors are closing, so we're forced to scramble upstairs to grab our seats in the balcony. I scan the audience for the back of Severn's head, but it's useless. She didn't inherit her mother's red hair, so she's much harder to pick out in a crowd. I can see only the first several rows of people on the orchestra level, but I hear hundreds of excited voices bubbling up from the seats under the balcony.

The chit-chat is definitely highbrow. The couple next to me are arguing about the function of critics in postmodern literature, while a man behind me is complaining about how much he paid to fix the transmission on his Lexus. I feel out of place in my borrowed sweats and day-old beard. I try to project a bohemian air.

The buzz of the crowd modulates as the house lights dim and a woman in a designer suit with an intricately patterned silk scarf draped over her shoulder makes her way to the podium. At first I don't recognize her, but when she welcomes everyone and introduces herself as the master of ceremonies, her voice envelops me like a plush bathrobe. I've heard her on CBC Radio, interviewing everyone from chicken farmers to prime ministers with equal charm and perspicacity.

"My first guest," she tells us, "has been a Canadian treasure ever since he burst onto the scene in the 1970s. One of his contemporaries described him early on in his career as the Oracle of the Alley. A man of the streets with the pen of an errant angel."

I recognize the hype only too well—although angel, no matter how errant, is not how I'd describe Jack Livingston. Something else with wings, maybe. An albatross. A vulture. A huge, ugly bird all too eager to shit on your head.

"His latest book, *Northwest Passage*," the emcee goes on, "has struck such a chord with the reading public that it's been on the bestseller lists since its release. One critic described the work as luminescent, a story that takes us on a journey as much into the human soul as into the glorious and terrifying solitude of the Arctic."

It occurs to me that Livingston has likely never bothered to travel to the Arctic, given its shortage of taverns. And I doubt that he knows much about the human soul, since he completely lacks one himself. Hardly surprising, then, that he sponges his material from others. What astonishes me is that no one but me has caught on after all these years.

The emcee pauses ever so briefly for dramatic effect before

welcoming Livingston onstage. The applause is surprisingly rau-
cous. There are several hoots from the audience as he enters from
the wings, wearing a faded denim shirt. He looks like a calcified
hippie with his grey hair pulled back in a ponytail. His nose is
more bulbous than I remember, probably the effect of nearly
twenty more years of booze. He smiles crookedly at the adoring
crowd. I notice Marla checking on me cautiously. She seems
relieved that we're so far from the stage.

The emcee greets Livingston and invites him to sit down. He
gives one last bemused look down his considerable nose at his
assembled fans. A woman in the audience has wandered to the
foot of the stage and is holding up a single red rose for him. He
bends over and accepts the flower, uttering a few words of thanks
that make the woman blush and slink back to her seat with an
embarrassed smile. Finally, he takes his place in the chair across
from the emcee, laying the rose at his feet.

"One of your female admirers?" the emcee quips.

Livingston says with false modesty that he didn't realize he still
had any at his age.

"So what's it like to be a national icon?" she asks with a grin.
She pitches it as a joke, but I can tell it's also an adroit poke at Livingston's vanity.

He says that in a country whose national animal is the beaver
and whose principal unit of currency is the loonie, the honour
seems somewhat dubious. Not that he ever made any effort to be
respectable, he adds. In fact, he's rather uncomfortable with how
accepted he's become lately. He interprets it as a sign of growing
decrepitude.

"Or," she says, "it may mean that it's simply taken us a while to
properly appreciate your talents."

An appealing notion, he says, but unlikely. He smiles at having
manoeuvred her into paying him a compliment. He crosses his
legs, resting his ankle on his opposite knee, and begins fiddling
with the tassels of his loafer.

I can see now that Livingston has left such a trail of discarded women in his life because they could never compete with his most ardent lover—himself. Women were simply pleasingly proportioned mirrors in which to admire his own reflection. Unfortunately, they all too often bent the light to his advantage, mistaking his bloated ego for svelte panache. I look around in disgust at the women in the audience as they titter at his deceptively self-effacing barbs. Even Marla is chuckling. She restrains herself after I give her the evil eye.

The emcee steers the conversation towards Livingston's latest work. She says that there are those who take exception when writers play with the facts of history. "*Northwest Passage* is a good example of this," she says. "You weave the nineteenth-century story of Franklin's lost Arctic expedition with the fictional present-day story of a girl's search for her mother. But you alter certain historical facts. For instance, you describe an affair Lady Jane had with an officer on one of the expedition's ships and leave us believing that she was more interested in the fate of her lover than that of her own husband. And yet there's no historical evidence that any such affair took place. In fact, history records that Lady Jane was enormously devoted to her husband."

He responds with predictable slickness, saying that shackling fiction to the limits of accepted truths would be like sending a runner into a race after busting his kneecaps. He says that his stories are works of imagination; he claims nothing else. He uses actual experiences as raw material, a starting point that readers can identify with. But from there, he wants to show us something about being human that we may not have imagined on our own. Just because there's no record that Lady Jane had an affair doesn't necessarily mean that one never took place. And anyway, what does it matter in the end? *Northwest Passage* isn't a retelling of the history books. It's a story about the guilt that comes with loss and the struggle we must endure to find a safe harbour for our grief.

There's enthusiastic applause from the audience. I wonder if everyone is taken in by his snake-oil salesman act, or if the thunderous clapping of a gullible few is forcing the remainder to politely join in, giving the ovation weight beyond its worth.

The emcee waits for the applause to die down, then asks him where he got the idea for the book.

There's really no one place, he equivocates. A novel is a coalescing of many different ideas.

I feel like waving one of Helen's crumbling notebooks in the air and calling him a plagiarist out loud. A thief. A looter. A grave robber. Marla gently lays her hand on my arm. I realize that I've mangled the program I was handed at the door. She reminds me to breathe.

The emcee continues, "But the main story—about a girl losing her mother—it's written with such genuine compassion and insight. I'm sure many people assume that you have gone through a similar loss yourself."

Livingston says that he doesn't need to experience something himself to write about it. In fact, it helps him to have a certain emotional distance from his subject.

I snort disdainfully. The man in the seat next to me half turns to show his annoyance with my little outburst.

"You don't have kids of your own," the emcee says, consulting the notes in front of her.

Livingston smiles ambiguously.

"And yet," she says, "it obviously didn't stop you from writing about what it's like to raise a teenager. Oh, and by the way, as someone who's living through it right now, I'd have to say that you're uncomfortably accurate on that score."

I can only assume that Livingston understands teenagers so well because he still behaves like one himself. As he sits there, smugly soaking up the plaudits, I see a balding and depraved Peter Pan in loafers.

At the emcee's invitation, Livingston goes to the podium and reads an excerpt from his book. He chooses a passage where Sally Campbell finds a baby photo of herself in the outfitter's wallet and confronts him with it. The outfitter claims to have got the picture in the mail many years before, when her mother was sending one to every friend and relative she could think of. Sally is unconvinced. She wants to know why he still keeps it in his wallet. He says that he simply forgot to take it out.

There's more over-the-top applause. Once Livingston is back in his chair, the emcee asks for the house lights to be raised and invites us to pose any questions we have. I feel like standing up and telling him to show us what baby photos he keeps in his own wallet. My hunch is that Severn's wouldn't be the only one.

The questioning from the audience is, for the most part, unbearably polite. A woman who reminds me of our school librarian gushes about the way Livingston captured the ambivalence teenage girls have towards their mothers, then asks him whether he has any advice for parents like her. A guy with a bad haircut asks him whom he'd cast in the movie version of his book. And a girl with long, scraggly hair and braces tells him how cool she thinks the story is, even though she hates history at school.

"Where are you going?" Marla asks, alarmed to see me getting up while Livingston is still onstage.

"You actually think that Jack Livingston is going to stick around to listen to other writers talk about themselves?" I say. "I'm going to see if I can catch him when he gets off."

"I'm coming with you," she says.

We manage to annoy half the people in our row as we squeeze past their knees and step on their toes. Marla follows me up the aisle and through the exit at the back of the balcony.

"What are you going to do?" she asks anxiously on our way downstairs.

"Livingston's the only chance I have of finding Severn right now," I tell her. "I'm not about to let him get away."

She scurries in front of me and blocks the steel doors that lead to the main level. "Have you even thought about what you're going to say to him?"

I sidestep her. "I'm sure something will come."

I enter and walk down the steep steps of the left-hand aisle towards a woman who's standing at her seat with her back to me, listening to Livingston's cleverly arrogant rejoinder to her comments. The audience chuckles in response, the woman along with them. She sits back down, and the emcee begins her wrap-up, thanking everyone for their interesting questions. As the crowd gives Livingston a warm round of applause, I approach the foot of the stage. I look up at him as he makes his triumphant exit to the wings. At the last moment, he sees me and hesitates. His eyes drift towards someone in the front row.

I follow his gaze and see Severn staring at me as if I've exposed my privates in public. She slides down in her seat, pretending not to know me.

Chapter 28

Most of the damage from the fire was to the front of the shop. Almost half the books in stock were salvageable. Insurance money covered the bulk of the repair costs; the rest came from what was left of Walter and Helen's savings. The place opened its doors again in January, having missed out on the Christmas shopping season. Nearly two years had passed since the day I'd come to solicit Farley Mowat and had ended up meeting my future wife.

Will knew they'd have to do something special to make people notice that they were back in business, particularly in the middle of the winter blahs. He got Helen to use her charms on Walter's fraternity of war buddies. Within a few weeks, she'd lined up a stellar cast of Canadian writers who'd agreed to come to London to help celebrate the reopening. Jack Livingston was among them.

Walter didn't actually know him. Nor did Helen at the time. He came as a favour to his publisher, who'd spent a week in a military hospital bed next to Walter. It also gave Livingston a chance to flog a collection of poems that he'd released the previous fall.

It was a Friday afternoon when he made his appearance at the shop. I was teaching, so I wasn't there to see him make what was surely a cocky entrance. An Alberta clipper hit shortly after he arrived, dumping nearly a foot of snow on the city in the space of twenty-four hours. Hardly anyone showed up to see him. Most people were more interested in finding a way home from work before the streets became impassable.

School closed early. I made it to our apartment building just after three-thirty, but the parking lot was already a mess. My day brightened considerably when I checked our mail slot and found a letter that I'd been eagerly anticipating. I ripped it open right there in the lobby. I was so excited by the contents that I raced up to the apartment and immediately phoned the shop to tell Helen the news.

Will answered. He told me that business in the shop was dead. Helen had taken their guest author across the street to the pub.

"In this weather?" I said.

Darkness fell and the blizzard intensified. By seven o'clock, Helen still wasn't home. I called the shop again, thinking she might have holed up there if she believed she couldn't get home safely, but there was no answer. I imagined her driving through a whiteout and running head-on into a snowplow. I'd get a call from the police any moment to inform me of the accident.

It was nearly eight when she finally walked through the door. A man in his forties with red cheeks, rakish good looks, and a full head of flowing black hair was with her.

"Jack is staying with us tonight," she announced, introducing me to my nemesis-to-be.

Livingston grinned and bobbed his head in greeting. He brushed past me, kicked off his boots, and followed Helen inside, the sour smell of bourbon floating in his wake.

"I was worried about you," I said to Helen, my annoyance overruling my relief.

"Sorry," she said, rubbing her cold hands together and sharing a coy smile with Livingston. "I guess we were having too much fun and didn't notice the time. What's for supper?"

Helen sat down to a round of beer with Livingston at our little dining-room table just off the kitchen while I pulled together supper from what I could find in the fridge. He proceeded to tell

Helen about his year in Tuscany, travelling the countryside, labouring in vineyards by day and practising his Italian on women in bars at night. Helen nearly peed her pants laughing when he described how he had inadvertently propositioned the wife of one of the local *carabinieri*.

In between anecdotes, Helen came into the kitchen to grab another couple of beers. She kissed me on the cheek and told me I was doing a wonderful job peeling the carrots. Just as she was about to rejoin Livingston, she noticed the letter on the counter.

"What's this?" she asked, examining the University of Alberta letterhead.

My eagerness to tell her had evaporated.

She read the letter. "Why didn't you tell me about this?"

I shrugged and started on the potatoes.

She turned to Livingston, holding the paper aloft. "It seems that my husband has just been invited on an Arctic expedition."

Livingston pretended to be duly impressed. He asked me to elaborate. I told him that I'd written to a professor who was doing a dig up north. I left it at that. I wasn't in the mood to explain everything to him. Helen, on the other hand, had no such reservations. She dug out the magazine I'd saved from two summers before and showed it to him.

"Irving's related to this guy," she told him, pointing to the coffin that the team of anthropologists had uncovered but had been unable to release from the ice. "What is he again?" she asked me. "Your great-great-great uncle?"

Livingston was clearly intrigued. He wanted to know more.

I wasn't about to explain to him that the head researcher, a forensic anthropologist at the University of Alberta, was testing a theory that Franklin's men had been poisoned by the lead used to seal their canned provisions. After reading the magazine article, I'd written for more information on the research findings. I hadn't realized that because I was an ancestor of John Hartnell's, my consent was required before further fieldwork could proceed.

The invitation to return to the gravesite with the research team that summer had come as a wonderful surprise to me.

Livingston considered the magazine photos of the corpse, whose leathery grimace had been preserved by the Arctic permafrost. "To have a chance to look into the eyes of an ancestor who lived so far in the past," he said. "That's almost beyond comprehension." I could see him turning the idea over in his mind like a diamond cutter examining a raw stone.

During supper, Livingston asked Helen about her writing, a topic that had obviously come up at the pub earlier in the day. He wanted to see her notebooks. Helen insisted that they were just random scribblings, but it didn't take much effort on Livingston's part to get her to accede to his request. He pushed his supper away half-finished when she brought them. She nervously watched his protruding lower lip as he read.

He declared that several of the passages in the notebooks showed promise, then said that she shouldn't let her experience at UBC discourage her. A writer's life was all about transcending failure and rejection. He was a classic example. People used to call his work unreadable. Some still did. He said that she should consider enrolling in the extension course he was offering in late February at U of T.

Helen was still giddy when she came to bed after settling Livingston into our spare room. I yanked off my socks and asked her if she'd had a good day. She immediately sensed the edge of resentment in my tone.

"You've been crotchety all night," she said, shucking her bra before climbing under the sheets. Normally the sight of her naked breasts would make me want to grope her, but I was too busy being sour.

"You could have called from the pub," I said, still unhurriedly removing my clothes.

"I said I was sorry."

"That's what you always say."

I'd cut her. She sat up in bed, her eyes smouldering. "Just because we're married doesn't mean I can't have a social life of my own."

"Did I say you couldn't?"

"Somehow I doubt we'd be having this conversation if Jack were a woman."

"I might not have minded so much if he hadn't flirted with you all night."

She jumped out of bed and pulled on her bathrobe, cinching the belt tight. "What do you want me to do? Ask your permission before I speak to another man?"

"Of course not."

"If this is how much you trust me, then I'm surprised you even let me out of your sight." She flung open the bedroom door and stormed out. I imagined Livingston with his ear to the wall in the next room, making notes for a future story about an insecure man who married a woman beyond his reach.

I waited an hour before I went out and apologized to her as she lay sulking on the living-room couch, watching TV. I admitted I'd overreacted, knowing that's what she wanted to hear. I asked her to come back to bed. She turned and looked at me, measuring my sincerity, her face a ghostly blue in the glow from the TV. She must have judged that even though I wasn't truly repentant, I was at least displaying a suitable measure of acquiescence. Mollified, she followed me back to the bedroom.

Chapter 29

The scene that Marla dreaded never materializes. Livingston catches Severn's eye as he glides towards the wings, motioning for her to come backstage with a subtle roll of his chin. She slips out of her seat, twists past me, and ducks through the side exit. Onstage, the emcee is introducing Roddy Doyle. No one takes notice of me standing there, stupidly watching the door click shut behind Severn.

Marla stops a few feet short of me, waiting to see what I'll do next. The audience members are on their feet now, welcoming the Irishman with a standing ovation. I look back at them in confusion, thinking that they're applauding Severn for jettisoning me, but then I see all their eyes directed towards the stage. I pull myself together and head for the side door. A man in a black shirt and black pants—a house staffer who reminds me more of a bouncer at a night club—blocks the way. He tells me that I'll have to use another exit.

"You just let my daughter through," I say, challenging the arbitrariness of his authority.

He tells me that she had a pass. Only people who have a pass can go backstage.

Marla is at my elbow. She tells the man that the girl he just let through is only sixteen. She questions the legality of issuing passes to minors without parental consent. She also mentions that her husband is a lawyer and asks the man whether it's necessary for her to call him to get this matter resolved.

The man stands his ground, but his eyes begin to search the theatre for a manager to save his neck. He's in the middle of repeating the party line when the door opens a crack behind him. A diminutive woman, also dressed in black, sticks her head and shoulders out. She instructs her colleague that Mr. Livingston has told them to let us through.

The woman leads us through the wings, where the curtains tower above us like sequoias. We pass within a few feet of the glare of the stage lights. Roddy Doyle is now settled in across from the emcee, his back towards me. I see countless faces staring at them from the twilight of the house, hanging on their every word. The world seems strangely refracted here behind the lens of the proscenium arch.

Severn and Livingston are standing off to the side, away from the action, next to a set of steps that look like they lead to the performers' exit. Our escort leaves us. Severn frowns at Marla as we approach.

"It's been a long time," Livingston says to me.

I look only at Severn. "Do you realize how worried I've been about you?" I tell her.

She stands there impatiently, suffering me as if I'm a bad black-and-white movie she's seen too many times before.

Livingston leans back on the metal handrail at the top of the stairs, observing the dynamics between father and daughter with detached fascination. "You're welcome to come to my place, where things are a little more private," he says.

"That won't be necessary," I tell him. "Severn and I will be heading back to London."

He shrugs and turns to head down the stairs. "Suit yourself."

"I'm not going back," Severn announces before he's off the top step.

"You have school on Monday," I say, as if I can't think of a better reason for her to come home.

Marla wades in. "Severn, honey, you and your dad have a lot to sort out. You need to give him a chance."

Severn resents the intrusion. Livingston, on the other hand, is intrigued by the added complication of Marla. He's trying to deduce her motivation, invent a back story for her, I can tell.

"The least you could have done was call to let me know you were all right," I tell Severn.

Livingston repeats his invitation to have us over to his place. "Seeing as how Severn doesn't seem particularly interested in being rescued from my evil clutches at the moment," he says. "You have a car? Otherwise, we'll all need to hop on a streetcar."

I'm loath to dance to his tune, but Marla nudges me to accept the offer. I stuff my hands in my pockets and motion for him to lead the way. Severn squeezes past him on the stairs, using him as her shield against me. We exit the theatre through a door next to the box office, then descend a further two levels past the glitzy shops and restaurants of the Queen's Quay Terminal. Severn orbits Livingston like a rogue moon, cautiously distant but undeniably drawn to him.

We finally emerge into the waning winter afternoon. We find the car, and Livingston climbs in front with me so he can give directions. That leaves the back for Severn and Marla. I glance over my shoulder and see Severn staring out her window, determined not to acknowledge her companion. Marla's eyes shift from Severn to Livingston. Like me, she's wondering what's passed between them.

Livingston directs me to head for Spadina. I keep the engine in Park.

"We're not going anywhere until you tell me what's been going on," I say.

He dips his chin and has a private little laugh. "Severn obviously thought it was time to meet me."

I tap the steering wheel restlessly.

He swivels around and smiles lopsidedly at my daughter. "She tried to introduce herself to me at my book-signing in London, but I was a little slow on the uptake. By the time I'd figured out who she was, she'd already beaten her retreat." He winks at me. "She has Helen's eyes, doesn't she?"

Severn looks down at her lap, embarrassed by how flattered she is.

"What have you told her?" I ask curtly.

Severn glares at me. "What you never bothered to tell me," she says.

"Perhaps it would be better to have this discussion somewhere other than a public parking lot," Livingston says. "My girlfriend, Katie, can make us all something hot to drink, perhaps with a little splash of rum for good measure. My place is less than fifteen minutes away." When I still don't move, he tells me that all Severn's things are there from her stay last night. Even if she was to go home with me today, she'd have to collect them first.

I pay the parking attendant and reluctantly follow Livingston's directions. As we drive through town, I overhear Marla asking Severn, "Are you okay?"

Severn is horrified by the intimacy of her tone. She slides closer to her door. I keep an eye on her in the rear-view mirror, worried that she'll decide to bolt at the next red light. Livingston takes it all in with the absorption of an anthropologist visiting a fascinating alien culture on the verge of extinction.

He explains to me that Katie answered the door yesterday afternoon and found Severn standing there asking for him. "Severn was quite persistent," he says, casting his words to the back seat as an accolade.

I park the car at the side of the road in a neighbourhood of narrow brick houses with modest wooden front porches and miniscule front yards, built in an era before cars demanded driveways, let alone garages. Livingston says that he's lived in more colourful neighbourhoods, but the rent's reasonable for downtown, and it's within walking distance of several good, cheap restaurants in Chinatown and Kensington Market. I realize that we're only a few blocks from where he once lived with Helen.

Severn is quick to get out of the car. She stands apart from us on the sidewalk, her shoulders to her ears, braced against the freshening wind off the lake. The timid winter sun has already slid behind the roofs of the neighbouring houses.

Livingston turns up the footpath of a cramped house with green trim. A petrified geranium sits in a snow-covered pot on the porch. As Livingston fishes for his keys, he looks down at Severn, who's hanging back on the sidewalk.

"Look at her," he says to me. "Like a lost pilgrim in search of a new faith."

The pain of Severn's situation appeals to his poetic soul, I realize. I would shove him down the steps right then and there but for Marla's reproachful gaze.

He opens the front door and announces he has company as he tracks clumps of greasy snow into the tiny living room. Marla and I follow cautiously, removing our footwear in the vestibule. In contrast to the house's stark exterior, the inside is warm and inviting. It smells of hot apple cider and baked bread. The living room is decorated with antique wooden pieces with quilted covers, a *Country Living* magazine spread realized in perfect detail.

Livingston stands in the middle of the living room, his arms outstretched, basking in the incongruity of his surroundings. "Very Anne of Green Gables, isn't it?" he says with an ironic smile. He assures us it's all Katie's touch. He calls to her again, telling her to put on a pot of coffee.

Severn closes the front door behind her. She unwraps her scarf from her neck, carefully wipes her feet on the hall mat, and shuffles in behind us. I can feel her gauging my reaction to this place, even though she diverts her eyes to the old fire grate when I look back at her.

A woman finally calls back to Livingston from upstairs. I hear a door close, then the thump of feet on the stairs. Severn suddenly can't decide where to put her hands or what expression to wear on her face. I catch her sneaking a last self-conscious glance at me just as Katie appears at the bottom of the staircase.

Livingston steps forward and introduces me to her as Severn's father. Katie pauses, sensing the delicacy of the situation, then reaches out to shake my hand. She remarks on how cold my fingers are and says she'd better get cracking on that coffee. She waits patiently for me to release her hand.

I watch her make her way to the kitchen. She elbows Livingston playfully as she passes him. I put her in her mid-twenties, his junior by thirty years or more. Even in her stocking feet, she tops him by at least an inch. And by the faded freckles on her skin, I realize that her hair is naturally red.

Chapter 30

Helen took Livingston's creative-writing course in Toronto that winter. It ran on Saturday afternoons to accommodate students with nine-to-five jobs. The first morning, Helen was as nervous as a kid before her first day at school. The omelette that I fixed her turned cold on its plate as she flitted around the apartment, stuffing extra pens and paper in her bag, fiddling with her mascara, and changing her outfit umpteen times. When I repeated my offer to drive her to Toronto, she pretended not to hear me. We both knew that my gallantry was just a facade.

In between classes, Helen was usually either writing feverishly, completing her assignment for the week, or poring over Livingston's collected works, seeking inspiration. In place of the garret, which was never rebuilt after the fire, she sealed herself in our spare room, leaving me to mark papers and prepare my lessons at the dining-room table.

In the final weeks of the course, Helen packed an overnight bag. She said that the drive back through the snow in the dark wore her out, and that she wanted to experience downtown Toronto instead of just commuting in and out of it. When I asked her for the phone number of the hotel where she was staying, she didn't bother to hide her annoyance. In fact, on her first weekend there, she made a point of calling at ten o'clock to inform me that—shocking though it might seem—she hadn't been invited to any wild parties and was lying alone in her PJs watching a cheesy TV movie in her room.

The second weekend she didn't call at all. I tried phoning her late, but there was no answer. When she got back to London, I asked her where she'd been. She said that she'd gone out for a night on the town with her classmates to celebrate the end of eight weeks of baring their literary souls to one another. It was two in the morning by the time she'd got in, and she hadn't seen much point in waking me up just so I could complain about how drunk she was.

It was UBC all over again. She'd given up her dream of becoming a writer for me then, and now here I was forcing her to make the same old choice. I thought things would smooth out between us once she was done with Livingston's classes, but she remained prickly to the touch. Apparently I'd broken our bond of trust, and it was up to me to repair it. Rather than fight the hopeless battle of getting her to admit some culpability, I embarked on a series of peace overtures—unsolicited foot rubs, flowers for no particular occasion, special weekends out of town. Although she gladly accepted my offerings, it was always with veiled scepticism, as if I were attempting to bribe her to commute my sentence.

The first sunny Saturday in May, I brought a picnic basket to the bookshop and walked her over to Victoria Park for her lunch break. I laid out a blanket by the daffodil bed where we'd first tussled and set before her a buffet of smoked oysters, artichoke hearts, potato salad, pickled herring, and finger sandwiches that I'd carefully trimmed of their crusts. As she ate, she kept glancing at her watch, claiming that she was concerned about leaving Will on his own too long.

"I've decided not to go," I announced.

"Go?" she said with an inquiring frown.

"To the Arctic."

She hesitated over the plate of finger sandwiches and peered at me suspiciously. "I thought you specially requested the time off."

"The weather's finally turned nice here," I said. "Why would I want to fly in a rickety plane to some dreary island where I have to wear a winter coat in June?"

"You were going to take lots of pictures, show them at school."

"I'd just end up boring the kids."

She pointedly laid down her paper plate. "What's this really about?"

"I don't know, Helen. You tell me. Maybe it's time you clued me in on what awful thing I did to piss you off for so long."

My sarcasm clearly didn't amuse her. She pulled the cellophane back over the sandwiches and started shoving food in the cooler. Lunch break was over.

"A few hours of this I could take," I said. "Maybe even a day. But it's been months now."

"You're exaggerating."

"No, I'm not. I've been walking on eggshells around you."

She snapped the cooler lid closed and drew herself to her full kneeling height. I sensed that I was about to be set straight. "You seem to think that marriage is all about compromise," she said. "About constantly making sacrifices to keep the other person happy. Well, it's not. Not always, at least."

I reacted to the recrimination in her voice. "What are you saying? That you're unhappy because of me?"

She shut her eyes and carefully measured her reply. "What I'm saying is that we shouldn't be jealous of the time we need apart from each other. That's all."

"I see."

"Listen," she said, still straining to explain it to me calmly. "I don't spend time away from you because I'm angry. I do it because there are things in life I still need to do for myself. Just as there are things you need to do for yourself. There's nothing wrong with that. It doesn't mean that we love each other any less. I just wish you'd see that."

She made it all sound perfectly grown-up, but I knew that when the dust settled, the blame inevitably would be pinned on me. "So," I said, "I'm possessive, is that it?"

She grabbed my face in both hands. I thought she was about to attempt to rattle some sense into my brain, but instead she looked in my eyes imploringly. "Go on your trip."

"Really?" I said, managing to sound sceptical even with my mouth puckered between the heels of her hands.

"Really," she said without a hint of guile. "You may never have a chance like this again."

Her sincerity caught me off guard. All at once, I felt remarkably adolescent.

"Besides," she said, her eyes searching mine, "I need to know you still trust me."

In the end, I decided to go despite my misgivings, aware that Helen would take it at as an insult if I didn't. Will came along when Helen drove me to the airport that Sunday in June. He was excited that I was going on a real, live expedition to the Arctic and insisted that I deserved a proper send-off, just like any other explorer. He presented me with a reproduction of a letter that Lady Jane Franklin had written to her husband. The letter had been sent to the Arctic aboard an American ship and brought back undelivered. No one knew then that Sir John had died two years earlier.

As Helen parked the car, Will helped me carry my gear to the check-in counter. "Don't worry," he said reassuringly, glancing towards the parking lot. "I'll keep watch over things for you while you're gone."

In the lineup for security, Helen hooked her arm through mine and reminded me what an incredible experience this was going to be. She told me that she wanted to hear about it in detail. I said I'd call her when I could, but I wasn't sure how good communications would be once we reached the research site. She handed me my camera bag and kissed me goodbye. Both she and Will gave me a thumbs-up as I collected my things on the other side of security.

When I arrived in Edmonton, the research team leader was there to greet me at the airport. He did his best to make me feel like less of a tourist among a company of adventurers, but I couldn't help noticing his hesitation when I identified the bulging gym bag on the luggage carousel as mine. On the drive to the airport inn, I quizzed him about his research into Franklin's ill-fated voyage. He got so caught up in telling me what he'd discovered on his 1984 expedition that he nearly side-swiped a pickup truck as he pulled into the parking lot in front of the inn.

Because he'd been able to autopsy only one of Franklin's men, he was eager to get back to Beechey Island to discover whether the same remarkably high levels of lead were present in the tissues of the other two members of the expedition buried there. He tried to help me imagine the bone-aching cold endured by Franklin's sailors as they dug the graves, their pickaxes sparking against the frozen ground in the endless night of January. Little did they realize that within another nine months, their two ships would become locked forever in the ice, where disease, starvation, and rats would relentlessly wear them down. By their third miserable year in the North, twenty-four men, including Franklin, were dead. One ship had already been crushed by the ice, and the second was sinking. They concluded that their only chance was to walk out of the Arctic. Dragging a heavy lifeboat across the desolation of King William Island, they hoped to find the mouth of the Great Fish River and forge upstream to the nearest Hudson's Bay Company post, a thousand miles away. But by that point, their brains were so addled that they included silver cutlery, plates, curtain rods, and a writing desk in their already back-breaking load. The only food they packed was tea and chocolate.

"You can't imagine what it was like the first time we were up there," he said. The two of us had been sitting in his parked car for almost fifteen minutes by then. "The complete sense of isolation. And we had a radio. We knew a plane would be coming to pick us up in a few days. Franklin and his men were there completely on their own, apart from their families. They had no way of calling for help. No way home."

The next morning, I met four more members of the research team at the airport. It took us an hour and a half to check in because we had so much gear. The airline actually had to hold the plane for us. It was a commercial jet, much to my surprise. I'd expected to board something smaller and more rugged. I buckled in next to the burliest member of our party, a Ph.D. who wryly introduced himself as one of the gravediggers.

We flew to Resolute via Yellowknife. The vast wilderness that passed below us seemed abstract to me as I sipped my tomato juice. From our altitude, the landscape was reduced to something almost benign, like a richly illustrated map. As we crossed the Arctic Circle, I contemplated the geometry of awe, trying to imagine myself alone on an ice floe, over a hundred miles from the nearest person on the planet.

The short flight from the base at Resolute the next morning more closely resembled my preconceptions of northern air travel. Seven of us loaded ourselves into a Twin Otter, along with our mountain of supplies. Although it was June and the sun no longer set at night, the snow had yet to leave the landscape. On the frozen gravel beach of Beechey Island, the glare of the sun off the white ground was so intense that it made my eyes ache. As we unloaded our gear, my friend the gravedigger pointed out three lonely headboards peeking out of the snow just a few feet away.

We all watched the plane take off and disappear into the sky. My ears were confused by the startling quiet after the droning of the engines faded away. I looked across the frozen bay at the enormous cliffs of Devon Island. I no longer had to imagine my insignificance.

We quickly turned our attention to setting up camp. We started with the two large tents—the kitchen tent and the autopsy tent—before pitching the smaller sleeping tents, pounding their stakes through the snow and into the permafrost. We even pitched tent shells over the two graves that we'd come to excavate, to protect their contents from the elements as work proceeded.

Chipping through the frozen gravel with pickaxe and shovel looked just as gruelling as I'd been led to imagine. Fortunately, my role was photographer and recorder. I took pictures at various stages of the excavation, but even with four diggers spelling one another off as their hands and arms gave out from pain and exhaustion, the coffin still wasn't exposed after almost twenty-four hours of hard labour. While the work dragged on, I wandered to the edge of the camp, pulled out my sextant, and took a reading. The cold metal stung my bare fingers. Our fearless leader spotted me as he left the kitchen tent and made his way over.

"I wouldn't wander too far away if I were you," he said. "We had a few run-ins with polar bears the last time we were here." He asked to see the sextant, and I handed it to him. "Interesting piece," he said, angling it towards the sun. Among his many skills, he'd been trained as a pilot, so he knew a thing or two about establishing his coordinates. "You have any family?" he asked me.

I told him I'd been married less than a year. He looked around at the barren landscape and said that field trips like this put things in perspective for him. It reminded him how much we took for granted, and how we deluded ourselves into believing we were self-sufficient. When you took away all the trappings of modern life, it became starkly obvious that we were completely unequipped to survive alone.

One of the diggers called out from the excavation tent. They'd reached the coffin. We headed back. Over the next hour, the team melted buckets of snow on naphtha stoves and poured the warm water into the grave to release the coffin lid from the ice. I perched on a ladder inside the tent, snapping pictures as the lid was lifted. I braced myself, expecting to see my ancestor's body, but the coffin was filled with a block of ice. More warm water was brought to the grave. And then a small hole in the ice opened up, and I saw him. An open eye, watery and opaque, gazed up. He clenched his teeth at me, his lips curled back.

Someone's hand shot up to steady me on the ladder. I crawled down from my perch, trying to find reassurance in the feel of firm ground beneath my feet. I watched the work proceed, the layers of ice gradually melting away to reveal the remainder of the contorted face, then the rest of the emaciated body. Here was my great-great-great uncle, a man whom I'd always thought of as generations removed from me, and yet all this time he'd remained twenty-five years old. His pain was still palpable. The ice had preserved it, refusing to release him, prolonging his agony.

Chapter 31

I watch Severn accept a mug of hot apple cider from Katie with both hands. Katie's red hair obscures her face as she leans forward, and for a moment, I can make myself believe that I'm sitting in my own living room, and Severn, Helen, and I have just returned from skating in the park. Except that Helen is as young as the year I married her.

"So," Katie says, "Severn tells me you're a history teacher."

I suddenly realize that she's talking to me. She sits in the rocking chair, curling one foot up underneath her. She's sensed the tension in the room and is trying to put me at ease. I feel myself staring at her and wonder if she realizes why. Meanwhile, Livingston studies me from across the room.

"What else did she tell you?" I ask, casting a sideways glance at Severn.

Katie is unfazed. "I know why she came here to see Jack, if that's what you mean."

Livingston tucks his hands behind his head. "Severn and Katie hit it off right from the start," he says.

Severn fidgets as we talk about her, but she seems content to let Livingston and his girlfriend run her defence.

"Would anyone like a scone?" Katie asks. "I just baked some this afternoon."

I get up. "Severn," I say, motioning for her to follow me. It's time for a private father–daughter chat.

Severn stays put. Marla stares at the potpourri on the coffee table, trying to ignore my humiliation. Livingston has no such compunction. He cocks his head, waiting to see what foolish thing I'm going to do next.

Katie stands up to alleviate my embarrassment. "Scones it is, then. Severn, why don't you come and help me put the jam and Devon cream in serving dishes?"

Severn avoids my gaze as she follows Katie to the kitchen.

I wait until they're both out of earshot. "Just what the hell are you trying to pull?" I ask Livingston.

"Pull?" he says, playing cute.

"This charade of domestic bliss," I say. "The red-headed girl-friend."

"You make it sound as if I concocted an elaborate scheme to lure Severn away. Remember, she came looking for me."

"Only after she read your book," I say.

He smiles indulgently. "If I'd really wanted to tell Severn about her mother's past, I could simply have written her a letter or called her on the telephone. A work of fiction is an exceptionally inefficient and ambiguous way of doing it."

Marla takes up my cause. "If that's so, why is Severn here?"

Livingston leans forward and pats her patronizingly on the thigh. "That's a very interesting question. Why would she think I was her father? In fact, how would she have figured out that I even knew Helen in the first place? I certainly never communicated with her in any way." His voice turns to a stage whisper. "Perhaps Irving told her about me."

I turn away in disgust.

"Ah," says Livingston. "I guess not. Which really leaves only one other possibility, when you think about it."

Marla looks at me. "Helen."

"Exactly," Livingston says. "Perhaps not a full account of our relationship. Maybe only a hint dropped now and then. Enough though to kindle a vague but nagging suspicion in Severn's mind. The book just set it off."

I snarl at him, sick of the tripe he's trying to feed us. "Helen's been dead barely a year, and already you're making royalties off her."

Livingston's smugness momentarily gives way to a hint of impatience. "I'm not the scavenger you make me out to be, you know."

I cast my gaze to the ceiling. "A girl loses her mother, then discovers that the man who's raised her isn't her real father. Geez, I wonder where you got the idea for that storyline."

"I'm hurt that you think I have so little imagination."

"Oh, come off it," I say. "We both know who the characters in your book really are."

"Fine," he says. "I admit there are certain resemblances."

"Resemblances! You hardly even tried to disguise them."

"I take it you're unimpressed by the thought that you inspired a notable piece of literature."

I don't know whether to laugh or spit. "The fact that you made me out to be an insecure asshole is something I can shrug off. After all, I could hardly expect you to cast me as the hero. And even though you exploited Severn, you at least portrayed her with a shred of compassion. But for you to represent Helen as a woman so callous that she'd abandon her own daughter, especially after what you did to her all those years ago . . . Well, I think that takes a special kind of gall."

Livingston looks up at me blandly, his hands clasped across his belly. "You're assuming that Helen didn't like the story."

I glance at Marla to see if I've heard him correctly, but she has the same perplexed look on her face that I know I must have on mine.

"She read my first draft," he says. "Her comments were quite encouraging. I think she was happy that some of the ideas she'd worked on with me so many years ago were finally going to make it to print."

I stand there like an idiot. I took Helen back on the condition that she never contact Livingston again. It wasn't something we'd agreed to, not in so many words, but it was understood—or at least I had always thought so. I wonder how many years they talked behind my back. If it was just talking. How many of those times, when she was away on shop business, she was really with him. I suddenly feel on the verge of throwing up.

Livingston mistakes my nausea for confusion. "The manuscript was already at the publisher's when she found out about her cancer," he explains. For the first time, I catch a hint of regret in his voice. "The story about the girl losing her mother was a complete invention. I had no idea it would come true." He attempts an ironic smile, but it fizzles. He's grown suddenly uncomfortable in his chair and gets to his feet. "My coffee needs a shot of rum. Anyone else interested?"

I feel a tear dribble down my cheek. I turn away to hide it from view.

Katie and Severn return from the kitchen with the scones. Katie lays the serving plate on the coffee table and peers up at me as she's bent forward. I see the freckles that curl around the base of her throat and plunge below the fringe of her camisole, just like Helen's. I picture Livingston and his sagging masculinity pressed up against her beautiful white flesh, mingling his sour sweat with hers. I suppress an impulse to take her by the hand and run as far away as possible. Severn reads the longing on my face as she sets down the jam and Devon cream beside the scones. For a brief instant, a flash of understanding passes between us, a shared yearning for Katie to be the woman we know she's not, but then it's gone.

Livingston is suddenly at my elbow, the bottle of rum in his hand. "Your coffee's getting cold," he tells me. He's seen me eyeing Katie and has decided to intervene.

"How many has it been?" I ask him.

His supercilious grin is back. "Just my third of the day," he says, clinking the bottle against his mug. "I try to avoid drinking before ten in the morning when I can help it."

"Women, I mean. Since Helen."

His eyes narrow to slits. He wags his fingers at me as if I'm being a mischievous little boy. Katie stares at me, stung by my callous comment.

"Your last girlfriend told me you never managed to forget Helen," I say, my focus still on Katie. "And now I can see that it's true."

Katie turns to offer Marla a scone, determined to ignore my remarks. I can tell that she doesn't entirely understand why I'm connecting her with Helen, though, and it bothers her.

Livingston hands me my neglected coffee. "The mythology you've built up around me is honestly quite intriguing," he says. "I suppose I should feel honoured."

I put my hand over his bottle and steer him to face Severn. "See that girl?" I say. "Did you even recognize her when she first came up to you? Do you have the least clue who she is? Do you know the name of her teddy bear from when she was six years old? Did you ever read her bedtime stories or sing her to sleep after she'd had a nightmare? Were you there to watch her leave home on her first date and wonder when she'd grown up without you noticing?"

Livingston waits for me to finish my little soliloquy with the imitation of an earnest look on his face. Severn crosses her arms, her head down, cringing at my desperate show of sentimentality.

I step in front of Livingston and stare him down. "What gives you the right to suddenly replace me as her father?" I say.

He shakes his head at me in condescending wonder. "Such strange ideas you have about me."

"I'm not about to be pushed aside like one of your throwaway girlfriends," I tell him.

My indignation amuses him no end. He speaks slowly so that

this simpleton in front of him will understand. "Whatever gave you the idea I was Severn's biological father?"

For a moment, I think he's trying to confuse me. But when I search his face for the guile I know should be there, I can't find it. He acknowledges my recognition of his astonishing sincerity with a smile. I turn to look at Severn. The shock in her eyes is already giving way to a look of utter desertion.

Chapter 32

Helen wasn't at the airport in London to greet me when I got back from the Arctic. I'd been away almost three weeks, counting my stopovers in Resolute and Edmonton, and I'd been looking forward to a homecoming. It had been impossible to reach Helen when I was up at the dig site, and I hadn't had any luck reaching her when I got back to Edmonton either. Still, I thought she'd be waiting for me. I called the apartment, but there was no answer. Maybe she'd got my arrival time mixed up, I told myself as I watched other passengers enjoying hearty welcomes from friends and family.

I caught a cab outside the arrivals area. It was a sticky summer evening. I laid the winter jacket I'd worn on Beechey Island beside me on the back seat and kept my camera slung over my shoulder, its lens cap and case securely fastened lest the souls of the frozen mariners I'd captured should try to escape when they sniffed the hot summer wind.

When I got home, she wasn't there. The air inside the apartment was stale and heavy. I opened all the windows and switched on our two electric fans. They offered only feeble relief from the mugginess. I hoisted my bags onto our bed but felt too tired to start unpacking them. The sheets were thrown aside, just as

Helen had left them. I could make out the imprint she'd left behind. I ran my hand over the wrinkles, trying to conjure up the sleek feel of her bare thigh.

On the airplane, I'd imagined Helen meeting me by the baggage carousel with a lascivious glint in her eye. I'd pictured us tearing each other's clothes off when we were barely inside the apartment, humping like rabbits before we made it to the bedroom. After sleeping on a windswept Arctic gravesite, I desperately needed the affirmation of her warm flesh.

There was no point calling the bookshop; it was well past closing. I went to the kitchen to grab myself a beer so I could wait by the fan in the living room for her return. In the fridge, I found a carton of milk one week past its best-before date. As I dumped the lumpy contents down the sink, I noticed a mouldy crust of toast sitting on a plate on the dining-room table next to a half-drunk mug of coffee. It was then I twigged that Helen wouldn't be coming home that night.

I went down to the front lobby. I hadn't bothered to check our mail slot because I'd been weighed down with luggage when the cab had dropped me off. Now I could see that the slot was jammed full. The mailman had left a note saying that all the mail he hadn't been able to deliver could be picked up at the local postal station.

I tried to rise above my humiliation, inventing innocent explanations for her absence. I told myself that I should be worried for her safety, that I should be ashamed for immediately assuming she'd walked out on me. I looked for clues in the apartment that would tell me where she'd gone. What I found didn't improve my state of mind. Most of the hangers on her side of the bedroom closet were bare. Her makeup and contact-lens solution were missing from the medicine cabinet.

I left my bags unpacked on the bed and spent the night on the living-room couch. Every car I heard in the parking lot and every person who walked down the corridor was Helen. My clenched gut wouldn't let me sleep, even after all the exhausting hours I'd spent in different planes and airport departure lounges. I'd believed the barren landscape of Beechey Island to be the loneliest place on earth. Now I knew it was my own living room.

I didn't leave the apartment at all the next day. I wanted to be there when Helen called from wherever she was. She owed me that much at least. But the phone never rang. Daytime became night again. I could only bring myself to eat crackers, cheese, and a tin of sardines. I left Helen's abandoned crust and coffee mug undisturbed on the dining-room table, preserving them like archaeological relics or, perhaps more aptly, forensic evidence.

The next morning I called Will, but he wasn't home. I looked at my watch and realized that he'd be at work already. I wasn't about to phone the bookshop. I knew that if Helen answered, I'd go tongue-tied. Even if I didn't talk, she'd recognize my pathetic silence and probably hang up on me in exasperation. I didn't want to give her the chance to dismiss me so easily. I was the one who'd been wronged. She should be the supplicant when we finally spoke. But I knew it would never work out that way. I spent the rest of the day watching cartoons and cooking shows on TV.

By the evening, I forced myself to shave and shower for the first time since I'd got home. I finally unpacked my bags and threw all my dirty clothes in the laundry hamper. Then I tried calling Will at home again. This time he answered.

"Hey, Will. It's Irving." I tried to sound casual, as if I'd called simply to tell him about my trip.

There was dead air on the line for several seconds before he spoke. "Irving," he said, the uneasy concern in his voice telling me that he already knew about Helen.

I kept up the charade. "Boy, it's a lot warmer here than where I was, I tell ya."

"Have you heard from Helen?" he asked, cutting through my false cheeriness.

"No," I admitted. I felt my chest sink.

Will fell silent again.

"Where is she, Will?" The despair in my voice disgusted me.

"I'm not sure," he said.

I could tell he was holding back. "You have a good idea, though."

"Look, Irving, I tried to stop her."

"She's in Toronto, isn't she?"

He hesitated. "I think so."

"Jesus," I said, my throat closing up on me.

"I'm sorry, Irving."

His regret was so heartfelt that I started to blubber. I thanked him and hung up. For a moment, I sat snivelling by the phone. In the living-room bookcase, Helen had devoted half a shelf to titles by Jack Livingston. I went to the kitchen and found a couple of plastic grocery bags. I returned to the living room, stuffed the offending books in the bags, and walked them to the garbage chute at the end of the building.

By the next morning, the apartment walls had begun to close in on me. I needed to get out. I dragged myself down to the parking lot, thinking that a drive would help clear my mind. I didn't clue in until too late that Helen, of course, had taken the car. I stood there like an imbecile, trying to figure out my next move. In the end I started walking, first a block, then another, until I found myself an hour later, dripping with sweat, on Richmond Street in front of the bookshop. Why my feet had carried me there, I wasn't sure. I supposed it was because the bookshop was the pivot point for my folly. As I stared up at its brick walls, it reminded me of the stone cairns that the hapless British explorers had built in the Arctic for those who one day would attempt to piece together the anatomy of their misfortune.

I sat down on the shop's front step like some kind of fallen gargoyle, watching with disdain the people walking by. Most of them gave me a wide berth, probably mistaking me for a panhandler or an alumnus of the psychiatric hospital. Prospective customers shied away when they saw me and went to spend their money somewhere else. I kept my surly vigil for what seemed like the better part of twenty minutes before the shop door opened behind me. I glanced at the two feet that appeared beside me. I'd expected to see Will's hairy toes in a pair of sandals, but instead I saw a pair of brown Oxfords. I peered up at their owner. It was Walter. In one hand he held a broom. He seemed ready to use it on me.

"She's not here," he said, sounding like his old severe self.

"I know," I said.

"So how long do you intend to sit here and scare off business?"

I looked away, making no effort to move.

"Hey," he said, poking me with the broom.

I grabbed the bottom of the broom handle and glared up at him. Walter's eyebrow cocked. He recognized my anguished look, I could tell. Slowly, he pulled the broom from my grasp and leaned it up against the door jamb. With joints creaking, he sat down on the step beside me.

"She'll be back," he said, as much warning as reassurance.

"Well, maybe I'm not the complete dupe she takes me for."

Walter shifted his weary bones on the hard step. The dark bags under his eyes had deepened in recent months. His cheekbones were sharper, his forearms thinner. He'd even begun to smell like an old man, sour and slightly fermented. I realized that we'd both been cast aside by the same woman. And there we sat, rotting on the same stoop together.

He wiped his nose with his hanky. A dried flake of snot hung in his nose hairs. "When Helen was a little girl, we went swimming once on this rocky beach," he said to me. "It was by a campground, so I told her to wear running shoes when she went in the water, just in case there was broken glass. Well, she thought I was just trying to spoil her fun. Of course, we weren't there an hour before she cut her foot on a broken bottle not far from shore. It was a nasty gash, and she was bawling her eyes out. I tried to stop the bleeding with a towel, but it just kept gushing. The nearest hospital was nearly fifty miles away, and she scowled at me the whole way, tears streaming down her cheeks, as if she was angry at me for being right. By the time she got her stitches, she'd worked it out that it was all my fault—first because I'd chosen the beach, and then because I hadn't warned her convincingly enough."

I stifled a bitter laugh. That certainly sounded like her.

Walter gazed blankly at the rooftops across the street. "Ever since that day, I've watched Helen do one reckless thing after another. If I try to discourage her, she just ignores me. I should be used it by now, but I'm not." His faded eyes slowly turned towards me. "I kept hoping that one day she'd meet someone who'd stop her from hurting herself."

I felt the weight of his regret being loaded on my shoulders. I looked at the pavement, trying to ignore his plea. My own failure with Helen was already too much for me to bear.

He picked a business card out of his shirt pocket and handed it to me. I hesitated, but he nodded for me to take it. On the back of the card, in Walter's shaky handwriting, was an address in Toronto.

I drove to Toronto the next day. The fan in my tiny, rented, non-air-conditioned Chevette was blowing full blast as I crawled through Chinatown, but the hot, thick air still closed in around me. The street smelled of barbecued duck and over-ripe melons, of jasmine incense and discarded fish guts. I rechecked the address that Walter had scrawled for me, but I couldn't turn left on to the cross street when I spotted it. The slow but relentless stream of weekend traffic carried me forward. As I looked in vain for an opportunity to double back, I nearly ran into a station wagon that had stopped to avoid running over a jaywalker. It wasn't until the jaywalker was nearly to the other side of the street that I realized it was Helen.

I watched her like a spectator in my own nightmare, unable to make myself yell out the window at her. Through the traffic, I saw Livingston standing on the opposite curb with two tall paper cups in his hands. She bounded up to him with the effervescence of a teenage girl out for a date on a carnival midway. An island continent of sweat stained the back of her sleeveless top. Slowly, she took one of the drinks from him and pressed it to her forehead, then her cheeks. The thought of his cup touching her skin, the trails of icy condensation dripping down her cleavage, was intensely obscene to me. I watched with dead eyes until Livingston finally took her by the hand and led her through the throng.

The car behind me blared its horn.

Like an automaton, I drove on. A part of me wanted to keep going, to get as far away as I could, to keep driving north until there were no more roads. But a block on, I turned into an underground parking lot. A few minutes later, I found myself picking my way through a surging crowd of Asian shoppers, searching for Helen's red head in a sea of black. I thought I saw her once and immediately ducked inside a Chinese grocer's, but it turned out to be a lanky girl in a long skirt and combat boots ambling beside a goofy-looking punker with a bad Mohawk. I stepped back out into the bustle of the sidewalk. As I did, I heard a rumble from the dark clouds overhead.

Each time someone stepped out of a doorway in front of me, I braced myself, but it was always a stranger. I hung back in the crowd, peering into bakeries, tea shops, newsagents, record stores, and restaurants, seeing no one familiar. Solitary, heavy drops of rain thunked on my head and on the roofs of cars parked along the curb. People held their hands out and tipped their heads towards the sky. And then, as surely as if someone had pulled a shower chain, the clouds burst. The thunking on the car roofs became rapid-fire. Everyone scurried for cover. I ducked under the awning of a smoke shop along with a horde of shoppers. Our wet clothes clung to us. The pavement hissed with driving rain.

A streetcar pulled up to its stop just a few yards away and discharged a handful of passengers. They dashed through the deluge, some holding newspapers above their heads in a vain effort to stay dry. Before the driver could close his door, a new set of riders darted out from the shelter of the storefronts. Those who arrived behind the others were forced to form a miserable queue in the downpour. After the last drowned rat stepped on board and the streetcar began to pull away, I heard a latecomer splashing through the puddles to my right. Somehow, even before turning to look, I knew it was Helen. There was something about the cadence of her stride that I recognized instinctually. As I watched her run out in front of me, I felt the panic of an exhausted swimmer too far from shore. The outline of her bra was clearly visible through her soaked top. She called for the driver to wait, but he didn't hear her above the moan of the electric engine. The streetcar gathered momentum, leaving her in the rain, her hands on her hips. Before I could gather the courage to call out, Livingston materialized next to her. He extended a scavenged sheet of corrugated cardboard over both their heads and tried to coax her back out of the rain, but she seemed more concerned with giving the streetcar driver the evil eye.

I stepped from under the smoke-shop awning and walked towards them. The rain beat down, flattening my hair and dripping off the end of my nose. Before I could reach them, Livingston put his arm around Helen's shoulder and steered her away. Neither of them seemed to notice me. My courage suddenly hit bottom, wrecked against the irrefutability of my own irrelevance. I sputtered to a stop and watched as they scampered up to a tiny discount clothing store. Livingston went inside, leaving Helen in the shelter of the doorway to wring water from her top. After a moment, he returned with a towel and handed it to her. Then an agitated shopkeeper emerged. Livingston reached for his wallet and stepped back inside to pay for the towel, leaving Helen alone again. Through the whole scene, I stayed rooted to my soggy vantage point. I could feel my shoes filling with water.

The rain had seeped into every crevice of my body by the time she finally noticed me. She was drying her hair with the towel, her back towards me. Given my angle to the store window, I doubted she could see my reflection. More likely, she simply sensed me watching her. She stopped what she was doing and slowly turned to look at me. Her gaze was unwavering but resigned, like that of a prisoner awaiting judgment. She made no attempt to explain, offered no excuses. I held her frozen in my eyes as the traffic whisked by indifferently in the street behind me. Then Livingston stepped outside again, breaking my trance. He squinted at me as if the rain had streaked me out of focus. Helen slowly handed him back his towel, her eyes never leaving me. I thought for a moment that she might step out from under the overhang and join me, but she never moved.

I realized then what I'd most feared: Helen didn't want to be rescued. Perhaps she never had.

I turned and headed back to the car before the rain could wash me away.

Chapter 33

Katie helps me gather up Severn's things. Strands of her red hair come free from behind her ear and dangle against her cheek as she bends forward. She smiles at me apologetically.

"You'll have to forgive Jack," she whispers. "He can be a little abrupt at times." Her eyes drift towards Severn, who is already on her way out the front door. Marla scrambles to get into her coat and follow.

"Why don't I pack some of those scones for Severn?" she says. "Something for the ride back home."

I decline her kind offer. As I sling Severn's bulging overnight bag over my shoulder, an old photofinisher's envelope slips from the outer pocket and slaps onto the hardwood floor in the front hallway. Katie crouches down, retrieving the pictures that have spilled out.

"What are these?" she asks as she picks them up. "Family photos?" She examines one. I see her turn pale.

I realize that they're the photos Severn stole from home, the ones of her with Helen. Katie picks up one picture after another, staring at each of them. The resemblance is unmistakable, even to her. She looks at me, at once shocked and embarrassed. Then her gaze inches towards Livingston, who has lost interest in the proceedings and is busy topping up his coffee with another splash of rum.

"I have to go," I tell her.

She passes me the remaining pictures, unable to look me directly in the eye. Livingston wanders out to see what's keeping me. He slips his arm around Katie's waist, oblivious to her growing unease as she forces herself to lean gently into his embrace.

"I don't envy you, Irving," he says disingenuously. "Raising a teenage girl on your own can't be easy."

I'm certain that once I leave, he'll jot down his impressions of the drama we've all played out for his benefit this afternoon. I wonder if he's keeping separate notes on Katie. He's sure to be fascinated by her reaction now that she's uncovered her role as surrogate in his obsession with another man's wife. As I open the front door, I can't help feeling that I'm abandoning her.

Severn is brooding by the car when I catch up with her, bracing herself for the lecture that she's certain I'll deliver. She's not prepared for the desperate hug I give her instead.

"Thank God I found you," I tell her, holding her tight.

I feel her sullenness slip, and for a moment I'm holding my little girl again. But then she stiffens, as if convinced that I'm trying to reclaim her like an umbrella from the lost and found. She straightens to her full height, dwarfing me by several inches.

"Come on," I say, undaunted. "Let's get you home."

I hustle her into the front passenger seat and throw her overnight bag in the trunk. Marla quietly gets in the back.

"You hungry?" I ask Severn as I slip behind the wheel. "We can stop somewhere on the way out of town."

I'm being too eager to show her how glad I am to have her back, I realize. Already I can see her eyes hardening against my affection. I sense Marla looking on from the back seat, waiting for me to talk to Severn where she hurts.

I draw a thin breath. "Nothing that Jack Livingston says matters, Severn."

She looks at me as if she's about to protest, but then falls into a moody silence.

"He manipulated your mom," I say. "You should be glad he didn't get his claws into you."

Her lips form a sour line. "You're just jealous of him."

"He's been stringing you along," I tell her.

"And *you* haven't?"

I feel my throat tighten. "I've always been your dad," I tell her. "I always will be."

She looks back at Livingston's house. I can tell by the pinched look on her face that she doesn't believe him. Maybe she thinks that his denial of her is a noble gesture designed to keep her from agonizing over her legitimacy. For my part, I'm not sure what to make of it. It's too much to hope that I could be Severn's true father after all these years of quiet self-immolation. Even so, I feel like a general whose sworn enemy has mysteriously withdrawn from the field to leave him uncontested. My victory seems fragile. I feel exposed, vulnerable to ambush.

Severn stares at me dully. "Jack told me you left Mom to go the Arctic."

"I didn't leave her," I say stiffly.

"No? He told me you were digging up frozen dead people the year before I was born."

I glance back at Marla in the rear-view mirror. She's looking out the window, pretending not to listen. "Can we not have this conversation right now?" I say.

Severn folds her arms and freezes me out again. I know I should have this out with her now, to keep it from festering any longer, but I'm afraid of what other mines Livingston has laid for me. I'm still reeling from his revelation that Helen communicated with him behind my back, reviewed his goddamned manuscript—gave it her blessing, even. I wonder what else she didn't tell me. The ground is still shifting beneath my feet. I'm not ready to go head to head with Severn right now. I need time to find a position I know I can defend.

Marla leans forward. "You can just drop me at a subway station," she says.

"Don't worry," I say, determined not to show how agitated I am. "I'll drive you back to Jay's."

As I'm pulling out into traffic, I catch a glimpse in the rear-view mirror of Marla digging in her knapsack. She passes something over the seat to Severn. When I realize what she's doing, I turn and flash a reproachful look at her, but it's already too late. For an instant, Severn seems reluctant to take the tattered notebook, suspicious of what strange debris Marla is trying to pass off to her. Then she recognizes her mom's handwriting and bites her lip. Her fingers trace the runs in the ink uncertainly.

"Where did you find this?" Severn asks in a brittle voice.

"Jack's old girlfriend had it," Marla says. "The painter you visited in the West End."

A tear from Severn's eye plops onto the open notebook. "What happened to it?" she asks, fingering the edges of the now crusty pages.

"Your dad was mugged last night," Marla says. "He did his best to save it."

Severn looks at me, confused by this piece of news, perhaps sensing for the first time that she's not the only victim of the past forty-eight hours. She seems simultaneously ashamed and annoyed, two emotions that I saw dance together across her mother's face on more occasions than I care to remember.

Marla says, "I have more notebooks back here, if you'd like to see them."

"Hadn't you better call Jay and let him know you're coming?" I ask her irritably.

Marla takes my not-so-subtle hint and backs off. She calls Jay's place on her cell and talks to Avery. She informs him that we've found Severn—good thing for him—and that she'll be by to collect him and the car shortly. My gaze drifts towards Severn to see whether her expression offers any hint of what went on between her and Avery the night she first arrived in Toronto. She immediately looks away. It doesn't matter, though. I can tell that she has something to hide.

As I drive to the Beaches, I find myself going back over the timetable of Helen's pregnancy in my mind, wondering whether I could have miscalculated—although for the life of me, I can't see how. Maybe it was me after all. Maybe all the time that I thought I was a fraud, I was the genuine article, Severn's father in every sense of the word. Even so, the idea isn't setting the world right like it should. I'm still a sap and a cuckold. What small comfort I can find in the thought that Helen and I actually made a child together is spoiled by the fact that she tried to convince me we didn't. In the end, I'm left to brood over her perverse reasons for keeping me in the dark. Was it simply to stop me from exercising too strong a claim over her?

Of course, there is another explanation—one that I've kept buried deep in the back of my mind all these years, hoping it would never escape. Livingston is telling the truth. My calculations aren't wrong. Someone else is Severn's father. Right now, my brain hurts too much to even consider the possibility, so I quickly stuff it back in the darkest recesses of my mind.

When we arrive at Jay's condo, I pull into the parking lot at the back and get out with Marla. Severn stays in the car, eyeing us impatiently from the front passenger seat.

"You didn't have to show her the notebook," I mutter, trying to maintain a veneer of tranquility for Severn's benefit.

"She needs to talk about Helen," Marla says, hoisting her knapsack on her shoulder. "You both do."

"I know," I say wearily. "I just need a little time, okay?"

She smiles back at me as if I sound like less of a lost cause than I did at the beginning of our trip. I get the sense that I've partially redeemed myself in her eyes and wonder why the thought comforts me so.

"Anyway," she says, "thanks for the ride." Before turning to go, she hesitates, then plants a kiss on my cheek. "Safe trip home."

Her kiss has a paralyzing effect on me. I feel the moisture from her lips tingling on my cheek like an exotic insect. The hard lines of my face melt just a little. I realize that it's the first truly warm touch I've felt from anyone since Helen died.

I watch Marla disappear through the condo's main entrance. As I turn back towards the car, I see Severn glaring at me through the windshield, making me feel as though I've just cheated on Helen.

Chapter 34

Helen never called from Toronto. And as far as I could tell, she never sneaked back into our apartment to pick up any of her things either. Meanwhile, I rattled around the place, eating microwave dinners from her plates with her forks in front of her TV. She'd made me throw out most of my stuff when we'd moved in together. Too grungy, she'd said. I felt like I was living a borrowed life. I knew that one day she'd come to collect it all, and I'd be left with nothing. I began browsing the newspaper for small furnished apartments that I could afford on my single salary, but I couldn't bring myself to visit any of them. Before long, ads for back-to-school sales appeared in the paper, and I realized that it had been six weeks since I'd seen her.

I should pack her things, I told myself. Save her the trouble for when she finally comes to retrieve them. I brought a bunch of old boxes home from the liquor store and started with the clothes in her dresser. It was no good. Handling her nylons and panties only made me feel like a fetishist. I gave up before I'd filled a single box.

I welcomed the beginning of the school year when it came—not that I was particularly well prepared for it after all the mooning around I'd done. I was teaching grade nine geography for the first time. The first week was a disaster, and I had to pull a series of all-nighters to improve my lesson plans. The advantage of my frenzy was that it gave me less time to think about Helen. Subsequently, I volunteered to help direct the school play and then offered to plan and escort a special field trip to Washington, D.C., for grade twelve students. I spent as little time in the apartment as possible.

My third week back at school, I arrived home one evening to find the apartment lights on. The place smelled of chlorine bleach. There were fresh vacuum tracks on the carpet. All the dirty dishes I'd been accumulating were cleaned and stacked in the drying rack by the kitchen sink. I stood there, afraid to move. I heard the sounds of the toilet flushing and the bathroom door opening. Helen stepped out, wearing one of her bulky sweatshirts. She paused a beat when she saw me, but then pretended she'd never left. She said she was thinking of making veal scaloppine for supper and asked me whether I'd like green beans or a salad with it. I stared at her, my briefcase still in hand. She made her way into the kitchen and asked how my day at school had been, then pushed up her sleeves and began pulling the makings for supper out of the now fully stocked fridge. She asked me to get a can of tomato paste from the cupboard and open it. I crossed through the kitchen and laid my briefcase on the dining-room table. I sat down unsteadily.

"Well?" she said, glancing over at me as she filled a pot with water for the pasta. "Are you just going to sit there?"

I said nothing. She shrugged and continued preparing supper.

I listened to her fill the void between us with chit-chat. She told me that the car had developed a rattle, and that she thought she was going to have to take it in for servicing. She lamented the state of her hair, especially the length of her bangs, and vowed to make an appointment to get it cut. After about ten minutes of this, I got up and went to the bedroom.

I'd waited for so long to have Helen back. I'd convinced myself that anything would be worth the chance at a fresh start, even a little swallowed pride. But whenever I'd imagined her return, she'd managed to show a crumb of contrition, a tiny bit of remorse. The sordid events of the preceding months were never dwelled on, but they weren't completely ignored either. Now that she was actually here, it was as if I somehow hadn't existed for her while we were apart. I'd been frozen out of time until she reappeared, when I could finally be reheated like a TV dinner.

When Helen came to tell me that supper was ready, I had my bags packed.

"What are you doing?" she said, the first real look of concern creeping across her face.

I found one of the empty liquor-store boxes at the back of our closet and took it with me to the spare bedroom. "This isn't the way it works," I said. "We don't just pick up where we left off by pretending nothing ever happened."

"Where are you going?" she demanded.

I packed all the things that I needed for school—my texts, my notes, my antique surveying instruments. "I don't know yet," I said.

She could have stopped me at any time, simply by offering me an apology. Even a half-hearted one would have done the job. But it never occurred to her. And I was damned if I was going to beg for one.

I went out to the living room and called myself a cab. Before I could give the dispatcher my apartment number, Helen clamped her hand on the phone cradle and cut me off.

"I just got home," she said, her voice trembling with anger. When I didn't cow, she quickly changed tack, softening her tone and trying to bargain with me. "At least stay for supper. I can't eat everything myself."

"We have Tupperware," I said.

It took me only three trips to get my stuff down to the cab. On my second trip, Helen was still trying to convince me to quit acting like a teenage drama queen and think things through. By the third trip, the door to our apartment was chained shut and my final load was waiting for me in the corridor.

I stayed the night in one of the old motels on Highway 22, lying in my clothes on top of the bed and listening to the lonely sound of late-night traffic on the empty road. Twice I picked up the phone to tell Helen I was sorry and beg her to take me back, but both times I managed to lay the receiver down before I could humiliate myself. The next morning, I showered, put on a fresh set of clothes, and showed up at school just as I always did.

I knew what would happen if I went crawling back to her. She'd offer me a truce, one that forbade any future mention of Livingston. She'd do me little favours to prove that I could trust her again, maybe even ravage me between the sheets for old time's sake. But after a while, her attention would wander, and she'd take another holiday from me, secure in the knowledge that I'd be waiting for her when her next affair flamed out. There'd be nothing of me left but a slowly decomposing man who lived simply to appease her.

When I got back to the room that evening, I circled the listings for a handful of prospective apartments in the classifieds and started calling landlords. I looked at three apartments, none of them very promising. University students had already snatched up most of the cheap furnished units in the north end of town. I spent the rest of the night propped up in my motel bed, marking a surprise quiz that, in my dark mood, I'd sprung on my grade ten history class earlier in the day.

Flowers arrived for me at school the next morning. They attracted a lot of attention at the reception desk. The secretary wiggled her eyebrows at me when I picked them up, asking me who my secret admirer was. Fortunately, the card that came with them was sealed in a tiny envelope. It simply said, "I miss you. Come home. Love, H." I couldn't tell whether it was meant as a plea or a command. At any rate, I wasn't about to let Helen tip everyone off that our marriage was falling apart and thus shame me back to her. I stuffed the card in my pocket and hid the flowers in one of the cupboards at the back of my homeroom until it was time to take them back to the motel.

That night, I looked at a couple more apartments. Desperate to get out of the motel, I signed a lease for the second one, even though it had tired green shag carpeting and a bathroom lit by a forty-watt bulb. I knew I'd be miserable there, but I felt that somehow I deserved it. For all my anger, I couldn't shake the feeling that I was somehow to blame for Helen's affair with Livingston, that I'd done something to drive her away but wasn't smart or grown-up enough to figure out what it was.

The middle of the next afternoon, just before my last class of the day, Helen showed up at school. She was standing in the middle of the corridor, buffeted by streams of students heading off to seventh period. She was wearing a baggy raincoat and looking washed-out, probably because she wasn't wearing any makeup. Her hair was hastily tied back, her bangs still uncut. When she spotted me, she tried to muster the indignant look of a wronged woman, but her unsteady chin wouldn't let her carry it off. She set her shoulders as I approached, waiting for me to say the first word. Seeing her there in front of me, I felt my resolve waver. If she hadn't been so defiant, I would have melted easily.

"I have a class," I told her.

"I want you home," she said.

A couple of girls on their way to my class looked at us curiously. They exchanged gossipy whispers once they'd passed.

I took Helen by the arm and led her off to the side. "Not here, all right?"

She twisted her arm free. "I'm not leaving until you promise to come back."

More students were looking our way.

"After my class," I said. "We can talk then."

"I'll be waiting here," she said.

My mind wasn't on teaching. As I delivered my shtick on the Riel Rebellion, I kept thinking about Helen standing out in the hall, attracting the attention of every staff member who happened by. If asked why she was waiting outside my classroom, she'd no doubt be vague but still come off sounding like the victim. She'd say just enough to leave them wondering how I could put seventh period history ahead of her when she so obviously needed to talk to me about something urgent.

I decided to assign my students their homework early and give them the final fifteen minutes of the period to get started. When everyone seemed settled, I drifted to the back of the room and glanced out into the corridor. There was no one outside. When I looked back at the class, all eyes quickly returned to the homework assignment.

I wondered why it surprised me that Helen couldn't wait three-quarters of an hour for me when I'd spent more than six weeks waiting for her. After the bell rang to end the period, I sat numbly at my desk and watched the students file out on their way to their next class. I waited until the chatter of young voices and the clank of shutting lockers subsided before I finally got up. The hallway had the eerie feel of a deserted freeway as I shut the classroom door behind me. I was done for the day. There was nothing left for me to do but check my mail and head home to my motel room. I was nearly to the front office when I heard the scuffle of footsteps on the linoleum behind me. I turned to see Helen trying to catch up with me.

"I was in the washroom," she said, annoyed that I'd given up on her.

It was a beautiful late summer day as we headed towards the school parking lot, but Helen kept her raincoat on. She marched ahead, apparently expecting me to follow like some chastened schoolboy whose mother had come to collect him from the principal's office.

"I'm parked over here," she said.

I stopped at the edge of the parking lot.

She looked back at me impatiently. "What?"

"I've rented an apartment." As angry as I was, I still couldn't help feeling ashamed to admit it.

She took me firmly by the hand and pulled me along. "Don't be silly."

"I signed a lease."

"Break it."

I dug in my heels.

"Jesus Christ, Irving. Why are you making this harder than it has to be?"

I'd had enough. She wasn't going to pass the fault for this off on me any more. I yanked my arm back so hard that she nearly toppled over. My violence startled me. I stepped away, afraid to touch her, not sure what I might do next.

She looked up at me, stung by my rejection. Her hand reached out again, hung uncertainly in mid-air, then dropped to her side. She closed her eyes tightly and drew a long, shaky breath. "Why can't you just come home?" she said, her voice cracking. "Please."

I stood there woodenly, the sound of her desperation making me feel like a monster. I teetered on the edge of apologizing for my eruption, but was determined not to let her sucker me into forgiving her out of pity.

"Why should I?" I asked, forcing myself to harden my heart. I looked around the parking lot to see who was watching. Lyle Spackling from the math department was leaving early. He squinted at us as he unlocked the driver's-side door of his car.

Helen wiped a tear from her cheek with the sleeve of her raincoat. "I promise not to leave you again," she said in a thin voice.

I stared at her impassively.

"You have to believe me," she said.

"Why?"

She took my hand again, but gently this time. She guided it between the folds of her raincoat and laid it on the swell of her belly.

I felt the blood drain from my face.

"I need you, Irving," she said. "I can't do this on my own."

I pulled my hand back stiffly. I felt my vocal cords constrict. "Livingston?"

She held me in her gaze, weighing her next words. "No one has to know."

My guts clutched as if I'd been run through with a shiv. "How can you even . . . ?" I was on the verge of tears. "Jesus, Helen."

She cupped my head in her hands and rested her forehead against mine. I felt her body shudder ever so slightly. She wanted me to rescue her after all, but it was too late. She'd gone past the point where I could ever find her again. I stepped back. The thought of Livingston's seed inside her repelled me.

"Please, Irving."

The panic in her voice made me shrink back even more. I'd been chasing an illusion all along. Helen would always live for Helen and no one else.

I didn't care whether Lyle Spackling was still looking or not. I turned and left my pregnant wife whimpering in the parking lot.

My new apartment was furnished with cast-offs that I suspected the landlord had picked off the curb on trash day. The couch reminded me of something from a sixties sitcom, with its stiff armrests and wooden peg legs. The shag carpet gave off the accumulated smell of every tenant who had come before me. I'd left all my books with Helen and had nothing to cover the depressingly bare white walls. I had no TV either, so I left my clock radio playing to keep myself company. All day long, I listened to pop singers croon about new love, true love, and blue love, their flashy voices echoing through the cavernous apartment.

As I stood at the kitchen counter, supping on a half-eaten pizza that I'd ordered the night before, there was a knock on the door. At first I thought it was one of my new neighbours, come to tell me to turn my radio down. But when I opened the door, I found Will standing in the hallway, his hands buried in his bomber jacket.

"Hey there," he said.

I asked him how he'd found me. He shrugged and looked past me into the Spartan interior. I stepped aside and let him in. He nodded as he looked about the place, as if the miserable circumstances were exactly how he'd imagined I'd be living.

"How much are you paying in rent?" he asked, implying that whatever it was, I was being fleeced.

I asked him if he'd come to offer me decorating advice. He buried his hands deeper in his pockets.

"You know that she's going to get an abortion, don't you?" he said, his eyes fixing on me for only an instant before drifting away again.

I didn't know how to react. "I hadn't heard," I said expressionlessly. As much as I despised the thought of another man's chromosomes propagating inside her, it was a brutal solution, even for Helen. Half of me knew that I'd driven her to it. The other half knew she was trying to force me into stopping her.

Will wandered into the kitchen and opened one of the cupboards, presumably to see whether the dishes were as tacky as the furniture. "So how long do you intend to stay here?"

"She sent you, didn't she?"

"Actually, no," he said. He opened the fridge and took a peek inside.

"But you're here because you think I should take her back."

"This carton of milk's past its due date," he said. "You should really dump it."

I thumped the fridge door shut, irritated with him for trying to restoke my guilt.

"You're angry," he said. "That's understandable."

"She couldn't wait for me to get out of town, Will. I was gone—what—maybe a couple of days, and she hopped into bed with another man. Now she wants me to raise this guy's kid for him. Please forgive me if I have a hard time accepting that I should be the one feeling guilty."

Will fell silent.

I dumped what was left of my cold pizza in the garbage. "I'm not some consolation prize that she can settle for when her boyfriend turns his back on her. I'm her goddamned husband."

He lowered his head. "You're right," he said. He zipped up his jacket and made for the door. "Sorry to disturb you."

He was almost out the door by the time I realized that he'd conceded our battle without a proper fight. He was letting me call Helen's bluff. The trouble was that I knew she still might go through with it. I felt the tide of my guilt rising.

"When is she . . . ?" I asked, my voice trailing off.

"Next Monday," he said.

My throat went dry.

I still had my key to our apartment, but I called Helen from the lobby. When she heard my voice over the intercom, she didn't answer. Several seconds passed before she buzzed me in.

She was wearing a rumpled flannel nightgown, even though it was five in the afternoon. Her hair was stringy. There was a pimple on her chin. I couldn't help looking at the gentle bulge of her belly, wondering how much it had grown since the last time I'd seen her.

We carefully avoided each other's gaze, and for a long time after I entered, neither of us said anything. Helen settled on the living-room couch and wrapped herself in an afghan. She glanced disinterestedly at the gardening show that was playing on TV. I sat down on the footstool beside her and watched the host demonstrate the proper method for making compost.

"Will paid me a visit," I said.

I noticed her neck stiffen. She kept looking at the TV.

"You don't have to do this, Helen."

She swung her dull eyes on me. "What choice do I have?"

"What about adoption?"

She turned back to the TV.

"Well, it's an option," I said.

"I'm not going through all of this if I have to turn the baby over to a stranger."

I was tired of trying to be sympathetic. I'd come to offer her an olive branch, and she'd snapped it back in my face. "Maybe you should have thought of that before you leapt into bed with Livingston," I said.

She replied numbly, "I never meant for things to go as far as they did."

"Well," I said dryly, "if you didn't mean it, I guess that's all right, then."

Helen clamped her eyes shut. I imagined the fetus shifting inside her, pleading its case. For the first time since she'd come home, I saw a look of genuine regret take over her face. When she opened her eyes again, they were brimming with tears. She looked straight at me. "I want to see this through, Irving."

I blinked at her, confused by her sudden resolve.

"I want to have the baby," she said. "But I can't do it without you."

I turned back to the TV, trying to find an empty space in my mind where I could make sense of my colliding emotions. She was blackmailing me, I knew, holding the baby hostage until I agreed to her terms. So why was I clinging to the sorrow in her words, to her admission that she still needed me?

"What about Livingston?" I said unsteadily.

"We're through," she said. "I promise."

I got up and wandered into the kitchen. I stood leaning over the sink, waiting for the whooshing of blood in my head to calm down. Within a few moments, Helen appeared in the doorway, watching me cautiously.

"I don't want this baby to have any other father but you," she said.

I knew that what she was offering me couldn't be real. Even so, it sounded so seductive. We'd be together again, but this time bound by an innocent that we'd both be obliged to protect.

As she stood there in her frumpy nightgown, I noticed a wholeness in her eyes that I'd never seen before. Her hand rested instinctively on her belly. I let myself believe that the hidden part of her was finally revealing itself to me. She was not a little girl anymore, but a woman—still selfish, and yet capable of unexpected acts of compassion.

"I'm sorry," she said. "What I did to you was . . ." She decided not to belittle her offence by attempting to classify it. She leaned back against the counter beside me and stared into space. "Motherhood terrifies me, Irving. The idea of being responsible for someone so helpless when I can't even be responsible for myself . . . Well, that's just beyond me right now."

I looked down at her hand. Even though she likely hadn't left the apartment in days, she was wearing her wedding ring.

"We'll be a family, Irving."

I knew that the future she was promising me would be a sham. But somehow I didn't care any more. It was enough for me to believe that she truly needed me, if for the wrong reasons. I let her take my arms and wrap them around her like the folds of a blanket.

Chapter 35

Of the many parties that went searching for Sir John Franklin, several had to be rescued themselves. They made the same mistakes that Franklin's expedition did, applying Victorian solutions to the problems of survival in an alien land. More ships were lost than just the *Erebus* and the *Terror*; more men died than just their crews. I remember seeing a grave marker for a member of HMS *Investigator*'s crew when I was on Beechey Island. He'd been laid to rest alongside my great-great-great uncle in the frozen gravel beach as an additional reminder of the folly of underestimating the High Arctic's harsh indifference to human ambition.

Severn and I are no different. We've both become lost searching for Helen in a landscape of bitter emotions that we can hardly begin to understand. It's about our own survival now. Even after I get Severn back to London, we won't truly be home. We'll still have to find a way of walking out of this alive together.

We stop off at a Tim Hortons on the 401, and I buy Severn a green tea and a box of her favourite Timbits. We sit down at a table. She doesn't touch the Timbits. Instead, she cradles the cup of tea in her hands and stares out at the highway. I study her face, looking past Helen's mouth and nose for hints of Livingston. I can't tell whether they're there or not.

"Severn."

I wait for her to look at me.

"You've been awfully quiet," I say. "I need to know what's on your mind."

Her eyes shift back to her cup of tea. "Nothing."

I can tell that she's still angry with me for humiliating her in front of Livingston, for tracking her down and dragging her back to London as though she were an escaped heifer. Perhaps she even thinks that if I hadn't shown up and spoiled it all, Livingston would have eventually conceded—perhaps truthfully—that she was his daughter. I've brought this all on myself, I know. If I'd been brave enough to tell her earlier, if I hadn't let her become a stranger to me since Helen died, she might never have felt the need to run away in the first place. If, if.

"Look," I tell her, "it's pretty clear that he doesn't want to have anything more to do with you. You're a passing curiosity to him, nothing more."

Her jaw tightens. She resents me for being so trite.

"It's true that your mom and I had a rough patch. But having you was what saw us through it."

My admission is too little, too late. She's not going to let me recast the lies of the past sixteen years so easily. I'm tempted to point out that if it hadn't been for me, she likely never would have been born, but I stop myself, aware that it would only make me sound like a martyr looking for recognition. More than that, it would leave her feeling that Helen had once considered her a burden she wasn't willing to bear.

When we get home, I follow Marla's painful advice and turn the conversation to Helen every chance I get, looking for an opening in the ice that Severn has let build up around herself. I make her pull out the old photos from her overnight bag and go through them with me, hoping that memories of happier times will heal the rift between us. She knows, of course, that it's a ploy on my part to make her blubber like a little girl, to take her back to a time in our relationship when she shared her triumphs and sorrows with me freely. She stays aloof, always remaining the gloomy sixteen-year-old.

The next morning, Sunday, I fix her a pancake breakfast and drive her to Victoria Park, where we watch the skaters for a while. I remind her of the figure-skating outfit her mom got her for Christmas one year and how she couldn't wait to come to the rink to show it off. She pretends not to listen. I suggest that we head across the street for hot chocolate.

As we wait for the traffic to clear on Richmond Street, I see the old bookshop just up the block. It's an upscale women's clothing store now. Before that it was a toy store, and before that a naughty lingerie emporium where you could buy ten different flavours of edible panties. Poor old Walter probably rolled over in his grave when that particular enterprise moved under his once-hallowed roof.

"Why did you take her back?" Severn asks me abruptly. They're the first unsolicited words I've heard from her all morning.

"What's that?" I say, caught off guard.

"What did she promise you?"

I smile nervously. "I'm not following you."

Her gaze meets mine unflinchingly. "What was the deal she made with you for being my dad?" She makes it sound like some job I applied for out of the classifieds. Wanted: One father. Long hours, no pay, promise of occasional sexual favours from spouse. No experience required.

"I don't know what you're talking about, Severn. There wasn't any deal."

"Sure there was." The bridge of her nose crimps into tight little ridges. "She must have promised you she was through with Jack."

"So he got in touch with her," I say dismissively, "used a few of her old notes."

"What if that's not the only thing she didn't tell you about?"

I stare back at her. "What are you saying?"

Severn's stony silence is confirmation enough.

"Jack told you another story, didn't he?" I say scornfully.

She looks away impatiently, as though I'm either incredibly stubborn or incredibly dense.

"Why do you keep believing him, Severn? He's a fiction writer. He earns a living making other people believe his lies."

Her eyes drill through me. "It wasn't anything Jack told me."

I feel my face go rigid.

She draws a deep, exasperated breath. "Mom used to tell me things," she says, her voice shaking with anger. "Talk to me like I was her girlfriend or something. Ever since I turned thirteen. She always said, 'Don't tell your father. This is just between us, all right?'"

I detect a ripple of shame in her words. For all my efforts to get her to open up to me, I don't want to hear any more.

"Mom told me that she gave up her chance at being a real writer because of you. She told me that after the bookshop went under, you never let her live it down. She said that if it weren't for me, she'd have left you long ago."

There's a sickly taste of rust in the back of my mouth, like old blood.

"Do you have any idea what it's like to hear your mother say things like that?" she says, unfurling her torment at my feet. "But you just carried on. Oblivious. Like there was nothing wrong. Couldn't you see how desperate I was for you to wake up so that Mom would stop telling me her goddamned secrets?"

That afternoon, I begin clearing Helen's clothes out of the bedroom closet, stuffing her dresses, sweaters, blouses, and skirts into green garbage bags for the Sally Ann. I don't bother folding them; I just grab them by the handful. I swipe the dresser clear of her knick-knacks. The framed photo of her toasting her literary success, which I reclaimed from Severn, pitches onto the floor, cracking the glass. I don't let the tears streaming down my face or the twisting sensation in my gut stop me. I'm a man intent on proving to himself that he isn't going to be a patsy any more.

Severn watches me warily from the upstairs hallway. She can see that I'm making a mess of it, but she doesn't offer to help. I get the sense that as angry as she is with Helen, she's still not ready to exorcise her from the house. She withdraws to her room, leaving me to finish the dirty work.

When I look in on her an hour later, she's nowhere to be found. I've been so absorbed in my private carnival of pain that she's slipped out of the house without my noticing. I immediately check for her overnight bag, but it's still on the floor where she left it after unpacking. Still not reassured, I go through the inventory of other items that I know she took with her to Toronto, eventually accounting for all of them. I wonder if disappearing and then waiting to see how long it takes before I call the cops is her new way of testing me.

I reluctantly phone Marla. "Is she over there?" I ask.

"Jesus, Irving," she says. "You've had her home less than twenty-four hours."

"Are you going to answer the question?"

"No," she says, dropping her facetious tone. "She's not here."

Marla offers to help me start another search. She and I call around town to all the places I usually check when Severn goes missing. We come up empty. I consider phoning Livingston but realize that I don't have his number—not that I would have stooped to ask for it, or that he would have given it to me.

At about eight-thirty, Severn stumbles in the front door, so drunk that she falls down in the front hall trying to kick off her boots. She glares up at me from the tile floor as if to accuse me of tripping her. She's wearing one of Helen's old coats, which she rescued from the front closet before I could bag it. I ask her where she's been. She staggers to her feet and brushes past me without answering. I catch a whiff of lavender mingled with the stale smell of booze. I follow her to the kitchen, where she throws up in the sink, fouling the front of the coat.

As I haul her upstairs to the bathroom, she upchucks once more en route. I soak a washcloth and scrub the vomit from around her mouth.

"Take off that filthy top," I tell her.

She looks at me wild-eyed, as if I've made an indecent proposal.

"Get it off so I can soak it in the sink," I say.

She moans at me to leave her alone. I yank her top off myself, then pull off her puke-stained pants.

"Listen here," I shout above her protests. "If you're going to act like a wilful little girl, then that's how I'm going to treat you."

I bat aside her drunken attempts to fight me off, force her under the showerhead in her bra and panties, and turn the cold water on her. She swears at me, but I swear back louder.

"I've had enough of your acting out, you understand?" I yell at her. "Whoever the hell your biological father is, you'll have to get used to the fact that I'm the only one who's willing to help you clean up your goddamned mess. I doubt Jack Livingston would ever wipe barf off your pretty little chin."

Once I've hosed her off and got her into some dry clothes, I make her help me scrub the kitchen, the bathroom, the stairway, and the upstairs hall. By the time I let her go to bed, she's sober enough to see the damage she's wrought. She cries when she realizes what she's done to Helen's coat.

"I need help," I tell Marla on the phone the next day. "Severn and I are eating each other alive."

She comes over to the house that evening after supper. Severn has sabotaged yet another one of my foolhardy attempts at a congenial family meal with her angry silences. When Marla arrives, Severn is sulking in her room.

As she enters, Marla notices the piles of green garbage bags in the den off the front hall. I explain to her what's in them and say that I haven't had a chance to take them to the Salvation Army drop box yet.

"Why the sudden urge to clean out Helen's stuff?" she asks warily.

I tell her what Helen confided to Severn about me. I try to relay the conversation matter-of-factly, as if I've dealt with the shock and already moved on, but the words catch in my throat. I'm mortified by the tears that sneak up on me. Marla takes me in her arms and lets me cry on her shoulder. When my water-works abate, she sits me down at the kitchen table and makes me tea.

I tell her about my fight with Severn after she came home drunk. "I just can't get through to her," I say. "I don't know what else to do."

"Maybe you're doing all you *can* do," she says, standing behind me and massaging my rigid neck while the tea steeps. "Just keep reminding her that you're there for her, no matter how hard she pushes you away."

"I'm not sure it's going to be enough."

"Give her time, Irving."

I shake my head. It won't be long before I lose Severn for good. I can sense it. I look at Marla. "Maybe you could talk to her."

Marla smiles uncomfortably.

"You understand what she's going through," I say.

"You can't be serious," she says.

I can see that as much as Marla is horrified by my request, a part of her wants to help. She cares too much now about what happens to Severn to keep a safe distance. The echoes from her own past are too familiar.

"You got through it somehow," I say. "She needs to hear that."

Marla laughs forlornly. "Think about it, Irving. I'm divorced. I've got a son who despises me. And I still have panic attacks more than twenty years after my mother died. Are you sure you want me talking to Severn?"

"I wouldn't ask if I wasn't sure," I say.

My unwavering vote of confidence disarms her. She sinks back in her chair. "All right," she says with a sigh and a shake of her head, still not convinced that my faith in her is justified.

I call Severn down from her room. When she finds Marla waiting for her in the kitchen, she flashes a look of protest at me. I've violated the rules of engagement in our private little war by recruiting this woman to my side.

"We were just having some tea," I say, trying to put Severn at ease. "You want some?"

Severn shakes her head. I busy myself making a fresh pot anyway, leaving her to Marla.

Marla leans forward in her chair. "Your dad says you and he had a bit of blow-up yesterday."

Severn slides another jagged look my way. She resents that I've been complaining about her to my new lady friend.

"I used to get into fights with my dad," Marla says. "Come home pissed. Have these big screaming matches with him. He always told me the same thing: smarten up; start acting like an adult. I thought he was such a prick."

Severn's eyes narrow. She's suspicious of the sisterhood act, I can tell.

"It was just him and me too," Marla says. "My mom died when I was still in high school."

"Geez," Severn says sardonically, "I'm sorry to hear that." I feel like swatting her.

Marla continues, undeterred. "My dad never talked about her. He just wanted me to grow up so he wouldn't have to deal with this mopey teenage girl any more."

Severn sees me watching her from beside the stove, measuring the impact of Marla's words on her face. She quickly refreshes her scowl, which has started to slip ever so slightly.

"You ever own a cat?" Marla asks her.

"No," Severn says, distrustful of the question.

"My mom had this calico cat," Marla says. "It used to sleep in the crook of her knees when she was sick at home. She'd rescued it from the animal shelter. Every time I came into Mom's room to give her a sponge bath or bring her some food, it was always there, keeping guard over her. I guess it was doing its best to return the favour."

Severn maintains her look of disdain, impatiently waiting for the moral of the story.

"Anyway," Marla goes on, "I inherited the cat when she died."

"I guess I'm more of a dog person," Severn shoots back.

Marla glances at me askew, as if to register the opinion that I've passed on my sarcasm to my daughter, if not my genes. She turns back to Severn and acknowledges her quip with a faint smile. "You must have something like that. Something special that reminds you of your mom."

Severn shrugs. For the moment, Marla's forbearance seems to have shamed her into silence.

"I couldn't wait to move away from home," Marla says. "Being with my dad was like living in a tomb. When I was eighteen, I loaded my bags and that cat on a bus and headed as far away as I could. I found a town where no one knew me, where I could make a fresh start all on my own. Things were pretty sweet for a while." She gives a little wince. "Then one day, the cat ran out in front of a car."

All at once, I'm back on Lakeshore Boulevard. Now I recognize the true nature of Marla's panic when she slammed on the brakes.

Marla clears her throat as though it's suddenly gone dry. "I'm not going to tell you that the pain fades with time, Severn. There's always going to be a piece of you missing because you lost your mom too soon. Just don't feel that there's something wrong with you because you haven't got over her yet. No matter how sad or angry you are."

Severn stares at her austerely, pretending to find the story maudlin despite all the hard swallows she's taken while Marla's been talking. "I'm not done my homework yet," she says. "Are we done here?"

Marla twitches her eyebrows and sinks back in her chair, as if Severn's reaction sadly isn't a surprise to her. I'm about to lambaste Severn for being so rude, but Marla gestures to me with weary eyes to let her go.

"I'm sorry," I say to Marla once Severn's back upstairs.

Marla shrugs. "I should have remembered: when you're sixteen, it's an inviolable law of nature that no adult can possibly understand you."

She gets up to leave.

"Finish your tea," I say.

"I have to go," she insists.

I follow her out to the front hall. "Thanks for trying," I say.

She retrieves her coat from the closet.

"So tell me," I say as I watch her bundle up, "am I as much a prick as your father was?"

She leans over and pulls on her boots. "You have your moments."

"I see."

"Not as bad as when I first met you, though." She squints up at me lopsidedly. "You almost seem human to me now."

I'm struck by how much I don't want to see her go. It's the prospect of having to face Severn on my own again, I realize. But there's something more than that, too, a reminder of what it's like to be known to someone beyond what the world at large sees. It's a feeling I haven't had since Helen died.

"Well," she says, slipping on her gloves, "I'm off." I catch her scanning my face, looking for signs that I'll be all right until the next time I have to call her. Even in her boots, she's no taller than I am.

"Thanks for coming," I say.

I lean across and kiss her gently on the forehead.

The moment is more awkward than I want it to be. Marla smiles nervously, as though she thinks I've mistaken her offerings of solace for something more. It seems I've failed to understand that it's safe for her to touch me but not the other way around. I feel my face go bright red.

"I've got to go," she says, shrinking back towards the door.

"Sure," I say self-consciously. "I understand."

Before I close the front door, I watch Marla get into her car, letting the winter wind invade the house. When I turn around, I see Severn watching from the stairs behind me. She stares at me as if she's caught me red-handed. Without a word, she heads back upstairs.

Chapter 36

After my reconciliation with Helen, neither one of us mentioned Livingston again. We simply wiped that part of our marriage from the history books, Helen likely out of a desire to expunge the man who had rejected her, and me in an effort to preserve the fragile peace. Without ever discussing it, we settled into an amicable arrangement. I would become the child's de facto father, thus removing the need for a certain party to account for indiscretions committed in the past. In return, said party would play the role of my devoted wife, thus preserving the conceit that I was a man to be envied. It was an illusion that seemed to hold this time. Helen grew less flighty and more maternal as her pregnancy wore on. I gradually became more secure in the knowledge that my loyalty was now a valuable asset rather than an embarrassing liability. I even felt traces of my old, unmitigated feelings of love for Helen creeping to the surface. Soon, it became simplest not to question the shaky underpinnings of what we'd built.

And so we masqueraded as typical new parents after Severn was born. Our circle of friends expanded naturally enough to include other couples with young children. We blended in with them, commiserating, sharing amusing anecdotes, passing without suspicion. Only Will and Walter knew the truth, but thankfully neither of them ever felt obliged to remind us of it.

Once Severn arrived, I never thought of her as Livingston's child, never searched for his angles in her face. His contribution to her life lasted only a few seconds; mine would last a lifetime. Her arrival only drew Helen and me closer together.

To her credit, Helen embraced motherhood with more sustained attention than I'd seen her give anything else. Sometimes when I watched her breast-feeding, still bleary-eyed from lack of sleep, she'd return my gaze with arched eyebrows, as if to mock me for doubting that she'd be able to rise to the occasion. Helen's dedication didn't waver, even through all the diaper changes and episodes of colic that followed. As Severn grew older and started to talk, Helen chattered along with her, amused to see how the world looked through such small, wondering eyes.

Severn dominated our schedule. Our joy became increasingly measured through her happiness. When other parents quietly confessed to us that their children drained them of all their sexual energy, we regretfully acknowledged the same experience. But the fact was that Severn had become a welcome buffer between us, letting us relate to each other simply as her sexless parents. We felt no obligation to mend our broken life as husband and wife. I satisfied myself with the achievement of finally securing Helen's unwavering allegiance, even if it was only as Severn's father. With her gentle touches and quiet smiles, Helen acknowledged my role in making our happy charade possible. Just the same, I couldn't help feeling that as much as she appreciated me, I was still playing a supporting role to her lead.

Severn was two and a half when Walter passed away. He continued to serve as book merchant emeritus at the shop right until the end. He'd become a fixture, like the pressed-tin ceiling. Most often, he could be found at the front counter with a vintage copy of *Ulysses* or *Heart of Darkness* open before him, although he rarely bothered turning the pages any more. He was content to keep greeting customers with his trademark scowl while his granddaughter hid under the counter and fiddled with his shoelaces. When things weren't too busy, he'd take her down the street and treat her to an ice cream, narrating his own version of the adventures of Peter Rabbit as they went. By closing time, Severn wouldn't want to come home. To protest, she'd lie prostrate on the floor and wail like a banshee. Helen would cringe, smiling painfully at the few remaining customers. Walter would just sit there, watching with amusement as his daughter turned successively deeper shades of red.

The day he died, Walter was scheduled to put in a couple of hours at the shop. It wasn't the first time he'd failed to show up. On at least three previous occasions, Helen had rushed to his house when he didn't answer the phone, only to find him sleeping on the couch or washing his underwear in the bathroom sink. When she showed her exasperation, he got snippy in return, claiming that she'd never told him to come in that day. Besides, it was her shop now. What did she need him around for?

It was only natural that she didn't drop everything to go and check on him that particular Saturday. After all, Will was off at a wedding, and she was tending the shop on her own. Business was so brisk that she didn't even have time for lunch. It wasn't until I carried Severn into the shop at about two in the afternoon to visit her grandpa that Helen remembered to try phoning him again. She rolled her eyes as she waited in vain for him to answer. After hanging up, she told me to look after the shop and took Severn with her.

We held the funeral at St. Peter's Basilica, within spitting distance of the shop. As I looked back from the front pew with Severn in my lap, I was astounded to see how full the church was. I'd forgotten how many people had come to know Walter over the years—long-time customers, fellow downtown merchants, local politicians, authors, publishers from Toronto, even the panhandlers who worked Richmond Street. To Helen, they were all just background noise. As the service began, she clutched my arm as if a sudden, unexpected breeze might blow her away.

The reception was held at the shop. Helen had arranged half a dozen framed black-and-white photos of her dad on the front counter. One showed him as a young man standing next to his Studebaker, his newly opened store in the background. Others showed him solemnly shaking the hands of various authors who'd passed through the place over the years, a veritable who's who of Canadian literature. Propped beside the pictures was a line from Milton that Will had written out in elegant calligraphy:

> A good book is the precious life-blood of a master spirit,
> embalmed and treasured up on purpose to a life beyond life.

A steady stream of guests offered Helen their condolences, each remarking that the place wouldn't be the same without Walter and asking her if she planned to carry on the business. She soldiered through the ordeal, summoning up one polite, noncommittal reply after another. I stayed at her side, trying to keep Severn from wandering out into the sea of adult legs. After a while, Will noticed my predicament.

"Hey, princess," he said, holding out his hand for Severn. "How's about we find you some nibblies?"

She clung to my leg. I crouched down and told her that Mommy and I wouldn't be far away. I said that if she was good, Will might get her some ice cream. Her eyes brightened, and after a little coaxing, she took Will's hand and let him lead her to the buffet table.

Helen's eyes followed them as they went. The broad-cheeked woman who ran the flower shop down the street was recounting one of her favourite memories of Walter, but her voice trailed off when she noticed that Helen wasn't listening. The woman smiled awkwardly, mumbled a parting platitude, and moved on.

"She had a big lunch," Helen said to me, her eyes still on Severn. "I don't want her getting sick."

Will had her up on his hip now. He pointed to each of the goodies on the buffet table, whispering in her ear to tempt her tummy.

"She'll be all right," I said.

Helen didn't seem convinced. She watched as Will's new boyfriend, Alan, fussed over Severn. Alan was a few years older than Will; he had salt-and-pepper hair and a runner's body. He owned a fashionable catering business in town. In fact, he'd supplied the spread for the reception at a considerable discount.

"You want me to get you something from the buffet?" I asked her.

"How long after I die would you wait before finding someone else?" she asked.

I refused to be baited. "I think it's great that Will's getting on with his life," I said.

She looked at me coolly. "So you'd wait—what?—a year after I'm dead? Or would it be even that long?"

"Helen."

She crossed her arms. "No, really. I'd like to know."

I chose not to remind her that she hadn't waited until I was dead before trying to replace me. "Those canapés look good," I said. "I think I'll get us some."

As we drove home, Helen kept glancing back at Severn in her car seat.

"You okay?" I asked her.

She nodded, even though it was obvious that she wasn't.

The fall colours had faded. Stacks of clear garbage bags stuffed with leaves lined the curbs, awaiting pickup by the city. The wind was shifting to the north. The first snowflakes of the year began falling from the slate grey sky.

"Look, Severn," I said. "Snow."

In the rear-view mirror, I saw her head swivel in her hood as she looked out the window. Her legs kicked excitedly.

By the time we pulled into our driveway, a carpet of wet snow had covered our lawn. Severn held her mitts out to catch the falling flakes as Helen carried her to the front door. Snow was still magical to her, a miracle from the sky. Once we got inside, Severn watched with fascination as the flakes turned clear and then dissolved on the sleeve of her coat. Before Helen and I could kick off our shoes, she ran to the living-room window to stare out at the new white world that our neighbourhood was becoming before her eyes.

"I'll start making supper," I said.

Helen took both my hands, not wanting to let me go just yet. Her fingers were cold, her cheeks sunken. Her eyes were hollowed from lack of sleep. "Promise me you'll take care of Severn if something happens to me," she said.

I laugh nervously. "What's that supposed to mean?"

"If I die before you. Just promise."

"Of course I'd take care of her. She's my daughter."

Helen held my gaze for a moment, then turned and went into the living room. She kneeled beside Severn, squeezed her tight, and gazed out the window with her. Within minutes, they were outside making snow angels on the front lawn. I watched them from the living room—Helen on her back, flapping her wings, and Severn squealing with delight.

Chapter 37

I get a call from Severn's school the next afternoon. She hasn't shown up for any of her classes, even though I drove her there myself that morning. I begin calling the same people I did the day before yesterday, and last week when she ran off to Toronto, but once again none of them have seen her. I sense their sympathy giving way to impatience. By suppertime, she still hasn't come home. I'm about to resign myself to another night of listening anxiously for her to come through the front door when the phone rings. It's the mother of one of Severn's former girlfriends. She tells me that she thought she'd better call me.

I find a parking spot on Richmond Street, near the store. There's a Closed sign hanging on the front door when I knock. A woman with stylishly coiffed hair lets me in.

"Mrs. Laviolette?" I ask.

The woman greets me with a tight smile. I look around the store, but we're the only ones there apart from several mannequins wearing the latest women's fashions. Mrs. Laviolette's eyes drift towards the ceiling. I notice that the pressed tin has been replaced by smooth white plaster highlighted by showy halogen lighting.

"She's upstairs," she says.

"Upstairs?"

"She came in just before closing. High as a kite." Mrs. Laviolette purses her lips at me before continuing, to make sure that I'm showing the appropriate amount of shame for letting my daughter run wild. "She goes, 'Where's your attic, Mrs. L.? Show me your attic.' I'm in the middle of serving this woman, a regular customer of mine, but she keeps going on about the goddamned attic. I try to settle her down, but she gets real agitated, like I'm trying to hide something from her. Starts opening all the doors at the back of the shop. Catches one customer in the change room with just her underwear on. Scares the hell out of her. If Severn and my Chantal hadn't been friends, I would've called the cops."

"I'm glad you called me instead," I say placatingly. We walk to the back of the store. The closet with the steep set of stairs is gone, removed during renovations to meet code requirements after Helen set fire to the garret. The way up is no longer obvious to me because of the numerous changes to the building . "How did she get up there?"

"Entrance from the side street," says Mrs. Laviolette. "The guy who owned this place before me planned to turn the upper floor into an apartment but never got around to it. It's just storage space now."

"You must keep the door locked."

"I let Severn go up and have a look," she says with a shrug. "Better that than have her scare away more customers. Besides, I thought it might keep her occupied until you got here."

"I appreciate that." I take one last look around the store before we exit through the side door. The place is hard to recognize. The uneven floors have been resurfaced and carpeted over. The dividing walls where the old, imposing bookshelves once stood have been torn down. The smell of books has been replaced by the smell of naked commerce. "I never realized that you owned this store," I say to her.

"This building has been a lot of different things over the years," she says dismissively. "So they tell me, anyway. I moved to London only five years ago."

I climb the stairs alone. At the top is an unlocked door. I open it and step inside. The first thing I notice is that there's no heat up here. The lingering smell of charred wood hangs in the air, even after all these years. As my eyes adjust to the dark, I see that the rabbit warren of small, musty rooms I remember is now one open space with exposed rafters. The floor is littered with store furniture abandoned by previous tenants—dented shelving units, an old refrigerator case, and cardboard signs advertising sales long past. In one corner, I make out Walter's old cash register sitting on a battered metal desk. Severn is curled up on the floor beneath it.

I crouch down beside her. She rocks back and forth with her eyes closed. Her chin is buried in the folds of her ski jacket, and her hands are clamped between her thighs for warmth. The stink of booze clings to her clothes. I'm not sure whether she notices me or not.

"Severn," I say softly, so as not to startle her.

She stops rocking but doesn't open her eyes. She draws her knees to her chest. I whisper her name again, gently brushing her sleeve with my fingers. She twists away from me.

I decide to soften her up with small talk. "This place has changed a lot," I say, glancing around us. "I take it that your mother told you what used to be up here."

Severn tries to fix me with a look of disgust, but her eyes won't focus. She snorts and gives up. Her gaze wanders to the cash register above her. She frowns, wondering how it got there.

"Jesus, Severn. How the hell am I supposed to talk to you when you're stoned out of your skull?"

She lets her head settle against the side of the metal desk with a clunk. "You just couldn't wait to replace her, could you? Dump all her stuff and pretend she never existed."

"It's time we moved on."

She sneers.

"Don't fight me this way, Severn. You're only hurting yourself."

Her eyes suddenly swell with tears. "I turn seventeen in a couple of weeks, and the only person who'll want to celebrate with me is my own father. Christ, how desperate is that?"

She can't stop crying now. I sit on the floor beside her and pull a Kleenex out of my pocket. Within seconds, it becomes a sodden little wad in her hand. I realize that Marla did get through to her after all, opening a tiny passageway into her pain for me to navigate.

"Sometimes I get so angry with her for leaving me," she says, forcing the words out between her jagged sobs. "And then I feel like a shit for thinking it."

I gently lay a consoling hand on her knee, hoping that she doesn't pull away. "I'm sorry I went ballistic on you the other night. Not that getting drunk like that wasn't a stupid thing to do. Still, I shouldn't have let myself lose it so completely."

She laughs pathetically, the tears still streaming down. "I thought you were going to kill me."

I pat my pockets for more Kleenex. "Sorry, I'm all out."

She wipes her cheeks with the edge of her palm and sniffles. "That's okay."

I squeeze her knee reassuringly. "Look, whatever awful things your mom did in her life, the one thing I know for sure is that she cared for you more than anything—even more than herself most of the time, which believe me is saying something."

She smiles weakly.

"We both want to remember her as the woman who loved us, not the one who hurt us," I tell her softly. "The trouble is, she was both. And until we accept that, we'll just live the rest of our days with a hole in our hearts that no one else can fill."

Her tears start up again. I put my arm around her shoulder, and she buries her face in the folds of my jacket like she used to when she was a little girl. After a while, she glances up at me, then meekly lowers her eyes.

"When I woke up that morning at Jack's, I went into the kitchen and found him reading the newspaper in his underwear," she confesses. She wraps herself a little tighter around me. "He looked at me like I was some stranger who'd snuck into his house. It actually took him a minute to remember who the hell I was."

I stroke her head and rock her gently. I can feel that my daughter's home now. She stays curled up against me under Walter's old cash register for a good long time. Eventually, Mrs. Laviolette comes up to ask us if everything's all right, a polite way of saying that she wants to go home already and would appreciate us clearing out so she can lock up.

I drive Severn home. The next day she helps me take Helen's things to the drop box.

Chapter 38

Helen did her best to keep her father's bookshop going after he died. She hosted book-signings, sponsored special readings at the public library, even resurrected my Saturday afternoon "famous person from history" gig. But no matter what she did, business continued to wane. Fewer people were coming downtown on weekends. All around the shop, retailers were folding. Even the big department stores on Dundas Street were closing down, consolidating their operations in the malls on the outskirts of town.

A couple of months before Severn's tenth birthday, the Imprint store opened in the north end of town. Helen was forced to cut back Will's hours even below the meagre number she'd been giving him. He didn't last long after that. Helen came home one day and announced that Will had gone to work for the enemy and his name was never to be spoken in our house again. I tried to defend him, arguing that he could hardly be expected to live on loyalty and pocket change, but Helen would have none of it.

She began to run the shop entirely on her own, spending more and more time there. As dedicated as she was to keeping her father's legacy alive, I think she resented the shop for forcing her to leave Severn with me more often. For my part, I enjoyed having the time alone with my little girl, free from Helen's scrutiny.

I always found it strange that other parents entrusted their children to my supervision without question, but Helen would radiate ambivalence about leaving our daughter in my care for a single afternoon.

After a trip to Pioneer Village one Saturday a few weeks later, I suggested to Severn that we drop by the bookshop so she could tell Mom about all the different farm animals she'd seen that day. She wasn't very enthusiastic. When I asked her why, she said that the shop was old and yucky and only ever made Mom unhappy. She said that all her friends had been to the big, new bookstore and asked me why I couldn't take her there instead. I warned her to be careful about saying that kind of thing within earshot of her mother.

When Severn's birthday rolled around that year, I found a card from Will in our mailbox. He'd always been like a favourite uncle to her, remembering her birthday each year with a little gift or offering her some treat from his pocket when she visited the shop. I supposed it was just another way for him to feel like a bona fide member of the Donnelly clan. Or maybe it was a sign of his friendship with me. At any rate, I was sorry that he wouldn't be allowed to join us this year to celebrate.

To compensate for all the time she'd been away from home, Helen went all out getting ready for the birthday party. She decorated the family room with balloons and streamers, set out party favours for Severn's friends, and even hand-made a piñata for the festivities. I was left out of the preparations. It was clear that this was to be Helen's special treat, and hers alone. My role was strictly to be a chaperone at the party.

Before any of the children arrived, she surprised Severn with a beautiful new party dress. Helen had me take a picture of the two of them all decked out. In the viewfinder, I could see mother and daughter reflecting each other's glow.

Within half an hour, the house was filled with excited nine-year-olds. I managed to play the jolly father of the birthday girl despite the restrictions placed on me, joking with Severn's friends and making sure that every child got included in the party games. Everything was perfect until it came time for Severn to open her gifts. As she peeled back the wrapping of her first present, she was delighted to see that it was a copy of *Charlotte's Web*. But just as she was thanking the girl who gave it to her, an Imprint book-mark fell from the wrapping. Severn looked hesitantly at her mom, her joy transmuted into guilt. Helen said nothing. She left the room and didn't appear again for the rest of the party.

The bookshop was insolvent by November. While fickle Christmas shoppers crammed the malls, I helped Helen stuff boxes full of books for shipping back to the distribution centres from which she'd received them only months before. Unlike Walter's funeral, few people came by to mark the passing of his shop. Perhaps it was because the place had already faded from people's memories, or more accurately, because the wonderfully quirky establishment that everyone had come to love had passed away with Walter. It was just as well that no one came to witness us clearing the shelves and packing away the last relics of Walter's legacy. Any mourners, no matter how well intentioned, would have simply deepened Helen's sense of failure.

Helen hung the black-and-white photos of her father in our den above the computer. With the shop gone, she defiantly resolved to bring a new focus to her life—or rather, to revive an old one. She declared that she would become a writer after all. I tried to sound encouraging, as was expected of me.

True to her word, she rose before dawn the next morning and plunked herself in front of the computer. She did this for three days running. Late each afternoon, I'd return home to find her still in her pyjamas, watching TV. When I asked how her writing had gone that day, she'd simply grunt and change the channel. Over the course of those days, her hair went stringy from not showering. She showed no interest in meals, even when I fixed them. On the third evening, she complained that she was coming down with something and went to bed early, skipping supper entirely. She stayed in bed for the remainder of the week.

"It's not your fault," I told her one night as she lay beside me in the dark, staring at the bedroom ceiling. "Lots of other businesses downtown are closing."

"I'd rather not talk about it," she said.

"Maybe you should get out of the house," I suggested. "Go for a drive or something. Do some Christmas shopping."

She said nothing, just kept staring at the ceiling.

A few hours later, when I was certain that she'd finally fallen asleep, I crept into the den and checked the computer to see what she'd been writing. All I could find was one page of errant thoughts. She'd made no attempt to revive the story that she'd been working on when she'd left me for Jack Livingston.

The next morning, I was surprised to find that she was already out of bed by the time I woke up. I shaved and showered, then knocked on Severn's door to tell her it was time to get up. After dressing for work, I went downstairs to fix breakfast. I checked the den on the way, but Helen wasn't there. She wasn't in the living room or the kitchen either. When Severn came down, I handed a bagged lunch to her and asked whether she'd seen her mom. Severn looked at me warily, as if I were trying to get her into trouble. She told me no.

The Toyota was missing from the driveway. I convinced myself that Helen had taken my advice and gone for a harmless early morning drive to clear her head. I drove Severn to school in the old Valiant.

I was only ten minutes into my first class when one of the vice-principals at my school pulled me out and told me about the accident. At first, I caught only snatches of what he told me—something about a car crash . . . Imprint Books. Nothing about whether Helen was hurt. What registered most in my mind was the solemn look on his face. It reinforced my worst fears.

As I rushed to the scene, all I could think of was the emptiness of Helen's voice the night before. I should have recognized just how depressed she was, just what she might have been capable of in her state of mind. Then I remembered how she'd made me promise after Walter's funeral to look after Severn if anything happened to her.

The first things I saw were the flashing lights of the police cruisers that were blocking access to the store parking lot. Then I spotted the ambulance in front of the store. I tried to drive around one of the police cars, but a cop in a fluorescent orange traffic vest stepped out in front of me. When he found out who I was, he asked that I get out of my car and walked me across the icy pavement to the ambulance. I could see the mangled remains of our Toyota sticking out of what had been the main entrance to the store. Upset books and broken bits of glass were everywhere.

"Lucky the place wasn't open yet," the officer said curtly. "A lot of people could've got hurt, or worse."

"What about my wife?" I asked anxiously.

"Seems she got off with just a few cuts and bruises," he said. "The paramedics are looking after her now."

Helen was sitting up in the back of the ambulance, wrapped in a blanket, while one of the paramedics treated a gash on her forehead. A second cop was questioning her about the accident and jotting down her answers.

"Helen," I said frantically, "are you okay?"

She shrugged noncommittally.

I turned to the paramedic. "Is she going to be okay?"

"We're going to take her to emerg, just as a precaution," he said. "You can follow us."

The officer escorting me headed back to direct traffic while his buddy resumed his questioning. Helen proceeded to tell him that she'd come to do some Christmas shopping, unaware that the store didn't open for another hour. She said that as she was turning to leave, her foot must have hit the gas instead of the brake.

"When the car jumped the curb, I guess I panicked," she said.

The second cop closed his notepad and gave us a moment alone. He walked back to his cruiser and got inside, keeping an eye on us as he sat there talking on his radio. I waited for the paramedic to finish treating Helen and disappear around the corner of the ambulance.

"What the hell happened?" I asked her in a hushed voice.

She grinned triumphantly. "I took your advice. I went for a drive."

"Jesus, Helen." I peered into her eyes. They seemed oddly serene, as if she was relieved to have executed a solemn duty. She patted my cheek to let me know that I needn't worry about her any more.

The paramedic reappeared and I made way for him. Several cars were now backed up behind the police roadblock. Staff members reporting for work stood at the edge of the parking lot, waiting to hear whether they'd be sent home for the day. Traffic on the street had ground to a crawl as rubber-necking drivers slowed down to take a look. A woman in a parka, her hands clasped in anguish on top of her head, paced outside the yellow tape the police had strung up. The officer who'd questioned Helen was out of his car now, trying to calm the woman down. I soon figured out that she was the store manager.

"Is Helen going to be all right?" asked a voice behind me.

I looked around and saw Will, standing with his hands in his coat pockets.

"I was the one who found her," he explained. "When I arrived to open the store."

I felt my face flush. "The paramedics think she'll be fine," I said.

He glanced towards his pacing boss, who was likely freaking out over the Christmas business the store would lose. He gestured for me to step behind the ambulance with him. "Don't worry," he said softly once we were safe from suspicious eyes. "I won't rat out Helen."

I looked at him, my embarrassment deepening. "She's been depressed ever since the shop went belly up," I tried to explain.

"I know," he said, resting his hand on my shoulder.

I heard the paramedics close the back doors of the ambulance. I thanked Will with a shake of the hand. He gave me an encouraging smile as we parted company.

"Take care of yourself, Irving," he said. "And that family of yours."

The store never pressed charges against Helen. The police didn't have the evidence to charge her with anything more than careless driving even though they clearly didn't put much stock in her account of the events leading up to the crash. Helen never went near the Imprint store again after that. I guess she didn't feel the need. Her message had been delivered.

Chapter 39

I go back to Imprint to pay Will a visit the Saturday after Severn and I return from Toronto. I find him at the back of the store, holding a group of cross-legged preschoolers spellbound with his reading of Dr. Seuss's *Horton Hears a Who*. He's wearing a pullover sweater that's a much better colour for him than his yellow Imprint golf shirt. I notice now that he's put on some weight since I saw him at Helen's funeral, especially around his face. It makes him look almost mirthful.

In the years following the closing of the bookshop on Richmond Street, Helen gradually relaxed her sanctions on Will. He was permitted to drop by our house on occasion, even babysit Severn a couple of times. Helen treated him civilly but always kept a wary eye on him, as though he was on probation. When she got sick, he took his turn at her bedside. He often read to her—using the same mellifluous voice he is using today—to keep her mind off the pain. I never heard them talk about the old days together at the shop, but I knew they likely were never far from their minds.

The children and parents clap enthusiastically when Will finishes his reading. He spots me adding my applause and dips his head in acknowledgment. As the crowd begins to disperse, he comes up to greet me.

"Is this a casual-dress day?" I ask, teasing him about being out of uniform.

"I do this for fun," he says. "I'm here on my own time today."

"I didn't realize you had such a way with kids," I say. It shouldn't have surprised me, given how good he was with Severn.

He shrugs, smiling at the excited, high-pitched chattering still going on around him. "Alan and I talk about adopting from time to time." A mother interrupts to tell him how much her daughter enjoyed his reading. He thanks her. "Say," he says to me as the woman moves on, "we should get you in here sometime. As Galileo or Alexander Graham Bell or . . . who was that guy with the big hat you used to do?"

"Lieutenant Henry Bayfield," I say.

"Right. Bayfield."

"I'm afraid my days as a performer are over," I tell him.

"Too bad," he says. "You were good at that sort of thing."

We make our way to the coffee bar at the front of the store. I ask Will what he'd like, then tell the girl behind the counter that I'll have the same thing. She steps over to the latte machine to fill our order.

"How's Severn doing?" he asks me. "I tried to call you after you dropped by here last week."

"We were away for the weekend," I say.

"Oh?"

"In Toronto, actually."

He frowns as he tries to decipher my meaning, then a look of comprehension washes across his face. "Livingston."

I study the concern in his expression.

"She went looking for him?" he asks.

I curl my eyebrow in the affirmative. "He has a new girlfriend now. A redhead."

The girl brings us our lattes. Will wants to pay but I insist it's my treat. We find a table in the far corner of the café. Will manages to spill half his coffee as he sets it down. He apologizes profusely and runs back to the counter to grab a fistful of paper napkins. I help him mop up the mess.

"Funny thing is, though," I say once he's finally settled in, "Livingston insisted he wasn't Severn's father."

"Huh," Will says. "Well, I guess that's good news for you, then." His cup rattles ever so slightly as he lifts it from its saucer.

"Of course, he's probably lying through his teeth," I say.

Will takes a tentative sip of coffee, then cautiously sets it back down. "What was Severn's reaction?"

"I think she realizes now that he's not the paragon she thought he was."

Will nods slowly. "She's okay, though?"

I'm not sure what to tell him. I still worry about her, still breathe a sigh of relief when she comes home for supper, still hope that the civility she's been showing me in the past few days won't suddenly evaporate. But at least I've begun to believe that she has a chance of surviving now. "She's better," I say.

Will tilts his head at me. "What about you?"

"Oh, I'm coming around, I guess."

He smiles encouragingly. I think he can see that I'm not lying to him this time. "You know," he says, "I could see about getting Severn a part-time job here. It might help her make some new friends. Give her a chance to build some confidence again."

I look at him incredulously. "Isn't she banned from the store for shoplifting?"

He winks at me and drapes his arm around the back of his chair. "Leave it to me."

He seems pleased with himself, more relaxed than when we first sat down. Relieved that I've let him steer the conversation away from Livingston. He's positioning himself as Severn's faithful uncle again, ready to step in wherever needed.

"What happened when I was in the Arctic, Will?" I ask, bursting his bubble.

His smile wavers. "What do you mean?"

"Helen didn't leave for Toronto right away, did she?"

His arm slips from the back of the chair. He begins fidgeting with the reading glasses hanging around his neck.

I keep my gaze fixed on him. "When I was looking for Severn, I started thinking about the things I've blotted out of my mind all these years. Like when I got back from my trip up north and phoned to ask you where Helen was."

"What about it?" he asks apprehensively.

"You weren't sure what to say to me. At the time, I thought it was just because you felt sorry for me. But now I wonder whether there wasn't another reason."

"Oh?"

"Severn means something special to you. You've never forgotten her birthday, even when Helen wouldn't let you in the house."

"What can I say? I got attached to her."

"When Helen was on the verge of getting an abortion, it was you who tipped me off and convinced me to stop her."

"You'd rather I hadn't said anything?"

"Maybe it's time you told me what really happened, Will."

He looks at me long and hard. After a tortured silence, he rakes his fingers through his thinning hair. "I'd just lost Kevin," he says. He waits for my reaction. I swallow sharply but say nothing.

"Helen was always trying to set me up with other guys," he tries to explain. "I kept frustrating her, telling her that it was too early, that I wasn't ready. The week you left, she got me a date with this guy—sometimes I think she knew more gay men in London than I did—but I didn't have the guts to go through with it and stood him up. Well, that was the last straw for her. She came to my apartment to tell me off. She said she didn't know why she was wasting her time on me. When was I going to realize that the best way to honour Kevin was to live life, not waste it feeling guilty for outlasting him?" He hesitates, nervously rubbing his thighs. "I was so numb, so desperate to feel again. Neither one of us was thinking." He turns his palms over in his lap and stares at them blankly. "The next morning, she left for Toronto. I guess she felt she needed to put some distance between us."

I should be jealous, but instead I feel a strange sympathy for Will. I hear the familiar pain in his voice that comes from carrying a dark secret for too long. I recognize now that while I was intent on protecting Severn with half truths, he was just as determined to protect me.

"I'm sorry, Irving. I never meant to drive her away from you."

I wonder what it must be like to watch another man raise a girl who could well be your daughter. To see her week in and week out, but never say anything. To work beside the woman who gave birth to her, but never treat her as anything more than your boss.

"We figured Jack would stay out of the picture," he says. "It was just simpler if you assumed he was Severn's father." He lowers his head again. "Not that Helen was ever completely certain one way or the other."

Now I begin to understand Helen's edginess whenever Will was around Severn. Perhaps she worried that he would let something slip and shatter the careful illusion we'd all created. Or perhaps she thought that he would prove himself to be a better parent than either of us.

I let my eyes drift to the window. It's snowing again. The parking lot is busy with cars competing for empty spots. Will sits with his hands resting gently on the table in front of him, awaiting my verdict. He seems thinner somehow, the guilt of so many years all at once showing itself in his face.

"It was a long time ago, Will. We both did what we thought was best for Severn."

He frowns, surprised by my lenience, perhaps even disappointed that his crime hasn't received the severe response he knows it deserves. "I should have told you before now," he insists.

"And chance me preventing you from seeing Severn ever again?"

He blinks at me as if there's something painful caught in his eye. I wonder if he thinks there's a chance even still.

I lean forward and lay my hand on his forearm. "Don't worry, Will. I'm not that spiteful. Not any more, at least. Severn's lost enough people from her life."

He looks down at my hand as though a rose petal has landed on his sleeve in the middle of a snowstorm. I can see the clouds lift from his face. He slowly raises his head and smiles unsteadily. A tear rolls down his cheek. "She doesn't need to know," he says.

He's wrong, of course. As traumatic as the whole ordeal with Livingston was, as fragile as the truce she's finally reached with me is, she still needs to be told.

But maybe not right away.

Chapter 40

Helen's short story was accepted by a fiction quarterly in the States. She showed up at school just before I went into my fifth-period class, waving the letter. This wasn't some rinky-dink university publication that had agreed to print her story, she hastened to inform me. This magazine had a circulation of thirty thousand. Over the years, it had published writers like Carver, McCullers, Welty, O'Connor, and Updike. And now her very first published story would appear on its pages.

I remembered her bringing the story to me several months earlier. She'd hovered in the doorway to the kitchen as I sat marking essays. When I noticed her standing there, she pressed the pages to her chest, swaying uncertainly before finally presenting them to me with instructions to check her writing for spelling and grammar. Then she proceeded to make Severn's lunch for school the next day, a chore she usually left to me.

The story was about a man who returned home from a business trip to discover that his wife had left him without warning. I stopped and looked at her sharply after reading the first few sentences, as she had to have known I would, but she ignored me, absorbing herself in the task of tearing shreds of lettuce for Severn's sandwich. I forced myself to read on, trying to reserve my judgment as any good teacher would. I was shocked to discover the abandoned husband's point of view told with surprising sympathy and compassion. How Helen had captured my tortured state of mind so accurately after all that time, I was at a loss to explain. I'd never dared describe to her the hell she'd put me through, worried that it would shake apart the delicate equilibrium we'd achieved. Yet somehow she'd inferred it from my silences. It was suddenly and astonishingly apparent to me that she'd been a faithful witness to my pain and its lingering effects, even if she had been the cause.

When I finished reading, I got up and slid my arm around her waist. I told her that it was the best work she'd ever done. She seemed surprised by, even a little suspicious of, my reaction. I insisted she get it published.

She didn't send the manuscript out for two more months. I wondered later whether I'd annoyed her by mistaking her story for an apology rather than a skilfully crafted piece of fiction. Perhaps I'd failed to understand that I'd simply been a convenient model for her little sketch. It seemed that any depiction of the torment she'd visited upon me, no matter how empathetic, was not to be construed as a display of contrition on her part. For several days she rejected my advances in bed, likely viewing them as unwarranted expressions of my forgiveness.

Now that the story was accepted for publication, I couldn't help feeling used, as if I were a mannequin about to be set out for public viewing. Of course, I quickly congratulated Helen on her achievement and insisted on taking her out to her favourite Greek restaurant to celebrate. If she saw through my duplicity, she didn't let on. Nothing was going to spoil her triumph.

Severn didn't want to come with us. She'd made plans to go with her girlfriends to see a movie—probably one of those inane teen comedies that Hollywood kept churning out. I told her that this was a very special moment in her mother's life, and that it would mean a lot to have her there to celebrate. When Severn still dragged her feet, Helen told me to cancel the reservation. If her own daughter thought that going to some lame movie was more important, then obviously she was making far too big a deal out of having her story published. Severn rolled her eyes but eventually gave in. In an out-and-out battle of the drama queens, she lost to Helen every time.

As any teenage girl would, Severn had begun to chafe under her mother's scrutiny. For months, she'd refused to continue with the daily creative-writing exercises Helen set for her. The works of great women authors, assigned for Severn's edification, languished unread on the floor of her bedroom. I found it ironic that Helen was putting her daughter through the same ordeal of expectations that she had suffered under Walter. I wondered whether the Donnellys were predisposed to pass on their obsessions to their offspring and thus perpetuate their frustration into future generations.

Severn refused to eat anything more than hummus and a little tabbouleh at the restaurant. Helen warned her that she'd turn into an anorexic if she didn't start eating more. I tiptoed away partway through the meal to check that the wait staff knew when to bring out the special cake I'd ordered as a surprise for Helen. When I got back, she and Severn were still arguing about what the daily caloric intake of a girl of fifteen should be. I called a time-out, reminding them this was supposed to be a celebration, not a rematch of suppertime bouts from evenings past. I lifted my glass of ouzo and proposed a toast honouring Helen's arrival as a published author. Severn grudgingly joined in, giving her glass of ice water a perfunctory jiggle.

The cake arrived at the table complete with sparklers, and I made sure to take lots of pictures. Helen wanted me to get one of her with the cake, then several of her with Severn. At first, Severn posed stiffly as Helen pulled her close, but eventually her irritation melted. By the last shot, she was leaning her cheek against Helen's shoulder, as if to show that—just for a moment, at least— she didn't mind being her mother's little girl again.

On the drive home, Severn made a tentative peace offering by asking Helen if she could read her story. Helen glanced at me. Sure, she said with a little catch in her voice. I could see that she was already working out what lies she'd tell Severn to head off any speculation about the origin of the story. In the end, Helen never did show her the manuscript. She pretended to keep forgetting, and Severn soon understood not to ask any more.

A few weeks later, when Helen began grumbling about feeling bloated, I ignored her, assuming it was the same complaint I'd heard almost every month since we'd been married. Then she started losing her appetite. By the end of the month, she was sufficiently concerned to visit our family doctor. When he did a pelvic exam, he felt a mass. He referred her to a specialist. More tests were performed. A needle was inserted to take a sample of the fluid that was causing her abdomen to swell. I was there when the oncologist told her that he was fairly certain she had ovarian cancer.

We delivered the news to Severn that afternoon. After she stormed off to her bedroom in shock, I contemplated the undiscovered horrors that lay ahead of us while Helen sobbed in my arms. As terrified as I was, a selfish part of me welcomed the fact that Helen needed me now as she never had before.

Helen was never entirely comfortable with my fussing as her health continued to fail. I liked to think it was because she felt guilty for having held a part of herself back from me ever since her failed affair with Livingston, but perhaps she simply sensed that she was losing her advantage over me. Whatever her misgivings, the night before she went into the hospital for surgery, she clung to me in bed as if I was her only refuge. I tried to soothe her with hopeful whispers. I still held out hope that the doctors would cure her and we'd emerge from this trial with a new, deeper connection to each other.

When the surgeon removed her womb and ovaries, he discovered that the cancer had already spread. After the first round of chemo, Helen showed no improvement. She began turning into the emaciated shell she'd been so concerned that Severn would become.

Severn was shattered by Helen's rapid decline, but somehow she managed to pull out of her spiral of self-pity just in time for her mom's return home. She took over cleaning chores around the house and helped me prepare meals that Helen could stomach, tasks she never would have dreamed of doing under normal circumstances. One time when I returned from the grocery store, I found her cleaning Helen's barf off the kitchen floor. Another time, I woke up in the middle of the night to the sound of Helen crying in the bathroom, only to discover Severn already on the scene, helping change her mother's soiled pyjama bottoms. Severn did these things without complaint. I should have told her how proud I was of her, but I'd become too preoccupied with the horror of Helen's deterioration to remember my imperatives as a father.

Whenever I held Helen, I could feel the pain vibrating through her, the pitch ascending with each passing week. Sometimes she'd still resist my attempts to comfort her, raging through her tears. She'd complain that she was too young, that she'd accomplished too little, that she wasn't ready. Other times, she'd wrap herself around me, begging me not to let go. I kept promising I wouldn't leave her, all the while trying not to think of what it must be like to sense your world coming to an end. To feel all control—all hope for rescue—slipping away. To feel your own body betraying you. But a quiet, less empathetic part of me wondered if she would have done the same for me, or if watching me die would have turned her stomach. After all, she'd left me for less before.

Eventually, Helen got so sick that she had to be readmitted to the hospital. I sat with her day and night, returning home only to shower and change my clothes, or to ferry Severn to and from the hospital when she wasn't in school. I came to know all the nurses, especially the ones whose children I'd taught over the years. They secured a cot for me and set it up in Helen's room. And so I learned the night sounds of the hospital—the gentle squeaking of the medication cart in the hallway, the rustling of a nurse changing Helen's IV bag, and the plaintive bleat of a call buzzer at three in the morning.

I recognized Helen less as the days went on. It was as if she was being displaced, squeezed out as the cancer filled her up. I searched for evidence in her eyes that she was still intact, but they'd glazed over, worn down by the escalating tug-of-war between pain and morphine. The only sign of life struggling to reassert itself was the hair that had begun to grow back on her head since they'd abandoned the chemo. It was duller than it should have been, almost brown instead of red.

In the few moments when her eyes seemed to clear, she'd grope for my hand, straining to lift her head, her lips moving wordlessly. I imagined that she was trying to communicate some profound truth she'd discovered on life's final precipice, or that she'd finally come to understand all that I meant to her. But in the end, her message remained unspoken, the words never finding form.

I was just as guilty of not knowing how to say goodbye. As it turned out, I wasn't even with Helen when she died. I'd sneaked home to get some real sleep for the first time in over a week, satisfied that her condition had stabilized. Waiting in the mailbox was a large envelope with her name on it. The literary magazine that had promised to make her a published author, and thus grant her words a sliver of immortality, was now defunct and was returning her manuscript.

The call from the hospital came just as I was finally drifting off to sleep. They told me that Helen had passed away less than an hour before. They asked me whether I wanted to spend time with the body, say my final goodbyes. As if she'd hear me now. As if I could ask her to forgive me for abandoning her at the last moment and letting her die alone.

I woke Severn and drove to the hospital one last time. As we walked up to the nursing station, I put my arm around her, squeezing her shoulder to assure her that she still had me, as little consolation as that was to her. When it came time to go inside her mother's room, she shrank back. I told her she didn't have to come with me if she didn't want to. Denise, a nurse whose son I'd taught only the year before, took her aside. She gave Severn her seat behind the counter, resting an understanding hand on her back as she broke down in heaving sobs. Denise nodded at me, letting me know that my daughter was taken care of. That I could go in on my own.

The nurses had cleaned Helen, changed her sheets, put her in a fresh hospital gown. I stood at the foot of the bed feeling strangely disconnected, as if I'd walked into a stranger's room by mistake. The twisted look on her face had almost completely receded. Her nose and forehead seemed disproportionately large, now that her muscles had slackened. She looked like a wax figure, a museum rendering of an ancient Egyptian queen in repose. It wasn't her any more. I snapped back in time to the graveside on Beechey Island. I felt hundreds of miles of Arctic desolation surrounding me in all directions.

Chapter 41

I often wonder what it was that made Lady Franklin so determined to find her husband. Her efforts far outstripped those of any merely devoted wife. For years, she exhausted her energies and savings trying to rescue him. She goaded the Lords of the Admiralty into action, badgering them even when their interest in the search flagged. If she'd been permitted, she might well have set sail for the Arctic herself.

Perhaps it was that she felt responsible for him. After all, she was largely the reason he'd made the epic journey that, in retrospect, he'd had little chance of completing successfully. He'd been a prisoner of her expectations, just as Helen had been a prisoner of her father's and, later, of mine. We'd both wanted her to be something she wasn't: a dedicated bookseller, a faithful wife. Her failure was as much ours as it was hers.

I realized long ago that I'd been searching for a Helen who never truly existed. And yet now that she was gone, I was tempted to hold on to the shining idea of her, to offer her up as some kind of tragic hero, to defend her memory at all costs. Better, I decide, to carry all the contrary pieces of her forward and sort through them over time, as painful as that will continue to be for me. Better to focus my efforts on the living.

I drive Severn to the Imprint store for her first day on the job. A fine rain is slowly dissolving the dirty mounds of snow left in the parking lot from previous storms. Severn surveys the front entrance apprehensively as I pull in. Her hair is tied back in a ponytail, just as Helen often tied hers when she was working in her father's shop. A yellow collar sticks out from under her rain jacket. She's wearing the shirt that Will brought over to the house so she would fit in with the other staff on her first day.

"I'll come in with you," I offer as I park the car.

She cringes the way any teenager would, embarrassed by my presence but secretly glad I'm there to see her through this.

We sit there quietly for a minute before getting out, the rain gently falling on the windshield.

"I wonder what Mom would think," she says timidly.

"Come on," I say. "Will's waiting for you."

We walk together through the doors that Helen once demolished. Will is tidying a display at the front of the store. He greets his new employee with a warm smile, trying to diffuse any fears she might have as the girl who was caught shoplifting only weeks before.

"Ready to get to work?" he asks, rubbing his hands together. He takes her rain jacket from her. "Hey, that shirt looks good on you."

She blushes. He's right, I realize. It makes her look all grown-up. I'm proud and a little sad at the same time.

"So, Dad," Will says to me archly, "I hope you're not planning on hovering. Your girl and I have a lot of work to do this morning."

Will and I haven't told her yet. We thought we'd wait a bit, let her recover from her ordeal with Livingston a little while longer.

"I'll just go check out the magazines," I say, taking his not-so-subtle hint.

Severn gives me an anxious little wave as Will steers her away. He swings her by the front counter and cheerfully introduces her to the people she'll be working with from here on.

This is what it will be like for me with Severn more and more, I recognize—fresh moments of discovery, followed quickly by a goodbye. Each chance I get to know my daughter a little better, it will be time to let her go.

I linger by the magazine racks for a while, then slowly browse through the rest of the store, catching glimpses of her as I move about. Each time I see her, I notice that her reticence has receded just a little more. From the travel section, I observe her laughing at something Will has said. From biography, I see her questioning him about the correct method for displaying books on the shelves.

"Hello, Irving."

I turn around to see Marla standing just a few feet away in the psychology section, looking up at me from an open hardcover. We both hesitate, uncertain what protocol we should follow. We haven't spoken for weeks, not since she was over at the house and I scared her away. I never found the nerve to call her after that.

"Good book?" I ask.

She closes it self-consciously. I notice the title now. *Daughters without Mothers*.

"I didn't realize I'd find you here," she says.

"Yeah, well . . ."

There's an awkward pause. I feel as though I should apologize for not calling, even though I know she's probably been avoiding me as much as I've been avoiding her.

"How's Severn?" she asks.

"Better," I say.

She nods. "That's good."

"She just got a job here, actually."

Marla frowns at me doubtfully.

"No, really," I say.

I can tell that she thinks I'm lying to put her off. She puts the book back on the shelf, then glances at her watch. "I should be going."

"No, wait." I grab her by the hand before she can duck away. "Just wait here a bit. You'll see."

She stares at me as though I've come unhinged.

"Look," I say. "Here she comes."

I turn Marla to see Severn striding by in uniform, her ponytail swaying behind her, absorbing the finer points of customer service from Will .

"It's just part time," I explain to Marla. "After school and on weekends."

Her look of stupefaction slowly gives way to a broad grin.

"It's a start anyway," I say. "She may make a few new friends this way. But I told her it can't get in the way of her schoolwork."

"How did you . . . ?"

"I have connections," I say impishly.

Her eyes stay on Severn to confirm that it's not just some trick of the light, but the longer she looks, the wider her smile gets. I think back to how our search for Severn began on her doorstep, with her as my reluctant guide. Witnessing this moment with her, I realize, makes that journey complete in a way that it never could have been if I'd been standing here on my own.

"Listen," I say, "Severn's seventeenth birthday is coming up. I'm trying to make a party out of it. Maybe you'd like to come? You and Avery, I mean."

She looks at me uncertainly. I wonder if I've stepped over the line again.

"A week Wednesday," I say. "But if you're busy . . ."

She squeezes my hand. "Of course I'll come."

We stand there together, contentedly watching Severn receive her reinitiation into the land of the living. I notice for the first time that the mouth and nose that were her mother's have become her own. And at that moment, I glimpse the woman she will become—capable of trust and compassion, still vulnerable yet self-aware. Someone who will go on to make her own mistakes in life, instead of her parents'.

Acknowledgements

Getting a first novel published is a journey which countless talented writers attempt only to find the odds stacked against them. I was extremely fortunate to have many of the perils of the route cleared for me by a competition called Lit Idol that was held for the first time in 2004 at the London Book Fair. It provided me with immediate exposure far beyond what any first-time fiction author could hope for. But even more importantly, it gave me the representation of literary agent, Ali Gunn, at Curtis Brown in the UK, who, along with Christy Fletcher and Emma Parry of Fletcher and Parry in New York, secured for me a publishing deal. To the organizers and judges of Lit Idol, as well as the other contestants, I present this book as a humble offering in the hope that it justifies the faith that was placed in me as a fledgling writer. I trust that this is only the first of many novels to be published by a pool of yet-to-be-discovered talent.

I'm indebted to a number of established authors who have helped me along the way: Paul Quarrington and the Humber School for Writers for starting me on the right path; George Bowering, in his capacity as writer-in-residence at the University of Western Ontario, whose incisive comments on my early chapters helped me sharpen my prose; and, most of all, Maureen

McKeon, from whom I learned so much about the craft of storytelling. Her keen insights into the heart of my narrative helped me tremendously.

Thank you also to my editors at HarperCollins*Canada*, Iris Tupholme and Katie Hearn. It was a joy to work with a pair of professionals who showed such enthusiasm for my story and helped me more fully understand what it could become. Credit also goes to my early readers, Julia Elliot and Scott McLean.

There were many sources that proved invaluable to me as I wrote this book. For readers interested in learning more about Franklin and his final voyage, I recommend Ken McGoogan's *Fatal Passage: The Untold Story of John Rae, the Arctic Adventurer Who Discovered the Fate of Franklin*; Owen Beattie's account of his scientific research (including his fieldwork on Beechey Island) entitled *Frozen In Time: Unlocking the Secrets of the Franklin Expedition*; and Frances Woodward's *Portrait of Jane: A Life of Lady Franklin*. The following books helped guide me through the emotional terrain of the story: Scott Campbell and Phyllis Silverman's *Widowers: When Men Are Left Alone* and Hope Edelman's *Motherless Daughters: The Legacy of Loss*.